A CONVENIENT PRETENSE

Elaine Violette

What the critics are saying ...

"Reading *A Convenient Pretense* was truly a joy. The pacing was excellent, and watching Emily and Marcus slowly change their views on love and marriage was a pleasure. Fans of historical romance and poetry would do well to pick up a copy today."

Long and Short Reviews

"This novel is very 'Jane Austen-ish' meets 'Agatha Christie' with a wink at some Historic New Englander appreciation

All Things in Between

"Elaine Violette presents us with strong characters that go against the grain, as well as an accurate rendition of the strict mores of the era."

Barnes and Noble Review

"A Convenient Pretense is an enchanting, bright, charming, well-plotted, and deeply moving sweet-romance novel."

Shirley Webb, Author

A Convenient Pretense
Copyright 2016 Elaine Violette
ISBN: 978-0-9966821-7-6

Cover Art by Harris Channing

Dedication
To my hero Drew, for all your patience and
understanding.

Chapter One

Foolish is a maiden who sets her heart a flight
with dreams of wedded bliss that surely lead to strife.

EMILY REREAD THE lines, her chin scrunched on her palm.

She might best consider a single life…

Snorting, she let the words flow from her pen with little thought to order or meter.

At her husband's beck and call,
if he is even home at all

She shall rue her chosen plight…

She brushed the feathered quill across her cheek before dipping it once again into the inkwell.

as he saunters off into the night.
A visit to his mistress
And he believes it is his right!
So foolish is the maiden who sets her heart a flight.

She lifted the vellum to reread the silly verse that spoke more truth to her than her more conventional creations.

"Are you composing, Emily Grace? You have that look of keen concentration," Randal Hughes asked from the doorway of the small sitting room.

"Mmm… Yes, Father." She glanced up from her near trance. "I was struggling with meter," she murmured, pushing her chair away from her writing desk. "How are you feeling this morning?"

"Better than yesterday, and no doubt, not as well as I shall feel tomorrow. We need to talk. See me in my study once you are sufficiently satisfied with your newest creation."

Emily's expression turned glum. "Not the same subject, I pray."

Her father gave no answer. His narrowed eyes said all that was needed before he turned and disappeared down the hall.

Pushing the poem aside, she dropped her head into her hands. Will he never understand? She had no desire to go to London or to meet an eligible bachelor. She wanted to write, to finish her book and to be left alone.

EMILY STOOD STIFF shouldered facing her father's large mahogany desk. "I beg you, do not force me to go."

"I prefer that it not be an order but you leave me no choice."

"You know my position on marriage. I am content here and my writing will suffer."

"Not another word about your poetry. You have an admirable hobby but a good marriage represents a secure future."

"Is there such thing as a good marriage or is it simply a necessity in your eyes?"

"So cynical, my dear."

Even her love for her father could not erase the unhappiness and strife she had observed in her parents' marriage. "A single life, Father, is… "

"Enough arguments." Her father slammed his hand on his desk.

She stepped back in surprise. He seldom lost his calm but lately had demonstrated greater impatience.

Her father leaned back in his chair and sighed heavily. "I will not allow you to avoid another Season. I must see you well settled before my time comes."

"Father, you are scaring me." Emily pressed a hand to her breast. Her father had been ill for the past few weeks and this morning he appeared unusually pale. "Are you truly feeling better? Perhaps I should talk to Dr. Howard."

"Dr. Howard is not overly concerned with my stomach problems."

"But you have lost more weight. How can I leave for London while you remain unwell?"

"Cutting back on the rich foods Cook serves may be the solution to my discomfort. I can afford to lose a few more pounds." He patted his stomach. "And you will not use my ailment as an excuse to miss an entire Season."

"It is not an excuse. I shall only worry about you."

"Enough about my health. I do not foresee a trip to heaven in the near future or a meeting of old friends in hell's fires just yet." He winked at her before lifting papers spread on his desk, shuffling them together and setting them back down in neat order, a clear sign of dismissal.

She turned to go, but paused.

"You have more to say, my dear? On a different topic, I hope."

Her lips twitched at her father's obvious

irritation. "Willard has visited twice in the past month, more than we have seen him in a year. Why the sudden visits?"

"Without a title, I suspect the London Season carries little interest for your cousin and few invitations."

"No doubt he is checking to see if the day of his inheritance might arrive sooner than later." Emily scowled as she twisted the fabric of her skirt into her tightened fist.

"As do many men who have not been born into wealth." Hughes pushed his papers aside.

Emily bit her bottom lip. The thought of her cousin inheriting the Hughes' estate made her want to scream out at the injustice.

If only I'd been born a male.

She willed herself not to rant on about Willard's offensive behaviors. She disliked him intensely and was not fooled by the disingenuous façade he wore in her father's presence.

"Emily, I realize you and your cousin have never gotten along... unfortunate. Though my wealth is not excessive, you have a sizeable dowry if you marry. If you remain single, you have only the cottage and a modest yearly allowance. I want more for you — a husband and family. Willard, I fear, will not be as considerate of your future."

"Father, you speak as if... "

Hughes raised a hand. "This mild infirmity has caused me to consider the future. I plan to be around until you are well married and I can hold my first grandchild. Allow me to have that honor. Now let us put this morbid talk aside. Your aunt is looking forward to your visit. It is time you embraced a Season."

"You mean find an eligible bachelor who will sweep me off my feet, and put me in my place after wedding vows are said."

Hughes raked a hand through his gray hair and heaved a sigh. "In your cynicism, you ignore the benefits of marriage."

"I shall be one and twenty in a few months. Please, allow me to make my own decisions about my future." She had been barely out of the schoolroom when she came to the realization that any mention of marriage left her depressed. She would not be a creature of convention.

"You are gambling with your future."

"Mother understood." Emily's hand flew to her mouth as soon as the words spilled out. "Forgive me. I am being impertinent."

Hughes nodded wearily. "Your mother's opinions of marriage should have been kept to herself. She was a bitter woman, God rest her soul. You were unable to finish your first Season because of her passing and have missed at least two since. I lose count since our arguments each Season have remained the same."

"For good reason," Emily muttered under her breath. "I despised my first Season. I found everything superficial and tiring." How could she make him understand that she had little empathy for debutantes who yearned for marriage and accepted their submissive roles, as well as their husbands' mistresses?

"As my only child, I have spoiled you and

given into your wishes, perhaps selfishly. This Season began weeks ago and because of your stubbornness, you are still here. You are leaving Sunday. I have told Maggie to begin your packing."

Emily opened her mouth for a final plea but seeing her father's stony expression she gritted her teeth and marched out of the study. The force of the door she closed behind her reflected her defiance.

Once in her room, she dismissed her maid and glared at the half-packed trunk on her bed. She pulled out a neatly folded gown and then another, tossing them to the side before collapsing on the bed, the tossed gowns crushed beneath her.

She groaned at the thought of primping and posturing, of dinners and dances, and worse, of the invitations and introductions that her aunt was most likely already planning. It was all a waste. She had only to think of her mother. No, she would never marry.

"UNCLE RANDAL, I am pleased to see you at your desk. You must be feeling better."

"A stomachache will not keep me from my duties. Have a seat, Willard. I am nearly finished."

"I took it upon myself to ask a maid to bring us tea, Uncle. I hope I am not overstepping. She told me that you have been closeted in your study for far too long."

"Fine, fine," Hughes huffed, pushing the paper he was reading aside. "Have a seat."

"You did not look well on my last visit. Seeing you busy at work gives me some relief," Willard said as he took a chair across from his uncle.

"Does it?" Hughes narrowed his eyes at his nephew.

Willard gave him an offended look. "Indeed, I have been deeply concerned. Has your doctor been back to see you?"

"Too often. I despise being probed and prodded."

"Dr. Howard, is it not? He is getting on in years. Perhaps we should call in another physician?"

"No, it is enough with my daughter hovering over me," Hughes growled, before rubbing his tired, strained eyes. "The sooner she leaves, the better."

Willard's brow lifted. "Is she taking a trip?"

"To London, for the remainder of the Season."

"Ah, perhaps she will find a husband who can tame her temper," Willard chuckled.

Hughes did not share his deprecating humor. He could not allow Willard and Emily's petty squabbles to interfere with what he needed to do. Whether he liked it or not, Willard was his heir and needed some direction before his illness took over his mind as well as his body. He leaned back and pressed folded hands to the back of his neck, his eyes shuttered.

"Uncle, you look fatigued."

"Been at my desk too long. I asked you to come for a serious discussion, but it may not be the best day."

Willard offered a grim nod of assent. "At least let me see you settled in the parlor to rest. I shall ask that the tea be delivered there."

Hughes gave a resigned nod. He pushed himself up from his seat only to grip his desk as a spell of dizziness overcame him.

Willard unfolded his long, narrow body and rushed to his uncle's aid.

Hughes waved him off. "Just give me a minute." Thank God, Emily would be gone soon. He did not know how much longer he could hide these spells of weakness. "Forget the tea. Come back next week." Hughes sank back into his chair.

"I shall not be content until I see that you are comfortably resting. Ah, here comes the tea now."

Hughes frowned as the maid set down the tray on a nearby table.

"May I pour, sir?" the maid asked.

"Allow me," Willard said, walking over to the table.

The maid stepped aside and glanced at Mr. Hughes.

"My nephew insists. You may go back to your duties."

Willard waited for the maid to leave the room before turning his back to his uncle to prepare the tea.

Chapter Two

MARCUS DEMING, EARL of Pembridge, cursed under his breath as he clambered up the steps of his London townhouse. He planned to tell his aunt in no uncertain terms to stop meddling into his affairs. He had experienced enough balls and soirees, dinners and outings, and every other event tied to the Season. His aunt's newest candidate for a future bride had giggled in his ear through most of last evening's dinner. When he awoke this morning, he could still hear the deafening sound of her atrocious cackle.

He thrust the front door open and nearly knocked his elderly butler off his feet. "Sorry, Jenkins." He grasped the servant's arm and steadied him. "I did not expect to find you standing just within the threshold."

"I was watching for you, my lord. I trust that you had a refreshing ride?"

"I found the morning air exhilarating." Marcus handed the butler his riding crop. "Has my aunt appeared yet this morning?"

"She is up and about in her usual morning spot in the rose salon."

Marcus grimaced. "No doubt writing acceptances to more invitations. Tell her that I wish to speak with her immediately. I shall be in the breakfast room."

"Yes, my lord. She asked about your whereabouts earlier. She seemed quite anxious to speak with you as well."

"Dear God, not another one so soon," Marcus mumbled.

"My lord?"

With a weary shake of his head, Marcus dismissed the butler and stalked off to the breakfast room and over to the sideboard. He poured a cup of coffee and turned his attention back to his objective.

He must convince Aunt Agatha to stop her attempts at matchmaking. *She can drag me by the ear next Season. I refuse to be cornered by one more blushing hopeful.* He continued to mumble in his mind as he took a gulp of coffee. *I refuse to sit beside another shy debutante who looks at me with glazed, pitiful eyes or those manipulating ones who simper and beg me to lead them to the balconies for air. There are those who have nothing to say and those who have too much to say!*

He knew his aunt meant well but his patience had grown thinner than a worn out sixpence. He pulled out his chair to sit only to jar the cup and spill hot coffee over his wrist. "Damn." His morning ride did little to calm his temper. Setting the cup down, he grabbed a napkin to blot his cuff.

"Marcus, Marcus, my dear." Aunt Agatha's high-pitched, warbling voice pierced his ears even before she entered the open doorway.

He tossed the napkin aside as Agatha swept into the room, her plump figure adorned in bright raspberry.

"I was aggrieved to hear that you had gone out before I left my bedchamber. I feared that you had left for the day."

"And what could possibly have caused such alarm that it could not wait?" Marcus pulled out a chair for his aunt and waited for her to be settled before returning to his seat.

"My dear friend Delia sent a note last evening and, oh, I cannot believe that I waited until this morning to open it." Agatha's hands flared out before she clamped them together and rested them on the white linen. "Why, I would have sent a messenger last night before we left for the Jamieson's."

"Mrs. Fenning's note could not wait until this morning for a response? After all, you do meet with her almost daily for tea. No doubt she is coming this afternoon."

"Indeed, but she was much too excited to wait until tea time."

Marcus rubbed his forehead. His earlier rage had left him with a blasted headache. "Pray tell me this news that has caused such elation."

Agatha smiled brightly, her round cheeks as rosy as the dress she wore. "Delia received a letter delayed in the mail from her brother-in-law in the country. He wrote that his daughter would be arriving in London tomorrow. She is delighted, naturally, and has invited us to Sunday dinner so that we might have the pleasure of meeting her. I dare say from everything Delia has told me, her niece seems an ideal candidate. Her family is imp —
"

"Stop!"

"But…"

Marcus rose from his chair and planted splayed fingers firmly on the table, his broad shoulders hunched forward. "I know exactly what you are about to say. 'She comes from an impeccable family, such superb breeding.' Am I accurate so far? 'She is certain to be the perfect match and she is lovely, of course. Why, all the other ladies will fade into the background at her appearance.'" He dropped back into his chair. The dramatic mimicking of his aunt's words had little effect. As usual, she graced him with a placating smile.

"I do realize that a few of the young ladies I have chosen have not been quite the ideal, however…"

"A few? You underrate yourself. Not a few, a dozen at least, this month alone."

"You are the Earl of Pembridge and eight and twenty years. Your father, God rest his soul, asked me to aid you in finding a suitable wife. I have taken that charge quite seriously."

Marcus' chest tightened at the thought of his father's last days. His sire had rejected life itself, dismissing his offspring and even begging for a premature death. Marcus understood his duty. He must eventually marry, but he would delay the inevitable as long as possible, and he would never make the mistake that led to his father's demise. He drank the remainder of his coffee in one gulp and set the cup down with a clang against its saucer. He had had enough of his aunt's meddling.

"Aunt Agatha, you have honored my father's

wishes to the extreme. I have attended more dinner parties than I can count on my fingers and toes." He rose from his seat. "I plan to wait until next Season to choose a bride. Now I am going up to change. I have business in town today."

"Marcus... Oh, dear."

He gained only a few steps toward the door before glancing back and seeing his aunt's distressed expression.

"What is it now?"

"I am afraid I have already accepted her invitation. You were not available and I assumed..." She stared meekly at her nephew. "How can I possibly send regrets after I so enthusiastically accepted?"

"Tell her that in your enthusiasm you did not check with me and that I have another engagement."

"She will only change the day. That just will not do. No, no, not at all..." Agatha shook her head from side to side, her gray ringlets bobbing.

"She is your dearest friend. She will understand." Marcus took another step toward the door.

"I give you my word that I shall stop my search... for the time being. I worry so about you, especially when you are out gallivanting until daybreak. Rumors do float about, you know. You must consider the need for an heir, in case..." She pressed a hand against her cheek. "I cannot bear to even think of it."

"I assure you that my habits are not life threatening. Next Season will be soon enough to consider a bride."

She tapped a finger to her chin. "If you would prefer to wait until next Season to marry and another year most likely, God willing, to have an heir…" Agatha sat back in her seat and clasped her hands neatly in her lap. "I accept your decision."

Marcus breathed a sigh of relief and nearly reached the door.

"I shall not press the issue until next Season if you would see your way to attend this one dinner. For if I send regrets so soon after accepting, heavens…" She raised a hand and pressed it to her throat. "I shall be humiliated." Pulling out a handkerchief tucked in her sleeve, she dabbed an eye.

Marcus raked his hands through his hair, now a cluster of black curls dampened from the morning mist. He glared at his aunt whose expression reminded him of a pouting child.

"I have truly upset you," she continued. Indeed, I have caused you nothing but trouble since I have arrived. If only my dear companion were still alive. I would be in Bath and not such a nuisance. But I did promise your father, and on his deathbed." She lifted her eyes to Marcus. "If you would prefer that I leave…"

"Nonsense, your home is here," Marcus said wearily. He felt honor bound to care for his aunt, but he had not expected her to take his father's final request so seriously, or to find such enjoyment in the quest.

After inheriting his father's title and property three years earlier, he had made wise financial decisions and despite his current choice of activities, he knew his responsibilities. Some might consider him a bit of a rake, but he was not the worst. He rubbed the back of his neck and groaned.

She had won again.

"I shall attend the dinner, but this will be the very last time. Do I make myself clear?"

"Indeed, I understand perfectly."

He glared into pale blue eyes that sparkled with too much pleasure. "For heaven's sake, Aunt, it is almost the end of the Season. Why is this niece even making an appearance at such a late date?"

"Delia had no explanation for the delay. Regardless, from her description, the girl seems a perfect match, impeccable breeding..." Agatha stopped abruptly, slapping her hand against her open mouth.

Marcus held his tongue, but his look said enough to silence even an apology. He stomped out of the room.

He did not need his aunt's help to choose his future wife. He already had a couple of women in mind. They were beautiful, refined and intelligent enough to carry on decent conversations. Both came from respected families. His title and affluence, no doubt, would be enough to keep either content. If they were not available next Season, he would have others to add to his list.

Most important, he felt no deep feelings for either one of his present choices. And that was the crucial measure. If he liked being in his wife's presence and if she was attentive in the bedroom, that would suffice. He refused to lose himself in love as his father had done. Love, Marcus had come to realize, created too deep a need and weakened a man, destroying his sensibilities.

When he felt impelled to marry, he would flip a coin and make his choice.

Chapter Three

"YOU LOOK ESPECIALLY lovely, Miss Emily." The maid stepped back to admire her handiwork.

"Maggie, you have emptied the entire tray of pins. I doubt a strand will dare come loose."

"Then I have accomplished my purpose. I shall be plucking them out soon enough."

Emily glared into the dressing table mirror. Her thick auburn hair was difficult enough to work with, but pinning it back so severely to mask its unruliness left her looking like someone else entirely.

"Could not Aunt Delia have waited a few days before inviting a bachelor for dinner? Her energy is being wasted."

"Not just a bachelor, miss, an earl." Maggie's eyes drifted upward, her smile wistful.

Emily's frown left little doubt what she thought of her maid's dreamy expression or her reminder.

"Is there anything else that you need, miss?"

"Yes, to spend the evening in my room."

"Come now, a smile instead of that dismal expression might lighten your mood. You should take a short rest. They shall be arriving soon."

Emily nodded, aware that her maid would not understand her dread of being primped for a possible suitor. "Thank you." She forced a smile. "I shall try to heed your advice."

Once Maggie left the room, Emily walked over to her bed, settling on its edge. She smoothed a hand across the cream and gold satin coverlet.

Perhaps if I write Father and plead to return? She had no interest in meeting an earl, or a viscount, or a duke for that matter. Even during her coming out Season, she had doubted a gentleman would pick her from the crowd of debutantes. Despite the tragic circumstances of her early departure, she was relieved to escape from the rituals and ostentatious manners of high society. She had stayed in the background at events and observed other debutantes' flirtations. Instead of trying to draw admirers, she spent her time scribbling poems in her mind that poked fun at her peers' silly behaviors.

She stood and began to pace. Passing by the mirror, she stopped to readjust the ecru lace bow beneath her midriff that wilted more from age than her maid's attempt to press it into place. Her outdated gown suited her purpose.

What she really wanted to do was work on her poetry book, not impress an earl. Many of her poems mocked the rituals of courtship. She wondered how many women, after marriage, would agree with her ironic twists to the hope-filled dreams of naïve girls. With scathing words, her mother had warned her that courtships never reflected the true course relationships took after the wedding vows.

Emily had witnessed, firsthand, her mother's loneliness and disappointments. She would not sacrifice herself at the altar and she saw it as sacrifice, not a woman's salvation from spinsterhood. She planned to find her own contentment and create her own livelihood if need be. There were moments when romantic imaginings stirred within her and curiosities about the intimacies of marriage caused her disquiet. At those times, she turned to her poetry. She could get lost in composing a verse or reading those of the published poets. Or she would take her horse, Sage, on a swift run through the fields. But most times, she envisioned her mother and recounted her words. She needed nothing more to sustain her chosen path.

A rapid tapping on the door aroused her from her thoughts. "Miss Emily, the guests have arrived."

She drew in a deep breath and exhaled with an exasperated sigh. "Thank you, Maggie, I shall be down presently." Brushing at the skirt of her gown and straightening her shoulders, she left the room.

When she reached the staircase, she attempted to glide down the steps slowly, elegantly, to please her aunt, though she found herself watching the steps rather than keeping her head erect. She knew Aunt Delia's suggestions for her entrance this evening were given with the best of intentions, but she had no desire to impress.

Further, she accepted that she was plain compared to the women of polite society, whose manners and dress were always at the height of fashion. She was certainly not someone an earl would have any interest in.

MARCUS STOOD IN the foyer near the bottom of the wide staircase with Mrs. Fenning and his aunt. When he looked up to see her niece coming down the stairs, he hoped his blank expression hid his first observations.

She was as stiff as a lamppost, her face long and her steps awkward. Though her dark reddish hair was swept up in a style women chose to wear, her dress, a rather dull shade of green, looked outdated. He closed his eyes briefly and swallowed, mentally preparing himself. Perhaps if he coughed his way through dinner, he could be excused.

When she took her final steps onto the foyer floor, her aunt gently grasped her shoulders and nudged her toward Marcus' aunt. "Agatha, may I present my lovely niece, Miss Emily Grace Hughes. Emily, I have written to you about my dearest friend, Agatha Trumbell."

"My dear Miss Hughes, I have heard so much about you," Agatha gushed.

Emily accepted her outreached hand. "Aunt Delia has mentioned you often in her letters. It is a pleasure to finally meet you."

"You must call me Agatha, my dear. Your aunt and I are as close as sisters."

While the three women conversed, Marcus took a step back and observed each of them. Mrs. Fenning carried her tall, slim figure regally. She wore her silver hair swept up in a bun, which enhanced her high cheekbones and gave an aura of elegance. His aunt stood a few inches shorter. She had a cheery demeanor, making a very good companion for Mrs. Fenning, who tended to be of a serious nature. Observing Miss Hughes with a more discerning eye, he had to admit that she had an attractive profile with delicate features. Dropping his gaze, he came to the conclusion that beneath her drab gown, which was the color of a wilted stem, she had a pleasing figure.

"How lovely you are," his aunt expounded. "Delia, she is quite lovely."

"Emily," Delia interrupted her friend's effusive praise. "May I introduce Agatha's nephew, Marcus Deming, the Earl of Pembridge."

Emily turned toward Marcus and offered a slight curtsy. When she raised her eyes, Marcus had a moment's pause before greeting her. Her face wasn't long but heart shaped, and her deep green eyes were mesmerizing. They reminded him of polished emeralds. He lowered his eyes to full lips that were slightly pursed rather than curved into the coquettish smile his aunt's hopefuls usually wore. Her complexion was flawless, but not pale. She had a healthy glow about her, most likely due to fresh country air, he mused.

"My lord," Emily murmured when he remained wordless.

Realizing he had been transfixed, he forced a tight smile. "Welcome to London, Miss Hughes. I hope your trip was pleasant and uneventful."

"Quite," Emily replied, her own eyes dwelling a moment too long on his features before glancing back at the aunts.

"Well now," Delia chirped, filling in the awkward silence that followed, "my cook was able to purchase splendid, fresh salmon and has warned me that all her delicacies must be served on time if we are to enjoy their full flavor."

Without further conversation, they were ushered into the dining room, Marcus following behind Emily, his eyes appreciating her lithe form that curved in all the right places.

DELIA'S FOOTMAN SERVED the first course, a fragrant vegetable and herb soup, while the aunts carried on a lively discussion about the goings-on in London circles.

When Aunt Delia began questioning Lord Deming on his interests, Emily observed him more closely. He was impressively dressed in a navy superfine coat that fit taut against his broad shoulders, though his white cravat was slightly askew. His nearly black hair was neatly trimmed and left longer at the nape of his neck. His square chin with a hint of a cleft reflected strength and confidence.

Was it simply his good looks that caused the odd reaction that coursed through her when they were introduced, or was it his eyes boring into hers? It was as if the sounds and décor around them had melted away and they were totally alone. For a brief moment, she had wanted to ignore her declarations and erase her fears. She had wanted to believe in romance and happy ever after endings. As she pondered her reaction, she found herself staring into narrowed, azure-blue eyes. Marcus' lips tilted up on one side, a sure sign that he was well aware of her examination.

Flushed with embarrassment, she focused her attention on her aunt's description of the best *modiste* in London.

"I only hope that she is not overly busy. I shall be so disappointed," Delia said with a sigh. "Her choices of fabrics and detail work are breathtaking."

"I suspect the gown Lady Sefton wore at the opera last week was Mademoiselle Rochelle's creation. Would you not agree?" Agatha asked.

"Indeed, I thought the same when I saw her walking about during intermission. Emily, my dear, women of the town place orders for their gowns months before the Season arrives. You may benefit from mademoiselle's most current designs. Her salon will be our first stop tomorrow morning."

Emily offered a brief smile. Extravagant gowns seemed frivolous since she would have little use for them in the country.

"Marcus, forgive us for going on about dresses," Delia said, turning her attention to the earl. "We women do carry on about such things. Perhaps you might know if the museums have special exhibitions that Emily might enjoy? I prefer the art galleries myself. Do you have a preference, Emily?"

Emily noted that Marcus looked relieved that her aunt's questions reverted to her. "I enjoy both."

"Splendid," Delia said, "and you must see an opera while in London. Agatha and I both adore the opera."

"Indeed and such an ideal opportunity to see

and be seen." Agatha looked at her nephew inquiringly. "Marcus?"

Marcus' eyes darted toward his aunt before he set down his spoon and turned his gaze toward Emily. "You are most welcome to join us in my box, Miss Hughes."

Emily groaned inwardly. The earl's aunt had just maneuvered him into an invitation that he doubtless did not want to extend.

When dessert was served, Emily picked at her slice of fruit pie. Lord Deming was as disinterested as she was in the two aunts' obvious matchmaking. He had said little during dinner and she had concluded that, despite her unusual reaction upon meeting him, he was a most boring dinner companion.

After dinner they moved to the drawing room where Aunt Delia's art displays became the subject of conversation. When the two aunts strolled across the room to the furthest side to discuss wall hangings, Emily suspected their motives. Sitting on the edge of a floral settee, she glanced up at Lord Deming who stood stiffly by the fireplace. Despite her desire not to notice, his presence seemed to fill the room. He was undeniably the handsomest man she had ever met.

He gave her a polite smile. "Miss Hughes, you have arrived quite late in the Season. Do you plan to extend your stay through the summer?"

"Heavens, no."

When the earl raised a brow, Emily realized she'd answered too emphatically. Measuring her tone, she continued. "I plan to return to the country at Season's end."

"Unfortunately, your late arrival has deprived you of opportunities to make new acquaintances. I suspect you will want to make an early appearance at the more notable social events."

Emily's lips twitched with a speck of humor. "I do not feel in the least deprived nor am I concerned about making an appearance, notable or otherwise."

"Really?" Marcus arched a brow, obviously surprised by her response.

Emily didn't miss his disbelieving tone. "Are appearances important to you, my lord?"

"I simply meant..." Marcus appeared thrown off by her brazen question. "I assumed that you hoped to..."

"Find a husband? No doubt you assume that I am as eager to marry as my aunt is in finding me a suitable match. I assure you, Lord Deming, you are quite safe." Emily offered a placating smile. "I am here at my father's request and plan to leave London as unencumbered as I have arrived."

Marcus looked stunned at her admission but was left no time to respond. The aunts approached, having completed their stroll.

Emily stifled a grin. She had caught him off guard and ruffled his arrogant self-assurance. To her relief, she had begun to recognize his flaws, freeing her from her previous discomforting attraction to him.

The aunts' return gave Emily the perfect opportunity to escape.

She stood just as the aunts settled in their seats.

"Please excuse me. I am feeling a bit overwhelmed with all our talk of the Season's events, and I do want to be rested for our shopping trip tomorrow."

Before her aunt could dissuade her, Emily turned to Agatha.

"Miss Trumbell, I am so glad to have finally met you."

"Please, you must call me Agatha, and it has been a delight, my dear."

Emily smiled gratefully, not missing the older woman's look of disappointment. Her aunt most likely was not happy with her either. She turned to face Marcus. "Lord Deming." She offered a slight curtsy.

"Miss Hughes." Marcus nodded, his expression a mixture of surprise and annoyance.

With a swirl of her skirt, Emily left the room without looking back.

He retreated with a sigh,
as she took her leave of him.
No doubt, she did surmise,
he would return again.
A rose bouquet in hand...

EMILY PAUSED AND reread the lines she'd begun once she had undressed and bid her maid good night. Her experiences had often been inspirations for her poetry, though the stirrings within her at this late hour were more disturbing than inspiring.

A grand bouquet would never please
Or words of flattery appease...

She stifled a yawn before placing her quill in its holder.

As she rose from her chair to prepare for bed,

her thoughts returned to the evening and to Lord Deming. She guessed that the earl must surely be the catch of the Season, and his aunt's remarks proved that she was on a crusade to match him.

Emily remembered how he fidgeted with his neckcloth each time the aunts began their effusive praise. Aunt Delia's overtures of Emily's own good breeding made her extremely uncomfortable as well.

We both seem to be in the same predicament, she mused as she doused her bedside lamp and snuggled beneath the covers. As she lay staring up at the ceiling, a spark of an idea formed in her mind. No, too impossible to think about...

Or was it, she thought, as she nodded off to sleep.

Chapter Four

WHY MUST WOMEN rehash every detail of an event, share every thought and expect you to do the same? Marcus thought as he recalled his aunt's constant chatter on the way home from Mrs. Fenning's dinner party the evening before. Thankfully, she was having breakfast in her room this morning.

He had to admit that Miss Hughes was not what he had expected. Surprisingly, the girl showed little enthusiasm for her aunt's plans and even less for a gentleman's attentions. He did, however, observe in her expressions thoughtful deliberation.

In fact, by the time dinner was over, he had felt as if he were the one being scrutinized and judged deficient. He was too accustomed to the opposite by marriage-minded women. *What is the saucy Miss Emily Grace Hughes all about?* He had felt oddly insulted that she had excused herself before he had prepared to leave.

Although he had thought, on first appearance, that she was a bit awkward and plain, he had changed his mind after looking into her eyes. Not only were they beautiful, but in their depths he saw more, though he found it difficult to put a name to the thoughts that flew through his mind. The truth was he had become lost in them for what seemed like minutes. Most likely it was only a few seconds.

At the dinner table, he had noticed that when she laughed, her eyes lit up and her smile, well, she was really quite pretty.

He straightened in his seat and chastised himself for giving too much thought to his aunt's newest hopeful. No doubt more time spent with Miss Hughes would prove as tedious as the other women Aunt Agatha had paraded before him.

Marcus grinned to himself, realizing that he did want to see her again, only to satisfy his curiosity. Her disinterest intrigued him.

Today, he recalled, Emily Hughes would be shopping with her aunt in the vicinity of his favorite tobacco shop. Though he had tried to shoo the thought away much as he would a disturbing fly, the idea of stopping at Fribourg & Treyer's for some fresh pipe tobacco had taken on more importance than usual.

"WOULD YOU MIND if I browsed the bookstore, Aunt Delia?" Emily asked after spying Hatchard's Bookshop. She hoped to add to her poetry collection while in London. They had already visited the *modiste* earlier in the morning and chosen materials for three lovely gowns.

"Of course. Perhaps I might find copies of *Lady's Magazine* that I have not yet enjoyed. Why, many of my entertaining ideas have come from them. I do so love to find a copy that I haven't read. And after the book store, we must go to the milliners'. Mrs. Buckley is only two shops over and has a grand collection of bonnets. I plan to buy myself one and, I admit, I try on every one that catches my fancy."

Emily smiled at her aunt's enthusiasm as she followed her lead into the bookstore.

MARCUS WALKED DOWN the thoroughfare, taking notice of the carriages parked about. Casting aside an odd feeling of disappointment upon not seeing Miss Hughes, he entered the tobacco shop and made his purchase.

Walking back up the street, he scowled at his uncharacteristic behavior. He had a plan for the day, fencing with an old friend in an hour and a visit later in the evening with an attractive widow. Why was he wasting time? Her behavior the previous night had been cool and unwelcoming. It must be his pride. Just as the thought passed, he spotted Miss Hughes and her aunt in front of the local bookshop. Marcus paused and waited for carriages to pass before crossing the street. He really should be on his way, but he had some time. Why not satisfy his curiosity about the new arrival?

When he reached the shop, he hesitated. Instead of entering, he perused the displayed books in the window, not for any particular interest. He was delaying, wondering if he should intrude upon their shopping venture. Or was it because his actions were beyond his normal behavior? Tossing aside his qualms, he entered. A gloomy-faced bookseller sat behind a high counter and lowered his spectacles. He nodded a weary greeting to Marcus before returning to the worn volume he had been reading.

Marcus spotted the aunt first. She was scouring

a collection of magazines. Emily stood behind her with a book in hand.

He looked out the cloudy windows of the shop and entertained the thought of walking right back out the door. Instead, he walked over to Mrs. Fenning who looked up in surprise at his appearance.

"Marcus, how delightful to see you."

"I was on my way to my club and decided to stop in for a… well, I looked up and there you were." He glanced over at Emily before refocusing on her aunt.

Delia's expression held a glint of humor. She was obviously aware that his interest stood beyond her. "I am sure Emily will be pleased to see you," she whispered. "She appears to have found a book to her liking. I am certain that she won't mind being interrupted." She smiled and lifted a magazine from the shelf.

Marcus stifled a grin. As he'd expected, Mrs. Fenning happily encouraged him in the hope he might have taken a liking to her niece. He took the few steps toward the back of the store, noting that Emily seemed quite involved with the book she held. He paused at the end of a stack of books and watched as she whispered the words of a familiar poem. He took a couple of steps closer. She remained absorbed and oblivious to his presence as she read just loud enough so he could make out the words.

…And the sunlight clasps the earth,
And the moonbeam kiss the sea

His eyes dwelled on her very kissable lips as they formed each word with tender intonation. Taking two quiet steps closer he completed the stanza.

What are all these kissings worth,
If thou kiss not me?

"Oh," Emily gasped as the book fell from her hand. Her eyes shot toward him and then at her aunt who gave her a quick smile over her magazine.

Marcus reached down and picked it up. "Forgive me for startling you, Miss Hughes," he said in the same quiet tone she'd been using in her reading. I happened to see you enter the shop." He held out the book to her. "Percy Shelley, I enjoy his verses."

"I had not expected..." She pressed a hand to her lips as if she wanted to catch her words before they spilled out.

"That I could recite poetry?"

"Your memorization is admirable." She accepted the book from his hand before peering anxiously toward her aunt whose eyes remained averted. Marcus sensed that she dearly hoped her aunt would join them. "I must say that it is a pleasure to see you today without my own aunt hovering nearby and ready to pounce on the occasion of a match."

Emily's eyes widened at his comment before covering her mouth to suppress a bubble of laughter.

Marcus grinned, pleased that his words had eased her anxiety at his appearance.

"You were no doubt aware that both our aunts were actively matchmaking last evening," she whispered.

"Much to my chagrin, my aunt has made it her goal of the Season."

Emily lowered her eyes and rubbed the binding of the book with one finger before gazing back up at him. "If you do not mind my bluntness, I did observe that you were, perhaps, slightly annoyed at her enthusiasm."

Now it was *Marcus' t*urn to laugh. "I assure you that my feelings on the matter go far beyond slight annoyance. Please do not take it as a personal affront to yourself, Miss Hughes. My aunt has been at it for months."

Emily glanced once again at her aunt who looked up for only a moment before returning to her magazine. She sucked in her bottom lip, a gesture that caused a stirring in Marcus' loins. The girl was a temptress, he thought, though he doubted she realized it. When she returned her gaze to him, her expression had changed. Determination, perhaps? The girl puzzled him and once again he felt impelled to know more about her.

"It appears that we are of the same mind," Emily whispered, wearing a hint of a smile. "My aunt and my father are bent on finding me a husband despite my disinterest."

"Your disinterest? That does surprise me."

"As it did when you assumed that I must regret my late arrival?"

Marcus gave her a sheepish grin, meant to

humor her rather than to appear apologetic.

"I purposely arrived late. I have no desire to attract admirers, Lord Deming."

Marcus raised a brow at her matter-of-fact announcement and her defiant stance. She was not being coy. He rubbed his chin, his eyes never leaving hers. "Since you are being so honest, neither do I. I rather enjoy my bachelorhood and prefer to plan my future in my own time."

Emily clutched the poetry book tighter to her chest and worried her bottom lip. Quite a lovely bottom lip, full and moist, he thought.

"What are you thinking, Miss Hughes? I see an unusual gleam in your eyes despite the poor lighting."

"I have an idea." Her soft tone held a nervous edge, her eyes darting back and forth from her aunt to Marcus. "You might find it quite absurd, even scandalous." She hesitated.

"Go on," Marcus urged, admittedly intrigued by her words and manner.

"Our aunts mean well, but my idea… it might protect us both from further interference during the remainder of the Season."

Marcus arched his brow. He took a step closer, partially blocking the view between Emily and her aunt "My curiosity must be satisfied, Miss Hughes."

EMILY LIFTED UP on her toes and looked over Marcus' shoulder, hoping that her aunt hadn't noticed the shift in his position. His close proximity to her caused her heart to beat faster, but wasn't that a natural reaction to being in a narrow space with a handsome gentleman? She could not allow her feminine reaction to his nearness stop her from achieving her goal. After all, she had decided last evening that he was arrogant and too self-assured and, therefore, not a threat to her sensibilities, and they did seem to be of the same mind. Did she dare suggest her idea? She raised her eyes to his. "Lord Deming," she whispered, "do you think we might be able to aid each other?"

She continued without waiting for a reply and before her anxiety stifled her. "I hope to stay in London for only a few weeks. By then, much of polite society will be off to their summer homes and there should be no reason for me to continue my visit. My aunt is a dear..." She paused and took in a deep breath. "I know what she has in store for me during my stay — balls, house parties, teas and numerous introductions. I admit my dread of them.

She sucked in another breath and looked up at him.

"Yes?"

"I was thinking, since you say you are of the same mind that we might create an illusion of, I mean... a pretense."

"A pretense?" Marcus' eyes widened.

She clenched the book tighter, her fingers turning pink against the brown binding. Why did his closeness cause her insides to quiver? And, doubtless, she could not ignore the scent of sandalwood that filled her nostrils, a pleasant scent she had to admit. Well, she had never denied male attraction, only her distaste for the journey women were expected to take to the altar. She forced her mind back to her brash utterance. She could not take back her words now.

"Miss Hughes, I await your explanation with bated breath."

Emily plowed ahead knowing she had little time to explain and while her mind questioned her sanity. "I propose that we might give our aunts a slight impression that we are interested in each other," she continued in a whisper. "After all, only a few weeks remain of the Season. I can return to the country as I left, free from attachment and you…" She stopped abruptly. She felt as if the muse had captured her tongue and inspired her into foolishness.

Despite her misgivings, she went on. "The appropriate formalities and expectations would be in place, of course. Just a month's time, or so, and little would be expected on your part, except to demonstrate an interest… on my part as well, in the presence of our aunts." Emily's cheeks reddened. She saw Marcus' lips twitch as she spoke and he looked especially rakish. Was he about to laugh at her? She knew she was talking too fast. She felt suddenly as if she might drown in her own stupidity, and the corner where they stood had grown exceptionally warm.

Marcus took another step closer. He heard the clearing of a throat behind him. Both he and Emily pulled back slightly and looked over at her aunt, whose eyes remained lifted toward them for only a second, a brief air of disapproval on her face before she returned to the magazine she'd been reading.

Marcus rested an arm on a rack of books above Emily's head. His lips curved into a devilish grin. He was obviously enjoying the girl's awkward verbiage while appreciating her aunt's, no doubt, feigned inattention to their whispers. She was far enough away that she couldn't have heard their conversation but she was aware of his movements. Fortunately, no one else but the shopkeeper was in the store.

"Miss Hughes, I am thoroughly impressed. You may have come upon a workable solution, saving us both from enduring more of our aunts' meddling."

Emily loosened the death grip on the book she held and let out a relieved sigh. "My lord, I assure you, I shall not impose too much on your time."

"First, might I suggest that you call me Marcus, and may I call you Emily? That alone should set our aunts' hearts aflutter."

"It would clearly be improper, my lord, to call you by your given name so soon. Indeed, it is appropriate for you to use mine."

"I respect your sense of propriety. In time, you might reconsider," Marcus said, his voice soft, caressing. "Our aunts are the dearest of friends. In their presence I doubt it would appear improper to them."

Before Emily could react to his rakish behavior, the rustle of skirts turned their attention.

Marcus offered Emily's aunt a welcoming smile as she joined them.

"Mrs. Fenning." Marcus nodded. "It appears both Miss Emily and I have an interest in poetry."

Marcus turned his gaze on Emily and flashed a crooked grin. "I was wondering, ma'am, if I might call tomorrow and take your niece for a ride through the park. Of course, you and my aunt are invited as chaperones."

"How lovely," Delia spouted too loudly, covering her mouth when the shopkeeper hushed her.

"I shall call at three, then?"

Delia nodded and smiled warmly. Marcus turned his gaze back toward Emily and gave her a roguish wink, before guiding them to the front entrance of the shop. He waited while Emily purchased the poetry book before accompanying them to her aunt's carriage. After helping the older woman into the carriage, he enclosed Emily's hand in his own and held it longer than was necessary before releasing it. "Until tomorrow."

Emily nodded with narrowed eyes, a blush rising from her neck up to her cheekbones. She turned away quickly and stepped into the carriage, her mind reeling.

Had she really asked an earl of the realm to participate in a ruse?

ONCE THE LADIES were off, Marcus walked the remaining distance to his club, his mind marveling at his encounter with Mrs. Fenning's niece. He could find no reason not to enjoy a fling with the country girl. The pretense might lead to a brief affair, one that would carry him through the remainder of the Season without having to deal with more of his aunt's good intentions. The girl's boldness might surface in other more intimate areas as well, he mused.

As he rounded the corner near his club, his fencing partner approached from the opposite direction.

"I say, Marcus, you look to be in good spirits this afternoon," Andrew Forrester said as they climbed the steps together.

"In good enough spirits to wallop you today."

"Want to make a wager on that?" Forrester joked, slapping Marcus on the back. "As I remember, you left our last game with your tail between your legs."

"Ha, I was dipping rather deep the night before, wasn't up to my usual finesse," Marcus countered as the two men nodded to other members and walked to the fencing room.

"If memory serves me," Forrester said, "you had woken up that morning with Lady Eliza Dunkirk in one of Lord Hadley's guestrooms. You had to climb out a window and down a thorny rosebush to reach the ground before old Dunkirk caught you with his wife."

"I had to have been skunked." Marcus tossed Forrester one of the chest pads hanging on the wall. "Otherwise, I would have left Hadley's party after my first encounter with Eliza in the servant closet."

"I suspect your aunt ambushed you into going to the Hadley's party to meet another one of her hopefuls," Forester taunted as he donned his fencing gear.

"True," Marcus grimaced. "When I disappeared with Eliza and did not return, she assumed I had left." Marcus tested his sword, whipping it in the air. "My aunt is insufferable. She is determined to get me leg shackled before the end of the Season."

"Your time is running out, Deming. Soon it may be my duty as a loyal friend to encourage you to marry."

Marcus glared, dropping the sword to his side. He and Forrester usually aided and abetted each other's attempts to avoid matchmaking matrons.

As childhood friends, they'd been partners in enough mischievous pranks to drive their parents to distraction. As they grew older they continued to help each other out of personal dilemmas.

In an especially memorable situation in childhood, they had both created havoc at one of the Deming family's summer picnics. An old maid who disliked children and shooed them off like garden pests, became their victim. Both boys decided a few days before the event to play a trick on the woman.

They scoured their fathers' barns for mice and collected half a dozen of them, securing them in a cage. On the day of the picnic, the boys waited for the woman to fill her plate with a mound of food, as was her custom. Hiding behind a bush near her seat, they released the mice just as she prepared to sit. As the mice scurried by her, a couple of them disappearing beneath the hem of her gown, she screeched, dropped her plate, lifted her gown and ran around in circles. The other startled guests stared in bewilderment at the woman's antics and not on the grass beneath them.

The boys nearly fell over each other, laughing with delight before racing from the scene. In fear of discovery, they tore around the side of the house to hide only to run directly into Marcus' father. With the cage in Marcus' hand and the guilty looks on both faces, they knew they were in deep trouble. For their prank, the boys received tanned behinds and were forbidden to see each other the remainder of the summer.

Marcus, however, could still recall not only his father's stern scolding with his mother in the background, but the quirk of a grin on his father's lips that he'd tried unsuccessfully to hide as he railed against his son's behavior.

"Has your aunt chosen another dizzy-eyed damsel for you to dodge?" Forrester's voice held mockery as he chose a sword and pulled down his face shield.

Marcus adjusted his chest padding and considered his friend's question. He thought of the very unusual and interesting Miss Hughes and the game they'd planned to play.

"I shall not be dodging any more dim-witted women this Season." Marcus flipped down his shield. "For the moment, Andy, I suggest you do the dodging."

"JENNINGS, IS MY aunt ready yet? It is nearly three."

"I believe that she is in the final stages of preparation."

Marcus knew what that meant. She probably could not decide what bonnet to wear or the color of her shawl. He had enjoyed a pleasant breakfast with his aunt and even had the patience to listen to her prattle on about her friend's niece and how thrilled she was that Marcus planned the afternoon outing. In fact, she was glowing.

"Please tell her that I shall be waiting by the carriage and if she does not present herself in the next ten minutes, I will be forced to leave without her."

"Yes, my lord."

Marcus grinned as his butler scurried off. Jennings had been in the Deming's employ since Marcus was a small child and he seemed old even then, most likely because of his prematurely gray hair and frail build. Now, the long, thin strands of white hair that remained were swept neatly over his mostly baldpate and his small stature gave him the appearance of being elfish.

Marcus turned his thoughts back to Miss Hughes and their conversation the day before. He found her to be remarkably discerning and her idea positively ingenious. The girl had a keen mind and even more intriguing, she had made no attempt to draw him into her favor as a candidate for marriage. To his astonishment, though gratifying, he found her disinterest a bit disconcerting. Ignoring the feeling, he rose to leave.

Within a half hour, they were on their way. When they arrived at Mrs. Fenning's residence, Agatha opted to wait in the carriage while Marcus collected the ladies. To his surprise, Emily greeted him at the door.

"Miss Emily, you are the picture of springtime

today." He reached for her hand, bending to brush a kiss on her palm.

Emily pulled her hand away, quickly raising it to brush a curl from her forehead, a curl that did not appear out of place. "Thank you, my lord."

"Marcus, remember?"

"Lord Deming," Emily responded, crossing her arms. She looked behind her, knowing it was improper for her to be conversing privately with a gentleman without a proper chaperon, even with his aunt so close. "I wanted a few minutes to speak with you alone before my aunt joined us," she murmured, her eyes still darting about.

"I could not be more pleased."

Emily did not miss his overconfident tone or his rakish grin. She looked at him suspiciously. "Please, I just wanted to thank you for agreeing to my idea. I beg you not to take my bold behavior as anything but my resolve to avoid being paraded before the *ton*."

Marcus brought a finger to her chin and smiled devilishly. "I am at your service."

Emily brushed his hand away while attempting to ignore that same shiver within her she had experience before in his presence. "Lord Deming, being in your company should be enough to keep my aunt content. I would appreciate it if you would save your rakish behavior for your more appreciative liaisons.

"If we are to appear captivated by one another for our aunts' benefit, you might be more accepting of my affectionate posturing," he said teasingly as his eyes traveled over her outfit of pale yellow muslin gown with a matching fichu.

"I suggest then that you save your flirtatious posturing for when we are in the presence of our aunts."

"I bow to your common sense, Miss Emily." He waved a hand in a flourish while his eyes glinted with humor.

Emily lowered her lashes and focused on retying the neatly secured ribbons of her bonnet.

MARCUS' LIPS SLANTED in satisfaction. He was enjoying the fact that he had flustered her prim façade.

He had been in the presence of more fashionable women who wore elegant carriage dresses to promenade about Hyde Park. Emily, in her simplicity and straightforwardness, charmed him. She carried no pretentious airs yet, she was willing to participate in a pretense.

"Good afternoon, Marcus," Mrs. Fenning said as she entered the hall. "I see my niece has kept you company." She raised a brow to Emily. "I went to your room to collect you, my dear, hardly expecting that you would be the first to greet Lord Deming."

Marcus sensed that her aunt had hoped Emily would make a late entrance as young ladies were urged to do. "I was delighted to be welcomed by your lovely niece. Shall we be on our way?"

Marcus walked to the door without delay to avoid more awkwardness. He ushered the women to his open carriage, its black door embossed with his family seal. His footman held the door open as

Marcus offered Mrs. Fenning a hand. After helping Emily into the carriage, he sat beside her, both of them facing their aunts. Once they were on their way, the aunts conversed continually, pausing only to wave to acquaintances.

"Such a perfect day," Emily said, gazing out of the carriage. She had barely looked his way since they'd left the Fenning townhouse. They were riding down Rotten Row in line with dozens of other carriages of varying sizes and styles. Horseback riders rode behind or weaved through the throng of coaches while other visitors strolled about on paths, arm in arm. All were taking advantage of the first day of sunshine after a number of days of rain and fog.

At first Emily appeared stiff and uncomfortable, but as they drove on she settled back into her seat. She wore a pleasant expression, often breaking into a bright smile as she looked about the park.

Marcus felt calm in her presence and enjoyed the occasional brush of her arm against his as the carriage swayed at bends in the road. In fact, he couldn't remember that last time he had felt such exhilaration. His reaction must certainly be the fun of outwitting his aunt.

"Oh, look!" Emily exclaimed gesturing toward a nearby pond. She pointed with gloved hands to a mother duck leading her tiny ducklings. "Why there must be close to a dozen of the little fledglings."

Marcus signaled his driver to stop so the party could watch the ducklings obediently follow their mother across the grass toward the water. He grinned as he watched Emily's animated expressions as she counted each one.

"Yes, there are ten and, oh, there's the father meeting them at the pond's edge. See how that last little one is trailing behind his siblings." Emily burst into laughter as it nearly fell over trying to keep up.

Marcus grin widened at the sound of her laughter. He was suddenly glad the ride brought her such pleasure. There was no doubt in his mind her joy was genuine and not meant to flatter him.

As they made their second trip around the park, he had to remind himself that today's outing was part of a pretense. She was saving him from his aunt's meddling and as she pointed out, saving herself as well.

Why is the girl uninterested in finding a suitable match? At the moment, he could find nothing about her that might be an obstacle to her marrying well.

The sound of bubbling laugher caused him to snap out of his thoughts. Three small children being chased by a tiny, shaggy-haired dog, giggled delightfully. However, it was Emily's radiant countenance as she observed the children that delighted him.

After driving only a short distance, he heard his name called out from behind.

"Say there, Lord Deming. Escorting the ladies about this afternoon?" Lord Haverly boomed as he led his horse to the side of Marcus' carriage. Tipping his hat to the aunts, he settled his eyes on Emily and lifted heavy brows. "A new face? Where have you been hiding this exquisite creature?"

Marcus forced a smile of greeting. "Miss Hughes is visiting her aunt. Miss Hughes, Lord Haverly," he said in a clipped voice. He found Haverly to be an annoying gossip.

Emily eyes widened at the appearance of the extravagantly dressed man on the large, sable brown thoroughbred. His shirt collar rose so high that he appeared stiff necked in the saddle. A double chin rested on its highest peak. The lapels and sleeves of his bright-green waistcoat that strained about his large waist were adorned with floral embroidery, and his leather boots were unusually patterned from the deepest brown to various golden hues. Several fob ribbons and other ornaments hung from the pocket that held his gold watch.

She nodded and offered a friendly smile. For the next fifteen minutes, Haverly carried the conversation. He asked questions and often answered his own queries, chortling loudly at some of his comments that he found especially humorous.

When Marcus finally broke free of his chatter and drove off, Emily turned to look at the aunts who were both clamping their lips together to stifle their laughter.

"My dear, you will find London full of surprises and eccentric individuals," Delia said as one of her hands held down her peacock-feathered bonnet.

"Eccentric is not the only word to describe Haverly," Marcus muttered. "He happens to be the worst gossip in London. I saw the look in his eyes when he realized your father is of the landed gentry. Expect to receive an avalanche of invitations by tomorrow morning."

"I am certain he can find other more interesting things to gossip about," Emily said with a careless shrug of her shoulders.

"You are too modest. He found you fascinating and asked enough questions to conclude family wealth and connections. He will pass the word, especially to mothers and aunts looking for a match for shy sons and obstinate nephews."

"He is quite right, my dear," Agatha agreed. "Delia, your niece's visit may create a stir."

Marcus felt suddenly irritated, realizing he had been looking forward to keeping Emily to himself. He'd noticed that she seemed to be unimpressed by even the noblest in polite society or by the high-fashioned ladies, some whose demeanors, despite the heat of the day, remained icy during their introductions. Emily seemed to have no idea of her allure or that she was being looked upon as a prime competitor, and in Haverly's eyes, a very eligible newcomer.

After another turn around the park and brief encounters, they left for the short ride home.

"Such a pleasant afternoon," Agatha chirped as the carriage came to a stop in front of the Fenning residence.

"And what an ideal environment for members of the *ton* to see Emily and to make her acquaintance," Delia added.

Marcus noted the sudden stiffening of Emily's

posture and the thinning of her lips.

When the aunts finished proclaiming the outing a success, Emily turned to Marcus. "Thank you for your invitation, my lord. It was a most enjoyable afternoon."

"I look forward to seeing you again."

Though Emily smiled in appreciation, Marcus saw that her aunt's comment had dampened her spirits. The woman most definitely was averse to the *ton*'s attentions.

After bidding Miss Hughes and her aunt a good evening, he rode the rest of the way home, half listening to his aunt's review of the afternoon and her effusive praise of Emily. Aunt Agatha did not need to convince him to see her again.

He had already begun to plan another excursion.

Chapter Five

MARCUS TOSSED ASIDE his paperwork, unable to concentrate. His thoughts were on the past two and half weeks spent courting Emily. He had taken her to the opera, art galleries, Kew gardens and three rides through the park, always with one or both aunts as chaperones. The pretense of a courtship was succeeding remarkably well. The aunts had ceased their matchmaking overtures and were beaming with satisfaction and anticipation.

Emily appeared to enjoy being with him and on occasion, he had wondered if she may have thought up the pretense as a game to draw him in. Other women had used a variety of tactics to trap him in the past. The thought of her using womanly wiles to snare him did not arise from her actions as much as from his reactions to her. Even when he chose to be with another woman, she invaded his thoughts.

He left his study and walked toward the rear veranda to breathe in some fresh air and to clear his mind. As he approached the open doors, he heard the aunts' voices. He had forgotten that Mrs. Fenning was coming for tea.

When he heard his name mentioned, he realized that he was the topic of conversation. Crossing his arms, he leaned against the wall out of the ladies' view. Might be helpful information, he thought.

"Delia, I do believe that my nephew and your niece may be the match of the Season," Agatha said, her face glowing as she sipped her iced tea.

"You could be reading more into their relationship than might be true."

"Come now. He has actively courted her over the past two weeks. Why just this morning he said he was planning a trip to Vauxhall Gardens. He may have already sent a note in that regard to your niece." Agatha paused, her lips drawing up into a bow and her pale eyes expressing delight. "He wanted me to tell you that we are both invited as chaperones."

"Splendid, I haven't been there in ages."

Marcus began to turn away, but paused at his aunt's next words.

"You must agree that they are attracted to each other."

Marcus watched Delia's reaction as she settled back in her chair.

"Your nephew has been a constant visitor and I must say quite charming. Emily appears pleased by his attentions, though she shows no signs of the giddiness that I remember at that age when a handsome suitor came to call. Regardless, what concerns me is that she has shown no interest in attending events where she might meet other available gentlemen, and the Season's parties will soon be coming to an end."

"Perhaps she needn't meet other gentlemen if she has settled her sights on Marcus. He is perfectly suitable," Agatha said as she plucked at the sleeve of her hyacinth blue dress.

Marcus grinned at his aunt's loyalty to him.

"Now, my dear, don't get snippy. Marcus is an admirable catch, indeed, and he and my niece make an attractive couple, but you do know how he tends to... he may not be as serious as you imagine."

"I admit that Marcus has shown a lack of interest in settling down to marriage," Agatha agreed, her eyelids lowered, "and he has been known to be a bit of a rake among polite society... "

"You are being too kind," Delia interrupted. "He has been dallying with a number of women's affections since he was old enough to realize that they had something to offer that his other sporting activities lacked."

Marcus nearly chuckled aloud at Delia's insinuation.

"I believe the right one had not come along," Agatha said, her voice clipped.

"Perhaps you are correct, but Emily Grace has not given any indication to me that she has become starry eyed. True, she has shown preference toward Marcus' invitations and avoided others and that concerns me."

Marcus rubbed his chin, feeling suddenly discomfited that Emily showed no signs of endearment toward him when they were apart. His aunt's voice drew him back to their conversation.

"Why in heavens should it concern you? She could hardly do better than marrying an earl." Agatha sniffed with annoyance and brushed a crumb from her skirt.

"My dear, I simply want my niece to be open to every opportunity before she leaves London. Her father will be less than pleased if I do not make the proper introductions. You must understand my position."

Agatha continued brushing at her skirt, her expression softening.

"And she must attend Lady Whittington's ball. It is the climax of the Season, after all! The invitation came in the mail yesterday."

"Ay, yes. We received ours as well." Agatha's eyes brightened. "Indeed, she must attend. No doubt Marcus will escort her and ask for the first dance."

"Indeed... What are you planning to wear?"

Having heard enough, Marcus strode back to his study. *Emily's plan seems to be working perfectly.* Since her arrival, his aunt hadn't pleaded with him once to attend another matchmaking function. She even scolded her friend for suggesting that he might not be sincere. He and Emily were succeeding in the ploy and it would be over soon. He should feel elated at the prospect.

As he walked over to his desk, his mood grew more somber. He picked up the note he had received from Emily that morning, thanking him for the roses he'd sent a day earlier. He ignored the tender feelings that the author of the note he held in his hand evoked.

If I could see the beauty she holds dear,
Would I choose her fancy for my own?
Or when youth fades will I succumb to

wearing purple bonnets as I age?

EMILY REREAD THE lines she had penned as she sat at her writing desk in her bedchamber. She smiled as she recalled her aunt's enthusiasm over her purchase of a bright purple hat with clusters of flowers and glittering feathers. Her aunt felt it complemented her silver hair. Emily's attempt to draw her eye to a less showy one proved fruitless. Delia would not be deterred. From the moment her aunt spotted it, she was in love.

She and her aunt had spent a good part of the day at the seamstress for the final fittings for two more gowns. After leaving the dressmaker, Aunt Delia insisted on buying her a new riding outfit since Lord Deming had offered to take Emily riding.

She found it hard to believe that three weeks had flown by since she'd arrived in London. Each day had been eventful with shopping, social visits or outings with Lord Deming. He was carrying through with their ruse expertly and with appropriate finesse, even sending her a variety of floral bouquets, a spring bouquet one day, roses the next.

Tomorrow evening they would be going to Vauxhall Gardens and she planned to wear one of her new gowns. Perhaps the cerulean blue and then the gold one for Saturday, she decided.

Although Lord Deming had been agreeable to her proposal, she had not expected him to be so accommodating, or that she would feel such an unsettling attraction.

Most distracting to her purpose.

Yet her lips formed a wistful smile when she thought of him. She thought of how the corners of his eyes crinkled when he laughed and how his lips curved into a lazy, lop-sided grin.

Best not to dwell on such dangerous musings, she reprimanded herself.

Her thoughts turned to her father. She had yet to receive a letter from him. She'd been angry at him for forcing her to come to London. After all, he'd practically pushed her out the door. In truth she'd used every excuse imaginable to avoid leaving. She regretted her angry noncompliance. A nagging worry remained. He still hadn't looked well when she left, though he insisted that he was improving daily. What if he had not been honest with her about how he was feeling?

Was her cousin Willard still making his weekly visits? She could not help but think he had begun buzzing around like a vulture when he'd heard his uncle was unwell.

Was she any less guilty than her cousin? He might be playing the devoted nephew to ensure his future inheritance, but she was deceiving both her father and her aunt in her collusion with the earl. A tinge of guilt caused her to wince before she lifted her chin obstinately. *They may believe they know what is good for me, but it is my life!*

Having no other poetic inspirations, she stood and walked over to the window. She pulled a pink rose from a vase set on a nearby table. While rubbing the soft, velvety petals against her cheek, she stared out the window.

The pretense with Marcus had been an ideal

plan to avoid meeting possible suitors, but she hadn't felt as detached as she'd expected, especially when his blue eyes sparkled with a hint of mischief. She felt certain her aroused feelings were simply a woman's natural reactions to an attractive male's attentions. She was facing the consequences of their ploy—consequences she had not considered.

She chastised herself for allowing her mind to wander to him once more. Her thoughts went to her mother's words, words engrained in her since she'd felt the first bloom of young womanhood. Men's adoration during courtship was fleeting. Once they conquered, their eyes wandered to another conquest.

"There shall be no conquest, Mother. I will not walk that path." She returned the rose to its vase. Fluffing her hair back, she willed away the warm feelings that thoughts of Marcus stirred within her. A nap before dinner might help to curb her conflicting thoughts.

Lying on her bed, she gazed at the gold-scrolled border that surrounded the ornate plaster ceilings. She tried to congratulate herself for accomplishing her goal. Instead, trepidation washed over her.

She twisted onto her side, clutching her pillow snugly to her breast. She'd found it more difficult to subdue unwanted desires. Desires best embraced or scorned in her poetry, not in her life. Thankfully, her mother's warnings that surfaced like ghostly scripts in her mind kept her from succumbing to the earl's charm.

MARCUS SURPRISED HIS guests by hiring a boat to ferry them over to Vauxhall Gardens the next evening. On their arrival they found the place booming with activity. Emily was in awe, especially by the thousands of gas lamps that hung from trees along the promenade and throughout the vast gardens. Bands were set up where couples could dance or sing along with the musicians. Minstrels walked along the Grand Walk serenading the crowd. The aunts expressed their delight, though before an hour was out, they were ready to find a place to rest.

Marcus had hired one of the upper-level supper boxes where waiters were available to serve drinks and take dinner orders. He ordered wine and a light fare of ham and cheeses. While they ate, he pondered how he might find some time to be alone with Emily. Though she surprised him with her daring when it came to their ruse, she followed other rules of etiquette. She wasn't going to take a chance of being compromised and, perhaps, forced to marry. He looked at the aunts who were both waving their fans and watching the goings-on below.

He had been planning this night for a week. Though he'd enjoyed their day trips, the thought of luring her into his arms and feeling the soft skin he wanted to touch in the most intimate of places had kept him awake at night. He wasn't surprised that despite her daring in suggesting the pretense, her behavior was most chaste. If one of the aunts even appeared inattentive as a chaperon, Emily appeared anxious. He understood. If she wanted to maintain her independence and remain single, her reputation must remain stainless. Unfortunately for him, she aroused a disturbing hunger. It was lust, of course. They'd been together often and she was lovely.

He was a man, after all.

Beneath her prim behavior, he detected a cloaked passion he wanted to be the one to uncloak in the most imaginative of ways. He loved a challenge. It was as simple as that. When he satisfied his curiosity, the pull he felt to be near her would diminish.

"Might I give Emily a tour of the gardens?" He asked finally.

The aunts looked from one to the other, neither appearing to want to leave the comfort of the box. "Oh, look, Agatha, Lady Fipps is coming our way," Delia beamed, adjusting her purple feathered bonnet and squaring her shoulders. "I have wanted to ask her opinion on my roses. She is such an expert on their care. Do you mind accompanying Emily?"

Agatha glared at her before rising from her seat. "Indeed, Emily must see the gardens." She followed Marcus and Emily as they descended the steps, stopping briefly to greet Lady Fipps, only to have her nephew wave her on. She followed at a respectable distance to Marcus' relief.

He folded Emily's hand in the crook of his arm and led her along the promenade, turning on to one of the less populated walkways.

As a Hayden concerto played in the background, they paused occasionally to admire splashing fountains and statues surrounded by fragrant flower gardens bursting with color. His chatty aunt began immediate conversations with other onlookers at each stop.

Rows of tulips, hyacinth and bluebells arranged in perfect order caused Emily to sigh with pleasure. While she gazed transfixed at the magnificent displays, Marcus watched her, mesmerized.

He had been with women who laughed airily as if it were expected in a light moment, pouted when disappointed like a spoiled child or behaved coquettishly to draw attention. Emily enjoyed the moment without making attempts to please or manipulate the situation to her benefit. Yes, she had suggested the pretense but he didn't feel like she played a role when they were together. If she was acting, he thought, she could be on stage. As he observed her, Emily's expression became wistful.

"Your thoughts seem far away at the moment."

"I was thinking of my father. His flower gardens are exceptional as well. Even the seedlings in his greenhouse flourish under his care. Though of late, he depends more on our gardener. Father has been quite absorbed in writing his second book on horticulture and his gardening techniques," she said with a note of pride before looking away. "I wonder at the state of his health since I have been away."

"I hear anxiety in your words. Are you planning to return to the country soon?"

"I plan to broach the subject of my departure

with Aunt Delia in the next few days. She has begged me to stay longer. I have realized that in my determination to avoid London that I have missed out on becoming closer to my aunt."

"Then why not extend your visit?" Marcus asked, surprised at his immediate response to her talk of leaving.

"I am concerned about my father. He was not feeling well when I left. He has always exuded such energy and life despite his age. He has put his malaise off to a mild stomach ailment, but he had lost weight. I finally received a letter from him today. Though his words expressed that he is well, they seemed to be chosen too carefully."

Marcus lowered his eyes. There it was again, even in her words. As she felt deeply about the beauty before her, she also read more through her heart's discernment, than from mere words or actions.

"You may be reading too much into his letter."

"Perhaps, he does write that he is feeling better. He has a tendency to overwork, either on his book or in his gardens. I shall feel better when I see for myself that his vitality has returned."

"I understand." Marcus took her arm, attempting to lead her on but Emily held back, waiting for his aunt to note their departure. Marcus grimaced while Aunt Delia finished her chitchat.

"You are obviously very close to your father," he said as they finally moved on.

"After my mother died, we grew closer. Before her death, he tended to close himself off in his study for hours on end or go off to London or to some other haunt. He seldom travels now and he has become more open to sharing his interests."

While Marcus listened, a wave of melancholy caused his chest to tighten. Emily's relationship with her father after her mother's death had turned out so differently than his own experience.

When his mother died, his father withdrew into himself. He locked his wife's bedchamber, leaving it as a memorial to her, and locked himself in his library. He seemed barely aware that his son grieved too, not only for the loss of his mother, but for the loss of his father's presence in his life. His father cast off most of his previous association and spent hours buried in one book after another. It appeared to Marcus that the books were used as shields to avoid conversation. No, they seemed more of a way to avoid facing the world without his wife in it. His father eventually succumbed, within a year of his mother's death.

Marcus believed he died of a broken heart. He still felt the anger and loss. He swore he would never love a woman so deeply that he could lose himself and desert his issue as his father had done.

"Are you all right? You looked suddenly sad," Emily asked, tilting her face up to his.

Marcus drew his thoughts back to the present. "I am perfectly fine." He gave her a reassuring smile. "You were telling me about your father. You spend a great deal of time with him?"

"I enjoy our daily chats and working with him in the gardens and..." She paused and brought a hand to her lips.

"Yes, you were going to say something else?"

"Reading," Emily replied, perhaps too abruptly. "We both love to read."

Marcus slanted his eyes toward her. He wondered if she used books to avoid looking at her own future, particularly a marriageable one.

"I find no shame in admitting that I am a bit of a bluestocking. We often read Shakespeare's plays together and argue our varied interpretations. Just before I left we were rereading Hamlet and arguing over the prince's irrational behaviors. We become quite adamant in our opinions, while at the same time enjoying our debates."

"And you thought that would shock me?"

"I am well aware that men are not always pleased with women who enjoy intellectual discussions or pursuits."

Marcus laughed. "And since you have no desire to wed, I assume that my opinion would be the least of your concerns."

"You are correct, of course. The single life offers the advantage of pursuing interests that a husband might scorn."

"Scorn? What an interesting word. I find it difficult to imagine you doing anything that might be so disapproving unless, of course, you desired to step into a man's shoes." One side of Marcus' lips lifted in a sardonic grin.

"And take on what would be considered a man's occupation?" Emily glared, pursing her lips.

"How on earth did we get on this subject? I realize you are an intelligent and independent woman. Any gentleman you might choose in the future would find you quite adequate."

"Adequate?" She winced. "I shan't be satisfied with adequate. If I planned to marry, and I don't, I would expect equal consideration in all matters and appreciation for my talents."

At that, a slow, crooked grin spread over Marcus' face. His eyes lowered to her lips and down to her low-cut gown. "I am certain your talents would be highly appreciated."

Emily blushed before giving him a scolding glance. Her eyes darted back to Agatha who'd met a friend along the way. She was talking gaily behind them and appeared oblivious to Marcus' flirtatious behavior.

Marcus gave an amused smile as they followed a narrow path cloaked in greenery. Turning around a bend, he spotted a row of benches. He paused, looking back at his aunt, who caught his eye. As he led Emily to one of the more secluded benches, Agatha and her companion sat a few benches away, still in sight of them. Emily waved to his aunt before looking about. He noted that his aunt waved back and immediately returned to her chatter.

He'd earlier admired the perfect fit of the blue confection she wore. As they strolled, the overdress of silk netting that wafted in the mild breeze did nothing to hide the way the blue silk beneath clung to her curves. The soft lighting added emphasis and allure. He turned his gaze up to the silky curls that framed her face. He wanted to pull out the pins that held the ringlets in place.

"You look especially lovely tonight, Emily." When she turned her eyes to his and lingered, he found himself immersed in them. The lighting caused her eyes to appear a deeper green, but it was more than just the color. When she looked at him, he felt that she was looking into his soul. What was she thinking? Most women he had met appeared to pose when they drew into conversation with him, as if they had practiced a specific gaze or an alluring expression.

He wondered how he appeared to her. Odd thought, he mused as he blinked and dropped his gaze. Seated, her cleavage was even more exposed.

Emily lowered her lashes and wrapped her light shawl more tightly about her.

"Our ruse has been extremely effective, you do agree?" Marcus brushed a curl away from her cheek, only to have it spring back. His thumb trailed down toward her chin and brushed gently over her lower lip.

"Yes... even more so than I had hoped." Emily's voice caught in her throat as her eyes darted towards his aunt. She averted his stare, her eyes following a butterfly that alighted on a nearby flowering bush. "My aunt has only demonstrated mild insistence that I attend a few affairs. I am truly grateful for your cooperation."

With his back twisted away from his aunt, Marcus waited for her to turn her face toward his. "Your eyes, they appear to absorb far more than common sight and your hair..." He lifted a curl and tucked it behind her ear before tracing the line of her chin with one finger. "I especially like it when it is not all tied up with ribbons and hairpins."

EMILY DARED TO look into his eyes and then wished she hadn't. They looked darker, more dangerous. She knew she should turn the conversation to their mission, but his words felt like lush velvet to her ears. He aroused her as if the butterfly she had observed was now flitting about in the pit of her stomach. She moved away toward the edge of the bench. His aunt could certainly see them, but she was more engrossed in her conversation than her nephew's actions.

Earlier, she had nearly told him about writing poetry. She often shared her writings with her father, but she had found that others looked upon her writing as a mere hobby, one to toss off after marriage or visit on occasion. She feared the earl too, might trivialize her passion.

Marcus drew closer, his lips inches from hers. She really needed to regain control of herself. The situation was getting out of hand. Fortunately, they were away from the watchful eyes of society, but his aunt was not being as observant as Emily hoped. She inched closer to the edge of the bench and nearly fell off the edge.

"Do not fear. I will not compromise you," Marcus teased. "But evening is upon us. The moonlight hides much and my aunt is only a few feet away."

"Yes, and paying little attention to your rakish behavior."

"Damn." This time he slid away from her.

Loud laughter had erupted along the nearby path. Couples were strolling too near to where they sat. Emily failed to notice that her wrap had fallen to the ground behind the bench.

"I... I believe that you may be carrying our ruse too far," Emily blurted out in a harsh whisper. "We need only to appear to our aunts that we have an interest in each other, nothing more."

"And my aunt is looking at us right now and smiling. I believe we are succeeding quite well. Further, I don't believe you are as immune to passion as you pretend. The look I saw in your eyes just a few moments ago was quite telling."

Color rose to Emily's cheeks at the truth of his words. Confused thoughts flew about in her mind like a flock of birds fluttering about on windblown branches. Taking a deep breath, she searched for a response. "I suspect it is in our primal natures to give into thoughtless behavior on occasion," she said in a more measured tone as she rose quickly from her seat. "We should seek out our aunts."

Marcus adjusted his cravat and stood, glaring at her. "Our primal nature?" He shook his head. "Indeed, we should return." He reached down and picked up her shawl. "Forgive me for taking advantage of the situation." He wrapped the shawl over her stiffened shoulders.

"I ask that it not happen again," Emily said more primly than she felt. She also doubted that he was sorry. Turning from him, she trotted off toward their chaperon who watched them while continuing her conversation. In two long strides, he reached her and grasped her arm. "I suggest that you slow down and appear as if you are enjoying yourself. We do not want to cause undue gossip, now do we?"

Emily slowed her steps while doing her best to rein in her flustered feelings.

Agatha stood quickly, as did her friend. "My dears, returning already? My friend Adelaide has been entertaining me with the latest gossip, but we must be on our way. We'll be right behind you."

"I must say, I am mystified that you choose not to marry," Marcus said as they rounded the path. "You possess all the attributes. You are well bred, intelligent, attractive… " Marcus gripped her arm more firmly, causing their steps to slow. He gave her a rakish grin. "And passionate."

She glared at him, her complexion reddening. "I have other interests," she said pertly. "And why do you have an aversion toward marriage? Ladies we have encountered flutter their lashes when you greet them, obviously eager for your attentions. In your position, no doubt, you have your pick of the loveliest in society. You must desire an heir."

"Ah, you have voiced my Achilles' heel. Yes, I desire an heir and, most likely in a year or two, I will choose a wife, one who is suitable to my station and undemanding of constant attention."

Emily huffed at his arrogance. "What you are saying is that you prefer a docile wife who meets your qualifications and allows you to do as you please." Her thoughts went to the coldness she had observed in her parents' marriage. She doubted her mother or father were aware of its effect on her. Had she ever observed a resolution to their issues or a display of love and loyalty? Marcus had just proclaimed his view of marriage and confirmed her mother's warnings. He wanted a marriage of convenience to procure an heir. *Does he even consider his future wife's needs?*

"And what of love?" Emily blurted, immediately wishing she could take back her question.

Marcus gave a jeering laugh. "Love is a weak man's downfall. Enough women desire envied positions in society and a few costly trinkets, not their husband's soul."

Emily gaped at him. "Do you actually believe that a man who marries for love will lose his soul?"

"Yes, his freedom, his allegiances and, perhaps, even his life, if he does not guard his heart."

A group of revelers strolled toward them, allowing her a few moments to digest his meaning. He had revealed his fear of love, not merely selfish pursuits as reasons to avoid a love match. She could think of no words in response. They were nearing the main thoroughfare where a crowd was gathered in front of a group of musicians. Marcus led her around them and to the spectator boxes.

"I enjoyed our stroll," he said with a half grin as they neared his reserved box.

Emily remained silent, still pondering his revealing words.

"I especially liked getting to know more about your passions," he whispered before delivering her to her aunt's side.

Chapter Six

A moment of weakness must not deter
my mind from its chosen path,
or create allure so great,
I thwart my heart's desire
and slow my gait…

EMILY BROUGHT THE top of the quill to her lips as she reread words that revealed more the trepidation she felt than a surge of poetic inspiration.

"Are you feeling any better, Emily?"

Emily jerked her head about as her aunt entered the sitting room.

"Did I startle you, my dear?"

Emily set her pen down and acknowledged her aunt with a brief smile. "No, please, join me. I do feel better."

Delia stood over her and looked more closely at her niece. "Your eyes look tired this morning. Are you having trouble sleeping?"

Emily averted her eyes, setting the pen in its holder and closing her notebook. She wished that her aunt was less discerning. Having feigned illness, she had managed to avoid Marcus for a couple of days. She wasn't proud of her farce, she had already felt enough guilt over their ruse. Now she had used pretense again, this time to avoid him. The truth was she feared seeing him again.

She had placed herself in a vulnerable position and had come close to wanting him to kiss her, right there in the gardens. What if she had allowed the weakness and they'd been seen? All her plans would be ruined. She would be ruined. Why were women held so accountable for a misstep while men who tossed caution aside?

He sensed her weakness and nearly took advantage. He was a man, after all.

She had spent two sleepless nights thinking about their encounter, coming to the conclusion that her near indiscretion was a typical situation that foolish women placed themselves and which too often leads to regret. Women are ruled or cast away by the very men they thought would adore them. Hadn't her mother warned her with just those words?

"Emily?"

"Forgive me. I am rested enough. I just become too absorbed in my writing." She settled back into her chair and offered a more welcoming smile. "I have written my father to tell him that I shall be returning home in a few days. I have enjoyed my stay with you more than I ever thought possible. You have welcomed me with such warmth and affection."

Delia tilted her head, examining Emily's features. "I had hoped you would stay longer."

Emily rose to give her aunt a warm hug. "Thank you, but I do believe I am ready to return home for the summer."

Delia nodded, settling herself on a nearby settee. She picked up her needlework and studied the threads. "I was concerned that you might not be able to attend Lady Whittington's ball tomorrow evening."

"Yes, of course, the ball." Emily had given it little thought. She took a step toward the door. "I should talk to Maggie about preparations, and packing as well."

"After the ball we shall talk of your plans to return home. And there will be plenty of time for packing." Delia patted the seat beside her to encourage her niece to join her.

Emily sighed inwardly, knowing her aunt was not easily accepting her decision to leave. "Lady Whittington's ball must be quite a lavish affair."

"A finale to a fine Season. All of polite society shall be there, including gentlemen who have remained unattached," she said with a wink.

Emily returned a tolerating smirk at her aunt's attempt to humor her. "I shall prepare for my departure next week then."

Delia drew a needle through fabric. "And what of Lord Deming? I am delighted at his attentions toward you. Not that you do not deserve such chivalry. It is just that in the past he has avoided all his aunt's attempts to encourage a courtship." She took another stitch. "Indeed, it is not up to me to draw conclusions, but his visits and the flowers alone speak volumes." Securing the needle, she set her work down in her lap and turned to her niece. "He may be falling in love with you."

Emily's lashes flared up. *We most definitely have carried our pretense too far.* "I assure you that his feelings do not go beyond friendship."

Delia waved off her niece's words. "My dear, do not think I have missed how he looks at you." She paused to draw in a breath before releasing it with a sigh. "Obviously, I had hoped you would have been open to meeting other possible suitors, but Marcus is an admirable catch." She reached over to pat Emily's tightly clasped hands. "He may be ready to settle down to marriage."

Emily fought to remain calm. She should say something, tell her aunt the truth.

"I would not be surprised if he offers a proposal," Delia continued, as she pulled the needle out once more. "Your father would most certainly approve of his only daughter marrying an earl."

"Aunt Delia, Lord Deming has not given the slightest hint of anything more. He is most likely preparing to leave for his own country estate." Emily plucked at the folds of her skirt. "And then there is the ball. I plan to wear the gold gown. What do you think?"

Her aunt blinked at the abrupt change in subject. "Yes, indeed." Her brows drew together. "The gold is exquisite and the perfect gown for the affair." She returned to her embroidery, pulling the needle through the fabric with an extra tug.

THE NEXT DAY was a flurry of activity for the maids in the Fenning household. Gowns were pressed and accessories chosen while the ladies painstakingly primped for the grand occasion.

After Emily's lavender scented bath, Maggie set out her chemise and robe, encouraging her to rest on the veranda with her eyes closed while her hair dried. "You want your eyes to be bright and sparkling this evening, miss, but that thick hair of yours needs the afternoon breeze to dry it."

"I shall take your advice."

Once Emily was settled on the veranda, she closed her eyes. She must speak to Marcus and end the pretense.

When Maggie returned an hour later, she helped Emily dress, first, an ivory-colored silk slip, then layers of fine golden netting delicately hemmed with lace. Rosettes of tiny pearls intertwined with thin gold ribbon edged the low, square bodice and puffed sleeves adorned in lace barely capped her shoulders. The gown was the most exquisite Emily had ever owned. Maggie styled her hair with soft curls framing her face and combed the remaining waves back into an elegant chignon weaved with ribbons and pearls.

When her maid left the room, Emily took a final look in the mirror. She felt like a princess. The only problem was her prince was only a pretense, and she was a fool.

Marcus had proved her mother's declarations when he had proclaimed his views on marriage and the desire for a docile wife. He could be counted among the men who saw their wives as necessary only to meet their needs and not as loving partners. Thankfully she had seen him in the true light, and they had accomplished their goal.

Shouldn't she be more content?

Tonight was the final affair, and it was now too late in the Season for her aunt to attempt any other match. She could return home, resume the life she had become accustomed to and complete her poetry book without her father pestering her about marriage, at least for a time.

Maggie's rapid knock at her door interrupted Emily's musing. Lord Deming and his aunt had arrived. She pulled on her long gold gloves and took a deep breath to prepare herself emotionally for, perhaps, the last evening she would spend with Lord Deming.

"AGATHA, DARLING, YOU look splendid. I don't recall seeing that gown before," Delia said as Marcus and his aunt were ushered into the drawing room.

"I have been saving it for the finale of the Season." Agatha stood preening in her new periwinkle gown with a matching lace shawl. "You look lovely as well. The silver embroidery is stunning with the royal blue."

"I do love Madame Rochelle's handiwork. Would you believe this gown is from last Season? It was one of my favorites." Delia spread out the skirt to give attention to the embroidered flounce that matched the elegant stitching below the midriff. "I simply asked her to change it up a bit. She added the embroidery and cording and puffed up the sleeves in the newest style. I feel certain everyone will think it is brand new. And wait until you see my new turban! The ostrich feathers are dyed the same royal blue with touches of silver beading about the flowers. Oh, you must come with me while I put it on. I do want the feathers to sit properly. You don't mind, do you, Marcus? We shall only be a few minutes and I must see what is keeping Emily."

"I am accustomed to waiting for ladies on their way to a ball."

Aunt Agatha wrinkled her nose at him as she followed her friend out the door. Marcus nodded in amusement though his expression turned serious once they'd left the room.

Tonight was the final affair and it was time for Emily to return home. He was ready for her to leave, more than ready. The woman stirred up feelings that reached beyond mere lust. He didn't like it. Not one bit. He had been with more women than he could count and none of them had left him with such inner disquiet.

He paced about the room, grimacing. He doubted that she had been ill, as she had written in her notes, having declined his offers to take her for a carriage ride twice.

Emily's desire to avoid her aunt's matchmaking was genuine and though she may have let her guard down, she had as quickly created excuses to avoid him since.

As he wondered what her reaction would be to him this evening, he paused at a writing desk and glanced down casually. Recognizing Emily's handwriting, he picked up the paper. He was overstepping his bounds, but the enticing words caught his eye.

Dear love,
In dreams last night, I saw you,
by the stream where we first met.

You dropped a note sealed with a kiss,
within its shallow depth.
I heard you pray to bless its path,
and wend its way to me.
A love-filled message, a reminder,
of dear promises we made,
before I took my leave.

Hearing a sound in the hallway, Marcus laid the paper down. *No wonder she desires to return to the country. A suitor is there waiting for her.*

He had kept himself overly busy since his last night with Emily. Despite the busyness, he hadn't been able to stop thinking of her. Now, he faced the realization that she had been dishonest all along.

How ridiculous that I should harbor feelings of betrayal. We have acted out a sham for God's sake, nothing more. But she lied. Why?

He was forced to turn from his thoughts as the aunts entered, still chatting away. Emily followed behind them.

His breath caught when he saw her.

Her auburn hair was swept up and adorned with ribbons and pearls and her gown looked like spun gold. She was breathtaking. What had happened to the awkward girl he had first seen on the staircase? Despite the turmoil in his mind, he was captivated. "Emily." He gave a sweeping bow. "You shall be the loveliest woman at the ball," he said, his voice not betraying the ragged emotions suddenly raging within him.

"I could not agree more," Aunt Agatha chimed in, beaming, "I fear you shall need to hover close, Marcus, or she may be snatched away."

Marcus' thoughts flew to the note he had just

read and its implications. His eyes narrowed toward Emily. Her lashes were lowered and she seemed preoccupied with fluffing a flounce of gold netting.

"We should be on our way," he said abruptly. Without another word, he took his aunt's arm and urged her toward the door. Delia and Emily followed suit, both wearing a look of surprise at his sudden haste.

WHEN THEY ARRIVED at the Whittington's ball, Marcus noted Emily's expression as a mixture of awe and trepidation. The country parties could not hold a candle to this extravagant London affair with its ornate décor and crystal chandeliers sparkling overhead in the vast ballroom.

Women dressed in elegant gowns and bedecked with their most impressive jewels stood about in circles. Gentlemen dressed in long-tailed coats and their finest breeches either stood staunchly by their wives or gathered in their own small groups. The men who had managed to remain unattached stood apart gazing about, some rakishly leering at the younger ladies dressed in pastel colors trimmed with lace and ribbons.

Delia and Agatha drew Emily immediately into a circle of young women. Marcus chose to stand on the outskirts of the crowd and watch. He usually found these affairs dull at best, and they too often meant being corralled by anxious mothers.

Tonight proved no different.

While observing Emily across the room, he didn't see Lady Castleberry coming toward him with her daughter in tow until far too late. Worse the music was beginning. He had been so wrapped up in his dark mood on the way to the ball, he'd neglected to ask Emily for the first dance.

"Lord Deming, what a delight to see you. I ought to scold you, young man, for not attending my party last month. You were sorely missed!" Lady Castleberry's high-pitched voice nearly pierced his eardrums.

"Unfortunately, I had a previous engagement," Marcus said, his voice clipped.

"Eudora, you must tell Lord Deming about the grand time had by all," Lady Castleberry chimed as she tugged at her daughter's chubby arm. "Oh dear, the first dance has begun and neither of you have a partner. Perhaps you might escort Eudora onto the floor? After all, it was I who pulled her away from admiring glances when I spotted you."

Marcus had been taking careful steps back while Lady Castleberry warbled on in her abrasive tone. He found himself backed against a wall, a large ornate sconce digging into his back. He looked over Lady Castleberry's head only to see Emily being escorted onto the dance floor with the worst rake of the Season, Gregory Dunstan.

Forced to be gracious, he gave Eudora a weak smile. Her mother had maneuvered the poor girl directly in front of him so that the girl's large feet were nearly toe-to-toe with his boots and her décolletage only inches below his chin. Since the girl looked mortified at her mother's forwardness, he led her on to the dance floor.

When the dance ended, Eudora's mother was

nowhere to be seen. The second dance, a Cotillion, began before he spotted the mother hiding behind a large fern. Irritated with the woman's manipulation and angrier still that Emily was being taken onto the dance floor by another less than deserving partner, Marcus chose not to play the mother's game a second time. He tugged Eudora to her mother's side, bowed, and took off before she could engage him in further conversation.

As he made his way through the crowd, he was stopped and forced to be cordial to other acquaintances, including the provocative widow he had spent time with on occasion. He finally made it to the area where the aunts sat just as the second dance ended.

"Marcus, where have you been?" Agatha asked, wearing a scolding frown. "Our Emily is the belle of the ball. You shall have to vie for her attention tonight."

"Yes, it appears so," Marcus muttered, knowing too well what the fellows who were surrounding Emily must be thinking. Most of them had grown bored with the usual female attendees grasping for a match.

"I shall ask if she might like some air before another dance begins, if I might have your permission, Mrs. Fenning?"

"I am certain she would appreciate a walk on the balcony and I could use some fresh air," Delia said, fanning herself. "It is dreadfully warm in here."

"Indeed it is," Agatha sighed, "and you must not let that annoying Lady Castleberry force her daughter upon you again, Marcus. That girl of hers will never make a match if her mother doesn't stop meddling into her affairs."

Marcus rolled his eyes, aware that his aunt remained oblivious to her own meddling. He waited for Delia to rise, wishing that he could sneak off with Emily without her aunt in tow, but he knew Emily would not allow a secret rendezvous. That thought added to his anger. Obviously, she'd participated in rendezvous in the past with her secret lover.

At what point had he lost control of the evening? Emily's note flashed through his mind. He gritted his teeth. She had fooled him from the beginning. He had believed in her apathy toward marriage, had treated her with the utmost respect and bought into her attempts to avoid introductions.

Approaching the group, he nearly stepped on the foot of Lord Cummings who tried to gain Marcus' attention. Offering only a brief nod, Marcus drew to Emily's side, easing himself between her and Gregory Dunstan.

"Miss Hughes, perhaps you might like to take a stroll on the balcony? He asked, while turning his back to Dunstan.

Emily smiled, visibly relieved to see him and her aunt. "Yes, I would be most grateful. It is quite warm."

Dunstan, slanting his eyes at Marcus, would not be deterred. "Miss Hughes, may I have the honor of the next dance when you return?"

"She has already promised it to me," Marcus

snapped as he took Emily's arm and led her away. *Where did that come from?* He should allow her to be set upon by the worst of the rakes.

"Deming, where are you going with this lovely creature?" Andrew Forrester asked, blocking Marcus' way. "I have only just arrived and you have made claim to this lovely lady before I've had a chance to meet her."

"Forrester, this is not the time," Marcus muttered before regaining his manners and remembering that Emily's aunt was standing nearby. "Miss Emily Hughes has arrived from the country. And may I introduce her aunt as well, Mrs. Fenning." He lifted a palm toward the older woman who stood behind them." Ladies, Andrew Forrester. He is an old friend of mine from our school days."

"A pleasure to meet you, Mr. Forrester," Emily said with a smile while her aunt nodded in greeting.

"Miss Hughes is visiting her aunt in London. I have been showing them about. There you have it. Now if you will excuse us, the ladies are in need of some air," Marcus said a bit too sharply as he gestured toward the balcony doors.

"Afraid I might turn Miss Hughes' pretty head in my direction, Deming?" Forrester murmured to Marcus before returning his gaze to Emily. He bowed graciously. "Splendid to meet you, miss. I hope our paths cross again soon." He raised his eyes, offering a sheepish grin to her aunt whose expression reflected annoyance at his flirtatious manner.

"Pardon my friend, Mrs. Fenning. He has failed to outgrow his boyish behavior." Marcus gave Forrester a steely glare. "As I said, the ladies desire some air." Brushing past Forrester, he ignored his friend's mocking grin.

ONCE OUTSIDE, THEY walked to a quiet corner on the large balcony. Delia took a seat nearby where another chaperon was seated. Marcus rested his arms on the marble railings and stared out at the perfectly manicured gardens separated by curving pebbled paths. He remained coldly silent.

Emily bit her bottom lip and watched him out of the corner of her eye. Their relationship had become more a complication than a solution. At least in her eyes.

"I appreciate that you came to my aid in the ballroom. I felt a bit overwhelmed," she said, attempting to move past the awkwardness she felt in his presence.

"Overwhelmed? At the male attention you were receiving?" Marcus glanced sharply in her direction before turning his eyes back to the gardens beyond the balcony. "Unattached men are curious when they see a new face, especially so late in the Season. You are an unexpected but pleasant diversion."

Emily's mouth parted in surprise at his callous tone. "Are you saying that their attentions are mere curiosity? Your friend Mr. Forrester seemed quite interested in furthering our acquaintance."

"Your appearance tonight, particularly your low-cut gown, captures their interest." He gazed boldly down at her cleavage. "Some of the gentlemen who were competing for your attention tonight are known rakes. I urge you not to encourage them."

His leering glare and harsh tone caused her to draw back from him. She certainly did not deserve such condescending words. "I am not naïve. Have you forgotten? I have no desire to be matched or to attract any one of those gentlemen. I am simply here tonight to please my aunt," she said matter-of-factly, her voice low, while her eyes darted in the aunt's direction.

"How could I forget? You invented our master plan, did you not?" His eyes delved into hers. "It must have been difficult to leave the country, especially leaving those of whom you are endeared."

"Yes... It was, actually," Emily tightened her lips at Marcus' cynicism and looked away for fear he would see the hurt she felt at his sudden coldness. "I plan to leave next week."

"You mentioned your anxiety over your father's health. Is that the only reason for the short visit?"

"I have my own personal interests that I have neglected as well." Emily looked away, confused by his suspicious tone.

"And these interests have more allure than what you have experienced in London?"

"I have enjoyed my visit. You have been most gracious and accommodating."

"Yes, I have played my part well. You have remained unencumbered by suitors vying for your hand."

"I believe I have also aided you in your desire to remain unshackled," Emily bit off, lifting her chin.

Marcus shrugged. "Quite true. My aunt has not made even one attempt to draw me into another match."

"Well then, we have been successful," Emily snapped, anger growing at his arrogance.

She hadn't seen this side of him before and it saddened her. She didn't want their last meeting to be hostile.

Despite the warm evening, the silence between them chilled her. She stayed focused on the clusters of daffodils, bluebells and primrose in the gardens beyond them, their colors muted by the moonlit sky and the lights glittering from the balcony.

She thought of the poets who wrote about lasting love. The reality, she knew, was far from their flowery words. She had witnessed her mother's pain and loneliness in a loveless union, and Marcus had made it very clear what he thought of love and marriage. His behavior tonight, so near to their parting, was more proof of a man's inability to be constant in his affections.

Probably best, she thought dismally. She had become caught up in feelings that would have only led to disappointment or even ruin. She just hadn't expected the icy reception from Marcus tonight. Obviously, he was ready to end the pretense. Why did she suddenly feel so miserable?

"You plan to leave next week," Marcus said finally.

"Yes, though my aunt is not happy about it."

"She may wonder why I do not encourage you to stay."

"I thought of that. I have felt quite guilty over our pretense, especially when I realized she had begun to think..." Emily paused and swallowed, coming too close to telling him what Aunt Delia had suggested.

Marcus snorted. "Our aunts, I believe, have been encouraged to think our relationship has gone far beyond friendship."

"Indeed, I fear we have played our parts too well. We must find a way to end this ruse," she said firmly, so unlike what she felt inside. She was truly playing a role tonight and not for the benefit of their aunts, but rather to save herself from falling apart.

"Before they begin planning the nuptials?" Marcus chuckled, wearing what looked more like a jeer than a jovial expression.

Emily glanced sharply at him. "Perhaps," she hesitated, "I shall tell her that we realize that we do not suit." While her words tumbled out, her insides grew taut.

"And that you are so broken up that you must leave?"

"Much too melodramatic," she said with a sweep of her free arm. She refused to reveal the hurt choking her heart.

"Or love unrequited?" Marcus lifted his brow. "You might tell her that I have chosen my usual path and prefer to remain unattached."

"I believe it best to keep it simple." She gazed

back at her aunt who smiled warmly at her. She returned a false smile, feeling traitorous and terribly sad. "We do not suit, that should suffice." She willed her heart to see him as an inconsiderate rake so she could walk away with pride.

"We should return to the ballroom, prepare the aunts to take our leave. I have become sufficiently bored."

Emily's lips parted but she could find no words to respond to his callousness.

"Once you are home, you might want to reconsider your other interest. I have my doubts that you have found fulfillment for your passionate nature," he said ruefully. "When I return you to your aunt, I shall appear disturbed. You can take it from there."

Emily willed herself not to cry. His words stung. He must see her as wanton, trying to control her impulses. She stiffened her lower lip. He had played his part well, she thought dismally.

She had almost forgotten that it was simply a role.

Chapter Seven

THE NEXT MORNING Emily hoped to speak to her aunt about her return to the country, but Delia chose to spend the morning in her room to soothe her aching joints. Emily's announcement after the ball that she and Marcus had argued and decided that they were not suited for more than friendship was ill received. Her aunt insisted that it was most likely a lover's quarrel. Emily's departure seemed the only answer to put an end to the fiasco she had created.

After a light breakfast, she spent an hour in the garden reading, but she couldn't stop thinking of Marcus and his callous indifference toward her at the ball. Had he grown angry because she had avoided him after their evening at Vauxhall? Or was it her behavior that night? Perhaps he had hoped to entice her into a more scandalous relationship. She had to protect her reputation and she had nearly succumbed to temptation. A woman who desired to remain independent must remain virtuous or be tossed off by society. More likely, he had tired of their game.

The Season was at an end and they had succeeded in their quest. He owed her nothing. But she hadn't expected his wrath and mockery. Picking up the book that lay in her lap, she tossed it to the ground. "Men! How foolish I was to even consider the pretense!" She dropped her head in her hands. How could she have allowed herself to become emotionally involved? She tried to ward off the one question that continued to tear at her heart.

Had she fallen in love with him?

She lifted her head and gazed out across the gardens, trying to hold back her tears. She needed to regain control of her scattered thoughts. Two house sparrows were building a nest on a branch of a large oak tree. Emily wiped her eyes and watched as the male sparrow nudged his orange beak caressingly against the female's neck. *They will be starting a family soon.* Had she been fooling herself? Is that what she wanted? She drew in a long sigh.

"How could I have allowed myself to get into this predicament?" She knew only one thing for certain. She could not see Marcus again.

"AUNT DELIA, HOW are you feeling?" Emily asked when she found her aunt sitting in the drawing room the next morning looking drawn and pale. "Perhaps you should rest in bed another day."

"No, my dear," Delia said quietly. "I feel much better today."

"I am unconvinced," Emily replied, looking into her aunt's eyes. "You look distressed. Is something wrong?"

"Come sit by me, Emily. I am afraid I have some upsetting news. I debated whether to wake you."

Emily took a seat on the couch by her aunt's chair. "What is it?" she asked warily.

"I did not go through my mail yesterday. I

wished I had." Emily stared down at the letter her aunt held in her hand. "Have you received bad news?"

"The letter is from your neighbor in the country, Mrs. Mosley."

"Mrs. Mosley? I don't understand." Fear crossed Emily's face. "Does it concern my father?"

"Dora Mosley and I are old friends, as you know. We spent much time together when I visited last year. She has been looking in on your father." Delia lowered her eyes to the letter. "He is quite ill."

Emily's hand went to her throat. "Oh, God. He has lied to me then. He wrote that he was improving daily."

"He would not have wanted to worry you, my dear."

"I had my suspicions and I ignored them." Emily clutched at her skirt, worrying a hank of fabric. "I should have paid attention to my misgivings. I should never have left him."

"You must not blame yourself. You were doing as your father wanted."

"Tell me what she writes."

"That your cousin Willard has moved in and is caring for him. When she found out that your cousin hadn't notified you, she felt compelled to write."

Emily groaned. "I am not surprised in the least that he would refuse to contact me. My father's illness has no doubt given him the opportunity to move in. I would not be surprised if he is waiting and hoping…" Emily stopped, the words caught in her throat.

"You must not think such a thing. Mrs. Mosley writes that he is attending to your father. He may not have wanted to alarm you."

"Or, may not have wanted me to rush home and be in his way," Emily scowled. "Willard is selfish and arrogant and my father's heir." Her voice rose in agitation. "I should never have left."

"Your father urged you to come. He will be pleased when he hears of Lord Deming's attentions toward you, despite your little spat the other evening."

"There was no 'little spat'. Lord Deming and I have no future," Emily blurted out. "Forgive me, I am so sorry."

"You are upset, my dear. I understand."

"No, you don't," she said with too much emphasis. "I know it was my father's hope that I come to London and find a husband. He refused to understand that I have no desire to marry." Emily turned her face away. She had to confess. She couldn't carry her guilt any longer.

She turned to her aunt and saw her perplexed expression. "Lord Deming, I realize, has an obligation to marry, but I saw on the night we met that he felt pressured. Oh, dear, how do I explain my defiance?" Emily squirmed, perched near the edge of her seat, her fingers still clutching her skirt. "When I met him at the bookstore the next day, we decided on a plan, a pretense... I am so ashamed."

"Are you saying that you and the earl have been pretending to care for one another?"

Emily lowered her eyes when she saw her

aunt's stunned expression. "It was all my idea. A convenient pretense. Marcus simply agreed to go along with it."

"Lord Deming does not simply go along with anything. He must have been attracted to you, though Agatha certainly wore out his patience. I suppose your suggestion brought some relief from her constant matchmaking." She exhaled a deep sigh. "Emily, it may have begun as a pretense, but I have seen the way you two look at each other. Indeed, I think you care more than you think and Lord Deming as well."

"You are mistaken," Emily said firmly, unwilling to admit to feelings she had only begun to question within herself. Her eyes went to the letter her aunt still held. "Now is not the time to discuss our relationship. Aunt Delia, you have been so kind and loving and I betrayed your trust in me. I pray that you will forgive me."

"No need for apologies." Delia clasped her niece's hand. "I admit I am surprised that you would go to such lengths to remain single. Most young women desire marriage and realize the need for security and a husband's protection." She looked deeply into Emily's eyes. "I must say, if nothing else, I have been entertained immensely by your visit and the earl's attentions. After all, I have been included in all of your outings. Furthermore, our shopping trips together have been a delight. I enjoyed spending your father's money and watching you blossom before my eyes."

Delia smiled as she reached out to wipe a tear that slid down Emily's cheek. "No, no, my dear, I am impressed by your ingenuity, though I find myself curious as to the reasons. But you are correct. This is not the time for me to question you."

Emily sighed. She owed her aunt more of an explanation, but her thoughts were with her father. "If I might beg the use of your carriage and coachman? I may not be able to hire a traveling coach to arrive at such short notice."

"Of course, I knew you would want to return home immediately. My carriage is being made ready and Maggie has been alerted to pack some of your things. I shall send your gowns later. Sit with me until your maid returns. You shall be on your way soon enough."

Despite her anxiety, Emily nodded and settled back in her seat.

"I only wish that I could accompany you. I am afraid my joints are not up to the journey today," Delia said, rubbing her knee. "Promise that you will write as soon as possible with news of your father's health. I am very fond of your father, you know. He was a good husband to my sister, though she did not appreciate him," she added, her eyes growing misty.

Emily's eyes widened. "I agree that they had a poor marriage. She held much resentment toward him and marriage in general."

"Your mother was never satisfied. Your father tried his best to please her during their first years of marriage."

"Aunt Delia, what are you implying? My father spent much time away from home or locked up in his study. Mother was very lonely. She told me it was expected in marriage. Women are not appreciated, suppressed in their desires and too often abused," Emily asserted, as if she were reading a text, rather than speaking from her heart, "and women must expect that husbands have certain freedoms that wives do not."

Delia stared at her niece, her mouth falling open. "What causes you to make those assumptions and to be so cynical of marriage?"

"My mother kept me well informed of the behaviors of men once they say their wedding vows as well as tales of her acquaintances' indiscretions. Though I do not know too many particulars of my parents' relationship, from what I observed of their marriage and from what she told me of others…"

"Were you truly close to your mother?" Delia interrupted. "I do not remember it to be so, though you were her only child.

"Not truly close. Mother always seemed so…distracted, in her own world." Emily stared straight ahead as she dwelled on childhood memories.

"Mother gave parties on occasion. She would dress in her best gown, primp and flutter about, quite lovely and gay as she prepared for her guests. She seemed like a fairy princess to me as a child. I was usually relegated to my bedchamber when her guests arrived. Too young to join in the festivities, Mother would say. The next day she would be angry and complain about the entire evening." Emily's voice grew softer, sadder. "Gone was the beautiful princess. She seemed old and tired at those times. Eventually the parties stopped and then she became ill and spent most of the time in her room or in a small cottage on the estate that she often used as an escape, I believe."

Delia reached for her hand. "Emily, I am not aware of what else your mother told you, and I certainly should not speak ill of the dead. After all, she was your mother. But I knew my sister very well. I can only imagine how she might have poisoned your mind."

"Aunt Delia!" Emily pulled her hand away. "She only wanted to prepare me. She didn't want me to make the same mistakes."

"Pshaw," Delia snorted. "Prepare you to distrust all men? I agree some men make very poor husbands. Your father, I believe, did not want to be among them. When they were first married, he tried in all ways to please her. She resented him for not having the wealth she had hoped for in a husband. Your father's income was handsome and his country estate small but elegant in its own way. Your mother, however, was a beauty and felt entitled since childhood to expect much more. Your birth brought such joy to your father, while my sister feared for her figure." Delia pressed her hand against her cheek. "I should not be telling you such things."

Delia closed her eyes and sighed. "I cannot let you go on thinking as you do. I should put a clamp on my mouth. Nevertheless, I feel I must speak to change your opinions of love and marriage."

Emily opened her mouth to reply, but the

anguish she saw on her aunt's face silenced her.

"My dear, your mother had been in love with an earl and expected that he would ask for her hand. She was certain he adored her and, at first, he lavished her with attention. But in the end, he chose another. Catherine, your mother, was devastated. The Season was nearing an end and she feared that she would not make a match. She was humiliated, for she had been brazen in her behavior in the hopes of a proposal.

"Your father fell in love with her at first sight. He was quite handsome. Another woman would have been delighted for his attentions." Delia's eyes brightened and a small smile appeared briefly before her expression turned serious. "He watched and waited while your mother spent her time relishing the earl's overtures. When it became obvious that the earl had lost interest in Catherine, your father asked for her hand. She accepted, but it was not for love. It was out of fear that she might be left on the shelf.

"I am speaking out of turn, but do not blame your father for all of your mother's bitterness," Delia said softly, her eyes pleading. "I agree that as time went on he became more distant and may have even strayed, but your mother pushed him away almost from the beginning. Oh, how he wanted another child, my dear," she smiled wistfully. "He loved you so much and wanted you to have a sibling, but Catherine refused to allow him into her bed." Delia raised a hand to her lips as if to stop herself, frowned, then continued. "You probably wonder why I know as much as I do."

Emily nodded, still too stricken to voice a reply.

"I grew up with your mother, so I knew her desires as well as her disposition. After your father and she married, they would come to London each year and stay with me. Your mother insisted on taking part in the pleasures of the Season. Your father cared little for balls and assemblies. He was quiet by nature, as I am sure you are aware. Your mother often confided in me, or should I say complained to me, incessantly, and your father, my dear Emily, confided in me as well to a lesser degree, though I admit, unbeknownst to your mother."

Delia's eyes became red-rimmed. Emily reached out for her hand.

"Forgive me, Emily. I just cannot bear for you to think badly of your father. He loved your mother deeply and suffered as well. Catherine could not realize her youthful dreams and she refused to accept new ones. She was to be pitied."

Emily watched as a tear slipped from Delia's eye. As her aunt reached for her handkerchief, realization dawned. "Were you in love with my father?"

Delia sucked in a shaky breath, her lips tightening slightly before she replied. "You are very perceptive, my dear. Your father was my first love, but he had eyes only for your mother. I was the plainer sister. She was radiantly beautiful and, in the beginning, your father could not see a fault with her."

"I never knew."

"Of course not." Delia gave a knowing smile. "It was all as it was meant to be. I met Mr. Fenning shortly after your parents were married. He was a good husband. We shared a wonderful life together and I loved him, much more as the years went by. The tears you see now are from old memories as well as sadness for my sister's inability to accept your father's love. I cannot sit here and let her foolishness ruin your life. To be well married to the right man is a blessing, and so much better than spinsterhood. Do not be afraid to love and be loved, or you may become like your mother, bitter and alone."

Emily tried to absorb her aunt's words and her warning. She had believed that a good marriage was the rarest of all life's events. Had her mother's warnings been conjured up from her own hurt and bitterness? "I… I don't know what to say. You have given me much to think about." Before she could say more, a knock sounded at the door.

Delia squeezed her niece's hand and wiped her eyes before turning her attention to the closed door. "Come in, come in."

Maggie entered and bobbed a curtsy to Mrs. Fenning and turned to Emily. "I have finished most of the packing, miss, but you may have some questions on what to send on later."

"Thank you, I shall be up in a few minutes." Emily waited until Maggie left before giving her aunt a hug. "I appreciate your concern and your candor. I just need some time to think."

"I understand. I see the worry and confusion on your face. Go, my dear. My prayers are with you and your father."

Within an hour and after a tearful goodbye, Emily and Maggie were on their way. As the coach passed through the streets of London and to its outskirts, Emily sat rigidly in her seat and offered little conversation.

She'd left the country confident about what she had wanted and now she was leaving London fearful and confused. Her aunt's words moved her to a place of uncertainty that left her dazed. And while she prayed for her father in one breath, she seethed at the thought of coming home to her self-seeking, loathsome cousin Willard.

"Good gracious!" Agatha gasped as she read the note from Delia.

"What it is?" Marcus asked, looking up from *The Republican* newspaper he had been reading.

"Delia's niece left London this morning. It seems her father's health has taken a turn for the worse."

Marcus' brow furrowed, his fingers tightening and wrinkling the newspaper in his hand. "She did mention that her father had not felt well before she came to London."

"Delia writes that she received a letter from a neighbor of the girl's. She gives no other details."

When Marcus remained silent, she tilted her head and looked at him quizzically. "Marcus, you have refused to discuss your unexpected announcement after the ball. How did you put it? Oh, yes, 'I should not have assumed that your relationship with Emily was ever more than friendship'."

Marcus glared at his aunt. "What has that to do with the subject at hand? I have heard enough of your opinion on the matter."

"I just do not know what to make of it all," Agatha frowned, shaking her head slowly from side to side. "Emily has left abruptly and your relationship has been downgraded to a mere friendship. I felt certain it was blossoming into... well, such an abrupt turn of events, I must say." She fell silent as if awaiting his response.

She received none.

Marcus tossed his paper aside and stood. He had been irritable all morning. Most likely too much whisky the night before hadn't helped his mood. His aunt's constant questions about his and Emily's decision did not help matters either. If she only knew that his courting of Emily was merely a convenient ploy.

He walked to the front window and looked out at St. Charles Place shrouded in a gray mist. The day was as murky as his thoughts. He rubbed the bristle on his chin. He hadn't even bothered to shave yesterday or today. Had he even combed his hair? He grimaced to himself. His appearance was the least of his concerns.

"Not a good day to travel, not good at all," he muttered aloud. He had spent the night angry at himself for even agreeing to the stupid pretense. He could have withstood his aunt's meddling for a few more weeks.

He had realized too late that Emily Hughes was just the type of woman he had spent years trying to avoid. She aroused feelings that he knew only brought weakness. He wanted nothing to do with the kind of love that yearned for another so deeply that it overwhelmed common sense.

Hadn't that been his father's ruin?

Fortunately, he had stopped the ruse in time. He just needed to get through the aftermath, the dwindling of that uncomfortable feeling each time they'd parted — an empty feeling. It was as if when in her presence, she fulfilled a part of him, a part that almost seemed to have been waiting for her. He rubbed his forehead as if to erase the insane thought.

A few more days and he would be fine. He just hadn't expected her to disappear out of his life today.

"Delia clearly addresses her concern for her brother-in-law. Perhaps you would like to read her note?" Agatha held it out to her nephew.

Marcus glared at the letter before walking over to his aunt and taking it from her. His expression turned grim as he read through it. "Emily told me that her father had written and that he was on the mend. It appears that he was not being truthful." Casting the note aside, he walked back to the window and stared out at the bleak day.

When Emily told him of her worry over her father's health, he had entertained the thought that she was using him as a reason to return home. As he mulled over their previous conversations, he unconsciously pulled at his neckcloth until it was as disjointed as the way he felt.

His thoughts turned to the words written to her

lover. He had convinced himself that her desire to leave London was because of this suitor. Yet despite Emily's declarations, she had responded to his overture, not in actions, but in desire. He was certain of it. He'd been with enough women to know. She was a mystery to him and no matter how hard he tried to thrusts thoughts of her from his mind, he failed.

"I must say I am surprised that Emily did not send you a note explaining her abrupt departure," Agatha said to Marcus' back. "After all the attention you bestowed on her, she should have felt some obligation to inform you."

"I am sure her main concern was returning home to care for her father," Marcus shot back. "She owes me nothing." Realizing his rudeness, he took in a breath, sighed and turned to face his aunt. "We enjoyed each other's company. There's nothing more to it."

"I simply find it odd that your attentions toward her should change so suddenly." She clasped her hands together and rested them on the table before her.

"Are you insinuating that I have run for cover?"

"Until you were introduced to Miss Hughes, you had avoided all my attempts to court an eligible candidate."

"Indeed. I found none of them suitable."

Agatha gave her nephew a weary look. "I am only questioning if you and she may have had a simple disagreement. A fit of jealousy, perhaps? Not uncommon, you know. She looked quite lovely at the ball and drew many admirers."

"I assure you, Emily and I did not have a simple disagreement nor was I disturbed that she was much admired," Marcus asserted, though his words lacked conviction. He tugged at his cravat, unraveling it further. "I believe it is time to prepare for our return to the country. The Season is officially over. You can stop your matchmaking until next year."

Agatha visibly scowled before she let out weary sigh of acceptance. "Then we shall be leaving for your country estate soon. Should I talk to the servants about closing the house?"

Marcus did not answer immediately. Instead, he paced and rubbed his chin thoughtfully.

He paused at the window. "I believe I shall go on ahead, by horseback," he said finally, still fixing his eyes toward the street. I should check on the improvements that were to be made in my absence. Yes, once everything is in order, I shall make arrangements for your travel." He glanced at his aunt. "Would you mind spending another few weeks in town?"

"Heavens, no," Aunt Agatha answered, eyeing him curiously. "I am quite comfortable here and Delia will appreciate the company."

"I shall prepare for my trip then."

As soon as Marcus left the room, Agatha hurried to the escritoire to pen a response to her friend.

Dear Delia,

You must come for tea today. We have much to discuss, indeed.

Chapter Eight

EMILY REMAINED RIGID and tense in her carriage seat though they had left London streets behind an hour before. Maggie's consoling words along the ride did little to allay her fears. Her maid confided some servant gossip concerning Mrs. Mosley, most specifically that she was considered a busybody and might tend toward exaggeration. Emily knew of her neighbor's reputation but also of her kindness. She appreciated Maggie's attempts toward consolation, but what she needed was time to think. The long, slow carriage ride was torturous when her emotions felt like needles prickling her insides. Soon Maggie maintained a respectful silence and dozed off, much to Emily's relief.

I should never have come to London, despite Father's insistence. He wasn't feeling well when I left, but he'd refused to take any more of my excuses. "Why?" she whispered aloud before bring her hand to her lips. *Did he believe even then that he was seriously ill? Is that why he sent me to Aunt Delia to find a husband? To safeguard my future?*

Emily closed her eyes as she remembered her father's pleas that turned into demands that she leave. *Father, did you not consider what a rebellious daughter you raised and my opinions of marriage?*

Her thoughts turned to Aunt Delia's admissions about her parents' marriage and especially her revelations concerning her mother. Her aunt's words cut into crevices of her heart where she had reverently stored her mother's words.

She had so yearned for her mother's love that when she gave Emily attention, seldom as it was, she listened avidly. Her mother was so pleased with her on those occasions. Now her aunt's words crushed the false image she had created of her mother as a victim, dependent on the whims of a husband.

She realized that her mother could never have taught her about love because she was never in love, had never experienced happiness in her marriage. Perhaps, she never gave it a chance.

When your father asked for her hand, she accepted, but it was not for love. It was out of fear that she might be left on the shelf.

Emily pressed her hand to her forehead as she remembered her aunt's words. She tried to recall times of devotion she had witnessed between her parents. Sadly, she couldn't. Most of their conversations, she recalled, consisted of irritations and expectations. In the public eye, they were gracious; in private, they tolerated one another. At night, they closed separate bedroom doors.

Catherine could not realize her youthful dreams and she refused to accept new ones. She was to be pitied.

She had wanted to believe that if her parents could have enjoyed a happy marriage, if her father had been more attentive, her mother might have been different—perhaps been more loving to her only child. Emily had to admit that she had seldom seen her mother offer affection to her father, only complaints.

She thought of her father. *How I have chastised him in my heart.* She had blamed him for her mother's disappointments just as her mother had blamed him. She accepted that it was men's weakness to become bored with their wives and to stray from their marriage vows.

As she reflected on her childhood with her new awareness, her mother's bitterness, not her father's inadequacies, took on new meaning. Since her father said little and never defended himself, she had reasoned that her mother's laments were well founded.

Do not be afraid to love and to be loved or you may become like your mother, bitter and alone.

Were the causes of her mother's dissatisfaction the outcome of her choices and her own misguided dreams? If so, was her own choice to remain single misguided? Would she become as bitter? Emily covered her face with her hands to suppress the desire to scream out to the heavens as questions bombarded her mind.

She remembered her earlier ride to London. She had set her mind to avoid the eye of any possible suitor who might turn in her direction. She had set the stage immediately after meeting Marcus to avoid any possibility of finding love. Yet when her thoughts wandered to Marcus, she unconsciously wrapped her arms about her.

I must stop dwelling on what could have been. He flirted with her, encouraged a more intimate exchange, but hadn't she heard of his reputation as a rake? Further, he had admitted that he planned to marry only for convenience. Despite her aunt's revelations, she realized her mother was right about men who lacked devotion to their wives, preferring their freedom to do as they pleased. Marcus said as much, though his reasons surprised her. 'Love was a man's downfall', he'd professed.

She thought of his coldness on the night of the ball and how quickly he had agreed to end their ruse. She suspected that he would be relieved when he heard that she had left London. She was the bigger fool for falling in love.

In love? The words and the passion behind them that formed in her mind were more powerful than any of her poetic inspirations. Had she truly fallen in love with him?

She looked out as rain drizzled on the coach's window. The sky was dark and dismal though it was early afternoon. Her weeks in London had been filled with so many pleasant days, and she had barely paid attention to the gray ones.

"How appropriate for the weather to be so miserable," she said softly. Fortunately Maggie didn't hear and except for an occasional snore, remained blissfully asleep.

She pulled a handkerchief from her reticule and wiped away tears that she could no longer hold back. She thought of Marcus when they'd first met. A brief smile crossed her face as she envisioned him sitting across from her at Aunt Delia's dinner party.

Her thoughts went to the next day when he'd

followed her into the bookshop and finished Shelley's poem. Memories of other happy moments flooded her mind.

She remembered how he would fiddle with his neckcloth at uncomfortable moments. How often she'd had the urge to straighten the crooked cravat. They had gotten along well for the most part, except for their last evening together.

Why even think of him? They'd both agreed to cease their ploy.

Lips may speak a thousand words,
Or grow silent with a kiss.
Yet in that kiss a thousand words
might speak in silence more profound.
What mystery is this?

Her brief poetic escape did little to ease the sadness she felt. As the carriage turned into the long drive that led to her home, Emily buried thoughts of love deep in her heart and bid a final farewell to Lord Deming.

"IT'S GOOD TO see you again, Miss Emily," Samuel, the stable hand, said with a broad smile as he helped the coachman remove the luggage atop the carriage. "You, too, Maggie," he said, with a wink, causing the sleepy-eyed maid to toss him a vexed glance.

"Maggie, take the coachman to the kitchen for refreshment and then go rest in your room until dinner," Emily said before hurrying into the house. Exchanging a brief greeting with Fitz, the butler, she headed directly to her father's study.

Just as she reached the door, her cousin Willard

stepped into the hallway. Emily nearly crashed into him.

"Cousin Emily, you've returned." Willard's expression revealed his surprise. "Your father said you would be in London for another few weeks."

Emily crossed her arms tightly against her. "I altered my plans once I heard of father's weakened state. Why didn't you write to me, Willard? If it wasn't for Mrs. Mosley's letter — "

"That impertinent woman," he snapped, not allowing her to finish. "It was not her place to contact you. I have been caring for your father since you traipsed off to London. I understand that your father was not well at your departure." He clasped his long fingers in front of his narrow waist and glared at her disapprovingly.

Emily froze at his less than subtle accusation. "I left for London at my father's request. Now, if you will excuse me, I must see him."

"You will not find him in the study. He has taken to bed. He tires very easily these days," Willard said, his narrow nose tilted up and his face pinched.

"I must go to him." She began to turn away, but paused, forcing a calmer façade. "I do appreciate your caring for Father while I was away. You must be anxious to return to your own home."

"My dear cousin, no doubt you will realize that my staying here may be for the best. Your father has agreed to have me oversee estate affairs during this unfortunate time."

Emily's mouth dropped open. "You talk as if he is on his death bed," she seethed. Even saying the words made her shudder.

"I suggest that you prepare yourself, Emily."

"I must see him." She turned away and hurried down the hall.

"You may find him asleep." Her cousin called after her. "Best not to wake him. He has bouts of severe pain."

Emily sucked in a fear-filled breath at his warning before she disappeared from his view and ran up the stairs to her father's room.

"I AM PERFECTLY fine, Heddy. I merely dozed off for a few minutes." Emily pushed a cluster of curls away from her forehead and tucked them under her cap as she looked up at her usually cheery housekeeper.

"Nonsense, miss, you have been sittin' by your father's bedside for hours and your eyes are beggin' for sleep. You need rest. The medicine Dr. Brandt gave him seems to have numbed the pain and put him in a deep slumber. I promise I will come for you as soon as he wakes. Come, missy, I'll see you settled in your own room for a nap."

Emily drew in a deep breath. "Oh, Heddy, everything is so changed since I've returned," she whispered wearily as she rose from her chair. "I feel at home only when I am close to my father."

"I understand, miss," she said tenderly as she took her arm and walked with her toward the door. "What with your cousin takin' over everything, and that Mrs. Hanover. Who could have known she'd be such a witch!"

Emily shushed her as they slipped out the

door.

"'Tis true, missy," Heddy said quietly, pursing her lips.

"I have not had the chance to observe the new cook for very long. Is she really such a shrew?" Emily had been surprised to find a new face in the kitchen, but she'd received only a brief explanation. Her mind had been only on her father's decline.

"She was hired as a kitchen-maid and now that our dear Ellie is gone, she thinks she owns the kitchen. She's been harpin' at Amy and tossin' her responsibilities off to her. Amy may not be the most efficient scullery maid and she is a bit dim-witted, but she takes her duties to heart. Mrs. Hanover's got her skittering about like a scared rabbit. I reminded Mrs. Hanover that I am the housekeeper here. She scrunched up those thin lips of hers and told me she's followin' Mr. Gates' orders."

"I shall speak with her. And my cousin. He had no right to force Ellie to leave. I have been so concerned about Father since I've returned that I haven't taken the time to address household issues."

"Listen to me goin' on and complainin' to you." The housekeeper shook her head fretfully. "As if you don't have enough to worry about. My mouth just keeps movin' even when my head tells me to be quiet."

"You need to tell me these things. I have wanted to visit Ellie to find out what happened. I refuse to believe that she was stealing our silver as my cousin claims. I know she is getting on in years and has become forgetful. She may have misplaced the spoons, put them in an apron pocket meaning to clean them and forgot they were there. I will address it. I have just had so much on my mind."

"I know, missy, what with your father ailin' so and your cousin nosing about in your father's affairs."

"Heddy..." Emily held a finger to her lips to remind her to speak more softly.

"'Tis true and you know it," the housekeeper declared in a passionate whisper. "Ellie ain't the stealing kind. Why she proclaimed her innocence over and over. Your cousin refused to listen. With your father bein' so ill, I don't know if he even realizes that she's gone. He would know it if his taste buds were back to normal," Heddy muttered. "Mrs. Hanover is far from the cook that Ellie was, though your cousin never complains about her bland tastin' meals. In fact, I've seen them talkin' together a number of times. It's as if he takes her counsel." Heddy's face tightened into a grimace.

"Perhaps he chooses not to get on her bad side. Firing another cook would be unwise in his position. He has already taken too much liberty. Father is still the head of this house."

Heddy heaved a sigh. "There I go complainin' again. I'll do my best to get along with her for the time bein'. I'm more worried about you. You're eatin' like a sparrow and up all night when you should be sleepin'," she scolded as they reached Emily's bedchamber door. "Now you go in and rest. I promise I'll have Maggie wake you if your father stirs. Meanwhile, I will face that shrew and see that she makes an adequate dinner for you when you wake."

"Thank you. I promise I shall talk to Mrs. Hanover. She may be taking her duties too seriously. So much has been going on since she arrived. As soon as Father is better... he will get better... " Emily bit her lip, trying to hold back tears that threatened.

Heddy reached out and cupped Emily's face in her hands. "We must pray, but worry will only give you wrinkles. Now off to bed with you."

Emily offered a weak smile of gratitude. "If only they knew the cause of his illness. My cousin, I understand, nearly tossed Dr. Howard out before calling in his own physician."

"I heard him tellin' old Dr. Howard they weren't in need of his services. Why the good doctor has been takin' care of your family for years. Didn't make sense to me but when I gave my opinion, your cousin put me in my place." Heddy clenched her lips together, the color rising in her cheeks.

"Willard insists Dr. Howard was not helping Father. And I was away." Emily cast her eyes down with regret.

Heddy reached out with a finger and lifted Emily's chin. "You stop that now. I heard Mr. Hughes demand that you go to London."

Emily nodded half-heartedly. "I wrote to Dr. Howard, days ago, against my cousin's wishes. He still hasn't replied, and his new physician, Dr. Brandt, doesn't seem to be any more knowledgeable about my father's condition. He continues to try new medication. Nothing seems to help." She fisted a hand and brought it to her lips. "I fear that Father is going to…"

"Hush now with such thoughts, you must not lose hope. Your father may turn the corner tomorrow. Please, missy, rest now. I'll sit with Mr. Hughes."

Emily clasped her housekeeper's hand with gratitude before entering her bedchamber and closing the door behind her.

Her housekeeper was right. She was exhausted but doubted she could sleep. She walked to her desk and sat down, folded her arms on the desktop and dropped her head into them. With eyes closed, she prayed for her father's healing. In minutes, she was asleep.

Waking a half hour later, she sat upright, nearly forgetting where she was. Regaining her equilibrium, she reached for her writing book. After a time, she dipped her pen in ink.

With bated breath,
Hope rests in Love's warm arms,
While Fear does tug and twist
my heart to harm.
Oh blessed Savior,
spread thy healing balm
upon your humble servant
that Hope may rise again.

She laid down her pen. Her poems had turned to prayers. Her verses were a mere distraction from the harsh realities she faced. The ink splattered on the page and mixed with her tears, tears she'd held in since her return.

She rose and crossed the room to her bed,

kicked off her slippers and lay down, not bothering to undress. She allowed more tears to fall, tears of sorrow and tears of anger. She cried for her father, for her misguided beliefs and for the loneliness she felt in her soul.

Her mother's words had left her fearful of a loveless marriage. Her father's strength and his love had remained constant through the years and she'd taken it for granted, even blamed him for her mother's misery.

As her father weakened, her own life felt more out of control. She had believed that his behavior was the cause of her mother's bitter outburst toward men. Better to be put on the shelf as an old maid than shelved by a husband who ignored his wife and did as he pleased.

So certain that she had planned the right direction for her life, she had rebelled against her father's wishes through deception. Now she wanted, needed, time with him to make up for the misguided beliefs she had held for too many years.

She could no longer blind herself to the fact that her father had shown no improvement. His stomach pain seemed only to increase. He had lost too much weight and was showing signs of confusion and disorientation. She felt only anxiety for the days ahead.

When her mind and body could take no more, she finally slept.

"HOW WILL YOU regain your strength if you do not eat?" Emily pleaded as she sat by her father's bedside the next morning.

"The only way I will regain my strength is to get out of this damn bed. I have about as much strength to stand up as a wilted dandelion."

Emily narrowed her eyes at his gardening humor. "Just a few bites of toast."

Hughes sighed in resignation. Reaching for his toast, he lifted a tired arm and tore off a chunk, grumbling as he chewed and swallowed. "Food has lost its taste, probably from all that medicine being poured down my throat."

"A sip of tea?" Emily reached for the small pot on his tray and filled the cup half full.

Grasping the cup, he lifted it with trembling hands. Emily folded her hands around his and held it to his lips until he drank it down.

"Enough. Get this out of here," her father snapped, pushing the bed tray away from him as he slumped back onto his pillows.

A rap sounded at the door as Emily grasped the tray that nearly tumbled to the floor.

"Come in," Her father growled.

Mrs. Hanover, the newly hired cook, entered. She gave a slight curtsy and eyed the breakfast tray. The expression on her thin face turned immediately disapproving. "Forgive my intrusion, Mr. Hughes, but for the past two days your food trays have been returned to the kitchen with your meal barely touched. That just will not do," she huffed, glaring at the uneaten eggs. "How will you get well if you do not eat?"

"My daughter's words exactly," Hughes grumbled.

The cook directed her upturned nose toward

Emily who was taken aback by the woman's surliness. "Miss Hughes, you must continue to urge him to eat." The cook walked to the tray and lifted a spoonful of eggs.

Emily held up a hand to stop the cook's attempts to spoon-feed her father. She knew the woman meant well but she was clearly going beyond her station. Her father, if he were well, would not have stood for such impertinence. "Mrs. Hanover, return to the kitchen and concern yourself with your duties. I shall return the tray later." She waved her off.

She had meant to have a talk with the woman the day before, but she had been surprised by a letter from her Aunt Delia. Her relief that her aunt planned to visit brought her consolation. She had concerned herself with sending a response immediately and notifying the servants to prepare a bedchamber. The remainder of the day was spent by her father's bedside. She would definitely make a point of speaking with her privately this afternoon.

She was pulled from her thoughts when she heard Mrs. Hanover clear her throat. She turned to see her standing militarily by the door.

"Mrs. Hanover, you are excused," Emily said, forcing a polite tone.

The cook stiffened her shoulders. "I apologize, Miss Hughes, however, Mr. Gates has requested that I look in on your father and encourage him to eat."

"Now that I have returned, I am seeing to his care." She wanted to send the overbearing servant on her way and came close to doing so, until she looked at her father.

His hand was raised as an order for both to stop their confrontation.

"Cook, return to the kitchen," he ordered in a feeble but firm tone.

Mrs. Hanover, wearing a tight-lipped scowl, nodded and left the room.

Emily swallowed down her irritation and touched her father's arm gently. "Father, she is right, you must eat more if you are to fight this infirmity."

"Later. We need to talk. I am not ignorant of my decline. We must talk, in case… "

"No, you must not say it! Your color is better this morning, I am sure of it." She touched his face tenderly.

Another knock at the door interrupted them. Emily sighed audibly and acknowledged the intruder.

"Emily, I must ask you to leave. Dr. Brandt is here to examine your father."

Emily's eyes narrowed at Willard's superior tone before gazing back at her father who nodded in agreement.

She reached out her hand to smooth back the wisps of his gray hair that had become disheveled by his restlessness. The change in her father's appearance caused a wrenching in her chest. He had always looked so stately, his hair neatly combed back and his beard perfectly trimmed.

Rising from her chair, she turned and met her cousin's stiff expression with one of her own. She squared her shoulders and walked out.

Chapter Nine

MARCUS RUMINATED ABOUT his decision to leave London immediately after Emily's departure. He hadn't actually lied to his aunt. He had planned to check on renovations to Hartwood Hall, his country estate. He simply avoided telling her that he had considered, perhaps irrationally at the time, to go to the Hughes' estate and confront Emily.

Now nearly three weeks had passed and he remained at his estate. Sitting in his study, he tried to blame his bad temper on estate issues but after another sleepless night he was forced to face the real cause. Emily's unexpected departure from London without a word to him still left him enraged. Obviously she was devoted to her father and he must be quite ill, Marcus thought, but not even a brief note?

He could not shake off his fury. She had deceived him unnecessarily about her reasons for the pretense. He had even come to imagine that he might change her thinking about marriage.

Not to him of course.

He agreed with her father's demand to send her off to London. No doubt women needed marriage for security and protection.

Indeed, he had his own selfish reasons for agreeing to the ruse. It saved him from his aunt's matchmaking. But in the end, the farce was at his expense.

And he wanted the last word.

He warred with his avenging thoughts. They had finished their business the night of the ball. He remained free of any attachments. He could continue on as he had before he met her. She was just one more chit of whom he had enjoyed a brief dalliance.

But there was more.

She intrigued him. She possessed a passionate nature and he'd admired her spunk and her independence, her desire to defy convention. He found her to be intelligent, unimpressed by the opulent world of the *beau monde*, and beautiful. Especially when she laughed. Her deep-green eyes sparkled with pleasure over a simple flower or a bubbling brook. And he missed her.

"Damn," he muttered aloud. She had gotten under his skin. He needed to confront her to be free of her.

She would be easy to forget once he had a final say in the matter. Perhaps he would get a glimpse of her lover. He refused to consider if that would be helpful or create more discomfort. He certainly could not be in love with her. She was a liar and a pretender. He simply felt used.

And he didn't like it one bit.

Rising from his chair, he left the room and walked out to the back patio, glad that the servants were off to other areas of the house. He needed some fresh air and did not want to answer questions or deal with any more problems.

He'd thought that his initial stop at Hartwood

Hall would be brief, but after meeting with his steward, he realized he needed to handle problems immediately.

Bad weather had caused delay in some renovations, and other repairs best done in the warmer weather needed his approval. His steward had been forced to discharge two skilled workers for drunkenness and tomfoolery, which caused added delays. Because they were tenants with families, much pleading and repentance on the part of the workers became Marcus' problem immediately upon his arrival.

He neither wanted to diminish the authority he had given his steward nor toss families with young children off the estate because of foolish husbands. After visiting with the families and seeing one of the husbands nursing a black eye caused by his wife's frying pan, Marcus decided the lost wages and their wives' fury might be punishment enough. He relegated the workers to cleaning out chicken coops and horse stalls for a time until they earned the steward's trust once again.

He handled estate business during the day and at night he reminded himself how much he enjoyed his personal freedom. He spent time making a list of plans for the summer. He wanted to purchase a couple of prime horses for mating purposes and enlarge the stables. He would certainly invite his bachelor friends for a shooting party. Numerous invitations had already arrived for sporting events and socials. Perhaps he would accept the invitation from a university friend to spend time at a seaside resort. His older sister Felicity had written insisting that he come for a visit. Her second child was on the way and he'd been errant in making time to see the family.

An invitation from a neighboring widow, whose company he had enjoyed in the past, arrived a few days after his return. He'd written an acceptance one morning after a sleepless night. A voluptuous and willing bed partner might clear his head. He'd ripped up the acceptance by evening, blaming his refusal on the need to handle estate affairs.

Despite all his attempts to return to his previous carefree endeavors, he had failed.

And it was Emily's fault.

Yes, he would have the last word. Once he faced the real Emily behind her deceptive mask, he would finally be free of her.

"MY LORD, IT is like old times seeing you in the kitchen," Mary, Marcus' cook, said with a bright smile. "Might you sit and chat with me? You so often came scurrying into the kitchen when you were a child, looking for a sweet or a warm biscuit."

"Your baking has always made it difficult for me to wait until dinnertime to be served."

Having just returned from a ride about his country estate, Marcus couldn't resist the smell of just-baked bread emanating through the house. He took a seat on a high stool, taking in a deep whiff of the golden loaf cooling on the counter before him.

Mary laughed gaily. "Ernest and I are so pleased that you've returned to the country. I hope you will stay longer this time."

Mary and her husband Ernest, the estate butler, had been with his family since he was a young boy. The couple had met and married soon after Mary had been hired as cook. Ernest was a footman at the time and had been given the position of butler as a wedding gift. Mary's hair was now gray and wound tightly in a bun. She'd become plumper over the years, but her jovial demeanor remained.

"I must go back to London tomorrow to complete some unfinished business, but I should be back by the end of the week with Aunt Agatha."

"Wonderful! Your aunt is such a delight to have about, except when she attempts to add more Seasonings to my already Seasoned stews."

"She loves to be helpful." Marcus gave the cook a knowing grin. "I plan to stay for the remainder of the summer, perhaps into the fall."

He had finally made the decision not to confront Emily, after changing his mind numerous times. He believed that his temporary lapse into insanity over Emily Hughes and his desire for revenge was beginning to diminish. Seeing her might stir up those unwanted feelings, rather than give him satisfaction.

"Since your mother's passing, your visits have been too brief, my lord. I understand the atmosphere about the place gave little comfort. Your father was in such a depressed state, but we have missed you." Mary's expression reflected empathy.

When Marcus' mother had become ill, Mary had devoted herself to her care. To Marcus, she had become more a member of the family than a servant. After his mother's death, he found little reason to stay at Hartwood, except to check on duties that needed his attention.

"My father hardly noticed when I was here." Marcus' words carried an edge of bitterness.

Mary's eyes widened at his tone. She took a long look at him, folding her arms across her plump chest. She reminded Marcus of his mother when she was about to scold him for some misconduct.

When she spoke, her voice softened and her words seemed carefully chosen. "True, near the end your father shut himself off from everyone, but he loved you dearly and demonstrated great pride in you. You must not forget all the years before your mother's passing. They were happy times. When you returned from school, all grown, I believe your father saw you as a man who no longer needed a father's instruction, or advice. You were, after all, quite independent by then, always off with friends. And, of course, all the ladies that vied for your attention kept you out many a night. No doubt they still do." Mary gave him a teasing smile before her expression turned thoughtful again.

"Your father was a desperately lonely man after your mother's death. He grieved for her until the day the Lord took him home. As you know, he managed affairs well enough over the years, enough so that his time was mostly his own. Being ten years older than your mother, he suffered aches and pains that come with age, though he seldom complained about them."

"No, Mary, there were no complaints, or conversations. Just dismal utterances."

Mary eyed him thoughtfully. "Unfortunately your father's grief not only added to his aging bones but also to his mind. He isolated himself from friends and drank a bit too much some nights. You were busy with your life and your sister was off and married with a family of her own. Too many memories of happier times, I think, drew him into a dark place. It was your mother who could bring him out of the doldrums when problems ruffled his reserve."

As Mary reminisced, Marcus tightened his grip on the counter's edge. Her words stirred his tightly controlled emotions. His long-held resentment was being over shadowed by a deeper, more uncomfortable feeling. Guilt.

She was presenting an image of a frail, old man, grief-stricken at life's losses. Had he simply stopped looking up to his father when age, illness and grief erased the strong, vital man he had known? Was he the one who had been selfish and uncaring, expecting too much from his sire, an aging lord who no longer demonstrated the strength of mind and spirit that gave his son a sense of security and pride?

His thoughts returned to his youth. He had been eager to enjoy his newfound freedom when his schooling was completed. He caroused with his friends recklessly, enjoyed hunting parties and late night revelries. He often left the estate to stay with friends for weeks at a time, not to mention nights spent with female companions he had cultivated to the extreme. His mother and father were simply at home living their lives. When they called him to task for his wayward behaviors, their remonstrations fell on deaf ears.

He was of age, after all. At least that was his excuse for his tomfoolery.

When his mother died, he delved into more activities to contain his grief. He found he became bored easily with his male friends and even more with the women he had previously enjoyed. Brief liaisons became preferable. But it was not only grief that caused him to busy himself to exhaustion. He had felt guilt too, that he hadn't spent more time or listened more to the wisdom of his mother's words.

His parents had nurtured him with a great deal of love during his childhood and seldom deprived him of anything. Had he taken them for granted and expected that they would always be there, that they would always be available to him? Had he expected his father to be strong for him when his wife died? The disturbing questions multiplied. He rubbed at his eyes and exhaled a long and deep breath.

He forced himself to look at Mary who had wisely stopped talking and simply watched him, her expression tender and caring. He cast his eyes down, feeling ashamed.

Mary broke the brief, heavy silence. "Your mother and father's marriage was built on love and trust and to be so envied. There was seldom a harsh word said between them. I admit their example caused me to clamp a hand over my mouth many a time when I wanted to give my Ernest a good tongue lashing."

When she chuckled, Marcus lifted his eyes. She wasn't looking at him, but seemed to be gazing off into distant memory.

"When your mother died, your father had little else to live for... " She stopped abruptly, covering her mouth. "Forgive me. I did not mean to say that you were not important to your father. I do not think he realized that you still needed him."

"I may have given him little reason to think I did," Marcus said despondently, his mind swirling with a new awareness that he found difficult to face. "I expected that he would know, reach out." Marcus sighed and sat back in his seat, realizing how he must sound. He had taken no responsibility for the gulf created between him and his father.

Mary reached over the counter and laid a hand on his arm. "You must not feel guilty, my lord. Keep in mind that your parents spent over thirty years together. I believe they are with each other now and proud of the man you have become. If you don't mind me saying so, they would want you to find a love as strong as theirs. There was no greater gift they could have bestowed than their example of a marriage built on lasting love."

Marcus wondered if Mary had planned this talk. The look on her face was one of satisfaction. He nodded. "Thank you."

The cook smiled knowingly and using a cloth napkin to hold the warm loaf of bread with one hand and a knife in the other, she cut into it. "Have a slice, my lord. Nothing brings more comfort than warm bread and butter.

MARCUS ROSE EARLY the next morning and gave final instructions to his staff. He rode off, taking the road that led away from London and toward the Hughes' estate.

Mary's wisdom had changed his course. He needed to see Emily, though he was not clear in his mind what he hoped to accomplish. He had felt superior to her and her actions and wanted to confront her about her lies. Now the truth of his own actions and misunderstandings about his father's last days caused him to question his motives.

Unfortunately, the long ride gave him too much time to think. The truth was that his avoidance of any relationship that hinted of love left him feeling empty. He had never admitted to loneliness before. In the darkness of his bedchamber he had faced the undeniable truth. Emily Hughes' departure had left him lonely and empty.

He needed to hear why she had deceived him from her own lips — those warm tempting lips that he'd been unable to forget.

As the road narrowed and he brought his roan to a walk, he envisioned Emily on that last evening in her stunning gold gown. She had been the most striking woman in the room. When she smiled at him her emerald green eyes had sparkled, and when he'd fingered a wayward curl, her auburn hair had felt like silk. He remembered how her long lashes lowered in contemplation when she became thoughtful and her moist lips pursed slightly. She had the habit of biting her lower lip, he remembered, when she pondered a decision.

The scent of lavender had filled his nostrils when he stood near her on the balcony that night. The desire to bed her had overwhelmed him, but the feeling of being made a fool of caused him to treat her with disdain and toss off their time together with an air of indifference.

As he rode closer to the Hughes' house, he thought about her father and how his unexpected visit might appear. His aunt would have surely sent a messenger to Marcus if Mr. Hughes had passed.

When he reached the road that led to the Hughes' estate, the sun had burned off the fog that lay heavy over the land for most of the morning. The sun's rays streamed through the heavily treed wood and across his path as he slowed his pace. He continued down the road until his horse sidestepped when a squirrel scampered across his path and down a ridge that led to a pond.

Marcus pulled at the reins, bringing Jericho to a halt and dismounted. He pulled off his coat, tucked it securely across Jericho's back and led the horse on a narrow path that bordered a pond and ran parallel to the main drive. Birds chirped in the trees while others flew from their nests at the sound of his presence. When he drew closer to the pond's edge, a different sound caused him to stop abruptly.

Tying Jericho to a nearby tree, he tread quietly until he spied Emily in the distance, sitting on a large rock that jutted out over the pond. Her skirt was lifted slightly and her bare feet dangled in water. Her hands covered her face and he could hear the sound of her weeping. His initial reaction was to go to her.

A male voice interrupted his thoughts.

Marcus remained behind a copse of trees and watched as Emily wiped away her tears with her skirt and turned toward the voice. Seeing the gentleman, she rose quickly, slipped on her shoes and rushed up the hill toward him. The man met her and took both of her hands in his.

Marcus watched as the well-dressed man, who appeared to be close to his own age, spoke a few words that caused Emily's shoulders to sag. The man draped his arm about her shoulders in a comforting gesture and led her up a path and away from view.

Is that him, her lover? Marcus nearly growled aloud as he went to retrieve his horse.

By the time he mounted Jericho and returned to the main road, his stomach was in knots. He had always thought of himself as sensible and unemotional. How could a woman affect him so?

He took a deep breath and urged Jericho on, despite a voice within him that questioned whether he'd chosen a poor time to arrive, especially unannounced. Emily was obviously grieving. Had her father worsened or even passed? He needed to see her, express his sympathy if necessary, and leave. Satisfied with his reasoning, he sat stiffly in his saddle and rode toward the Hughes' house.

The treed path opened to an impressive vista of

manicured lawn. The large red brick manor house with a Georgian façade sat on the top of the hill. Groves of greenery neatly clipped and flower gardens bursting with color greeted Marcus. Though his estate, Hartwood Hall in Yorkshire, was grander, he could see why Emily longed for home. The setting before him with its groves and gardens presented an immediate welcome. He wondered if he would feel the same welcome when he appeared at her door.

Chapter Ten

EMILY BID DR. Brandt goodbye and waited until his carriage drove off. She turned to enter the house but stopped at the sound of a horse's hooves. As she watched the rider come closer, she gaped in recognition. Her hands flew to her mouth.

It couldn't be, Marcus?

She tucked in the careless curls that escaped her cap and looked down at the drab navy day gown she had put on hurriedly this morning. *I must look a sight.* Chastising herself for the vain thought that entered her mind, she waited for him to draw closer. She had more important things to consider.

The news Dr. Brandt gave her was grave. Her father showed no improvement. The doctor administered more medication and told her that hope for recovery was dimming. She needed to return to her father's bedside and will him to get better. And yet, her heart wanted to burst with expectation as Marcus drew closer. She wanted to run to him, plead with him to hold her and give her his strength.

Again, she chastised herself. She needed strength, but it was her own she had to reclaim. She blocked out the thoughts that rushed in as he called her name from a short distance away.

Marcus dismounted, retrieved his jacket and slipped it on before walking toward her, reins in one hand. He wore a white cambric shirt beneath the jacket, fawn-colored riding breeches and his brown Hessians. The shadow of a beard only enhanced his appeal. She could not help thinking that he was even more handsome than she'd remembered him in her dreams.

"MARCUS," EMILY SAID, one hand pressed to her chest, her eyes wide. Her lips parted as if she wanted to say more, but no words came. She accepted his outstretched hand.

Marcus hoped he successfully masked his alarm at her appearance. Her face was pale and she looked thinner, almost fragile in her loose-fitting dress.

"I was returning to London," he said finally. "I thought your aunt would want me to look in on you." What else could he say? That he hadn't had a decent night's sleep since she'd left London? That he needed to see her for his own sake? "Forgive me if I am intruding."

"Your visit is welcomed," she said softly.

"You've been crying." He dropped his horse's reins and looked deep into her eyes. Tired eyes, he noted.

"I just received news from my father's physician. His condition has worsened." Her voice quivered.

A physician, not her lover. Marcus had passed the doctor's carriage on his way to her door. "Is there anything that I can do?"

"There is nothing anyone seems to be able to do. His physician can find no cause for his decline.

Less than three months ago my father was robust, healthy. How do I comprehend what is happening to him? He... " Emily stopped abruptly at the sound of a door creak. She stepped away from Marcus.

"I hate to break up this heartwarming reunion but luncheon is soon to be served, cousin," Willard said, standing above them on the porch. "I thought you might want to attend to your father unless, of course, you would prefer to entertain your gentleman friend." Willard eyed Marcus coldly.

Emily opened her mouth as if ready to snap at her cousin, but appeared to collect herself with an indrawn breath. "May I present Marcus Deming, Earl of Pembridge. We met in London. He is the son of my aunt's dearest friend. Marc... Lord Deming, may I introduce my second cousin on my father's side, Willard Gates."

MARCUS NODDED AT the man that stood above him on the steps, not having missed the chilly exchange between cousins or Gates' reaction to him. It looked as if the man had hurriedly put on his coat since the collar stood up carelessly behind his neckcloth. Tall and thin with narrow shoulders, he looked to be in his middle thirties, perhaps older. His black hair was sleeked back and receding, emphasizing a high forehead and a long face. He wore a stern expression that was far from inviting.

"Lord Deming," Willard acknowledged, "have you ridden out from London?"

"Returning. I was at my country house and decided to take a detour to see how Miss Hughes' father is faring."

"At this time of year, I would suspect you would be leaving London for the country, not returning," Gates said, raising a brow.

"Indeed, I was seeing to maintenance. I shall return soon for the remainder of the summer."

"How thoughtful of you to visit, your lordship," Emily cut in, interrupting her cousin's abrasive interrogation. "You must give your aunt my sincere apologizes for not saying goodbye."

"She quite understood your immediate need to return home."

Emily smiled gratefully. "We are being impolite. I shall call for a stable boy to care for your horse." She turned to her cousin. "If you would please show our guest into the parlor, I will notify the cook to expect another visitor for luncheon."

With only a nod from Gates, Marcus tied his horse to a nearby post. He followed Gates' lead into the main entrance while his opinion of the man formed in his mind — a very poor opinion, indeed.

"LORD DEMING, I do not believe we received an announcement of your arrival, unless my cousin refrained from telling me," Gates inquired as he strode over to the liquor cabinet. He poured a glass of brandy.

"A last-minute decision. Miss Hughes' sudden departure from London caused us great concern."

"Yes, as sudden as your visit," Gates said as he capped the bottle of brandy, his back to Marcus. "We are under a great deal of stress. I fear it is not the best time to entertain guests."

"I understand, of course."

"A glass of brandy?" Gates turned about and held out a glass.

Marcus held up a hand in refusal.

Gates gave a half smile. "Of course, strong drink might impede your travel. I assume that you will want to reach London before dark. A glass of lemonade, or iced tea, perhaps?"

"No thank you. My visit will be brief." Marcus couldn't miss the man's eagerness to be rid of him sooner than later. "Might I inquire of Mr. Hughes' condition? Miss Hughes appears distressed and seems to fear the worst."

"My uncle's condition has deteriorated over the past few weeks. Hope is dimming for a recovery." Gates lowered his eyes to his glass and took a sip.

Marcus studied the man, sensing little warmth or genuine empathy. "Are there any siblings in residence?"

Gates looked up, quirking a brow. "It appears that you do not know Emily as well as appearances demonstrate. She has no brothers or sisters. I am her closest male relative. When I found my uncle seriously ill and my cousin off to London, I offered aid immediately. I assure you that I will see to her welfare when her father passes."

"How dare you proclaim such a dire prediction?" Emily demanded as she stood in the doorway, her face ashen.

Marcus darted a glance toward Emily and then to Gates who offered no reply. "I fear my visit was poorly timed. I do not want to intrude."

Emily shook her head briskly, an obvious

signal to Marcus that this was her battle and not the time to offer apologies. Taking a few steps into the room, she stopped and grasped the top of a high-back brocade covered chair, her knuckles turning white as she fisted her hands into the tapestry.

"My father has been more alert the past couple of days, cousin, despite what his doctor says."

"Forgive me. I did not see you enter." Gates set his glass down carefully and steepled his fingers to his thinned lips. "I know how difficult it must be for you to accept, Emily, but his alertness is most likely due to the medication to relieve the pain. Unfortunately, I speak only what his physician has told me. He told you the same, I believe."

"My father's will is strong. He is sitting up in bed right now and he has eaten most of his lunch."

"He is eating better? Excellent," Gates said, reaching for his brandy.

Marcus weighed the interchange between Emily and her cousin. His opinion of the man had already been ascertained. He doubted he could be trusted to look after his cousin if her father should die. The man's sympathetic words sounded strained. Yet he seemed pleased that her father's appetite may have improved. *Perhaps, he is simply arrogant and enjoys his position of control.* A tap on the open door interrupted his thoughts.

"Luncheon is ready to be served," Heddy announced.

"You will stay for a meal, my lord?" Emily asked. "We have become accustomed to having only a light repast at this time of day, but I have asked cook to offer a heartier lunch since you have been traveling some distance."

"If I am not imposing." His cook had packed sandwiches for the journey back to London and he had no appetite, but he could not refuse her. His visit was turning out much different than he had imagined.

"You are most definitely not imposing," Emily insisted. "Do you not agree, cousin?"

"Indeed, you must join us."

"My pleasure, then."

Emily smiled for the first time since Marcus' arrival. "Heddy, please set an extra plate for our guest."

"Yes, miss." The housekeeper offered a slight curtsy and retreated.

Marcus ignored the frown that appeared on Gates' face. He admired Emily's brave standoff with her cousin, though it appeared that her father might well be on his deathbed. Emily desired him to stay and he was sure he saw more—a need, perhaps, for a friend amidst the tense atmosphere. The friction at their last parting in London had faded, at least for the present. He wondered only briefly if her lover offered her comfort and if Gates welcomed him in the house.

"Let us remove to the dining room," Gates said. "Your friend still has a long ride ahead of him, Emily. We must not cause him added delay."

"YOU SAID EARLIER that your father's appetite has improved?" Marcus asked, setting down his fork.

"He ate most of his meal before I came down, which is not often the case."

Marcus noticed that she had barely touched the sliced meat or cheese in her own dish.

"He has lost a great deal of weight and suffers much abdominal pain," Emily continued. "His physician continues to try different medications. Father has not responded well."

Marcus saw her bottom lip tremble slightly.

Gates cut in. "As I said earlier, though I may have done so with little tact, it is a melancholy and anxious time in this household. We are all on edge. We appreciate your visit and your concern." He looked about the table as he dabbed his mouth with his napkin. "Well, it appears that everyone has nearly finished." Tossing his napkin on the table, he pushed his chair back and stood up. "I must get back to my obligations."

Marcus, taking Gates' lead, stood. "I appreciate your hospitality."

"You are not leaving so soon?" Emily asked, her face clouding in disappointment.

Before Marcus could respond, a flash of lightning lit the room that had grown dimmer over the past few minutes. A loud clap of thunder followed.

Gates walked to the window just as the rain began, pelting the glass with greater intensity as he stood staring out. "The storm is unexpected. No doubt, it will pass within the hour."

"You certainly cannot leave now in the midst of a storm," Emily said, walking past her cousin to a second window. Another burst of thunder hit. "Look how dark the sky has become. If the rain continues with such force, our deeply rutted roads will become mud holes and too dangerous for travel, especially on horseback."

"Perhaps your cousin is right, Miss Hughes. It may just be a passing shower." He had not missed Gates' narrowed glare toward Emily and he didn't want to add to her problems.

"Nonsense," she scoffed, "and, please, call me Emily as you did in London. It is at least four hours to London and with this downpour the roads will be hazardous. Your horse could slip and break a leg. Do you have pressing business in London that could not afford you to stay for just the night?"

"No, I cannot say that I do," Marcus shrugged, impressed at how she stood her ground despite her cousin's obvious desire to see him gone. "Aunt Agatha writes that she has been entertaining herself with shopping and teas. I have given her only a tentative date for my return."

"That settles it then. I shall have our housekeeper prepare a room for you."

Marcus nodded. "I would prefer not to subject my horse to dangerous travel." He glanced at Gates, who wore a tight-lipped grimace.

"You do agree, Willard?" Emily asked, lifting her chin to her cousin.

"Yes...of course," he answered flatly. "The morning should be soon enough."

"Then it is settled. I must tell Father that you have arrived. He will most likely want to meet you." Before either man could protest, she walked briskly to the door. "Your room will be ready within the hour. Please excuse me while I make arrangements."

Emily took a step into the hallway, but swiveled about and stared at her cousin who hadn't moved from the window. She folded her arms at her waist and drummed one foot on the floor. "Willard, you are not going to leave Lord Deming standing in the middle of the dining room, are you?"

"See to your father, Emily," Gates muttered through barely parted lips. "Deming and I will be in the parlor."

Emily smiled smugly and left the room.

Marcus grinned inwardly. Emily and her cousin were at odds and she was not going to give him the upper hand.

He considered Emily's invitation for him to stay. She wasn't just being polite. She seemed relieved by his presence. After their bitter exchange at the Wittington's ball, he had feared she would leave him standing at the door. She may have resolved that their relationship in London served its purpose and though it ended less than pleasantly, it had to come to an end. She had greater things to worry about.

And, of course, there was her lover.

With her father's life so tenuous, Marcus knew he'd be the selfish one to demand any more from her.

He followed Gates into the parlor. Though they were well into July, the housekeeper had ordered a fire in the hearth to alleviate the harsh damp air created by the storm. The room was comfortable and welcoming with fine furnishings, classic ceramic vases on marble-topped tables, an ornate plaster ceiling and well-chosen artwork on the walls. The chill in the room, in Marcus' perception, seemed to radiate more from Gates' barely cloaked hostility than the dampness.

Gates led Marcus to a comfortable leather chair by the fire before offering him a glass of port. This time Marcus accepted more for cordiality than desire.

Gates poured two glasses and handed Marcus his drink before taking an identical chair across from him. "You must excuse my cousin. If you have come to know her at all, you must be aware that she is highly emotional and accustomed to her own way. As an only child, her father has spoiled her."

Marcus' brows furrowed. He didn't share Gates' opinion of Emily. Emotional wasn't the word he would use to describe her. Passionate, yes, independent and determined in her pursuits, unquestionably. "She obviously fears for her father," he replied, deciding it best to avoid a confrontation.

"Indeed, it is a trying time for all of us."

"No doubt."

"I have gone out of my way to be of service to her father during this difficult time, Lord Deming. Emily has shown little appreciation for my efforts. If I have appeared distracted or unwelcoming, I assure you, these unfortunate circumstances have weighed heavily on my shoulders." Gates stared at the glowing embers. "I have much on my mind, keeping my uncle's affairs in order and his servants on task."

"Understandable." Marcus took a slow sip of his port. "Has Mr. Hughes an efficient steward to alleviate some of your concerns?"

"I dare not interfere with his steward's responsibilities. I am here to assure my uncle that nothing goes amiss and none of his staff takes advantage."

Marcus took another sip of his drink while Gates folded and unfolded his long, thin legs. Gates' shallow attempt at hospitality or to win favor for his service to his uncle had no effect on Marcus. Furthermore, his edginess disturbed him.

"I appreciate your concern for my cousin's welfare, Deming, as well as your good wishes toward her father," he hesitated, "of which you have had no acquaintance, I believe?"

"I have not had the pleasure of meeting Mr. Hughes."

"My uncle has discouraged visitors. He is a proud man and has had no desire for others to see him in his present state. I am sure a man of your regal standing would understand."

Marcus gave Gates a sideways glance. "Indeed."

"I attempt to cater to my uncle's wishes regarding visitors. My full attentions must be on the matters of the household of which he has entrusted me. If I have offended you, please accept my apologies."

"No apologies necessary. As you said, it is a trying time." Marcus felt certain Gates' lack of hospitality had more to do with his own inconvenience.

With little more to say to one another, the two men sat in an uneasy silence as they sipped their port and gazed into the fire.

Marcus was grateful for the unexpected storm. He wanted to find out if there was anyone else who Emily could count on for support. She wouldn't receive any from Gates. Where was this man of whom she wrote those tender words of love? The mere thought of the letter disturbed him, but better to know if she had someone to turn to in case his intuition concerning her cousin proved true. As he pondered the predicament, he watched Gates drum the fingers of one hand on the arm of his chair.

"If you don't mind my asking, where do you reside when you are not visiting your uncle?"

Gates' hand stilled and his brow lifted at the unexpected question. He took a sip of his port. "Most recently, I have been spending time in London. I have found we enjoy city life… Ah, I see you are almost finished with your drink. Let me fill your glass."

We? Marcus thought, aware that he had avoided additional details or given a home address.

Before Marcus could press the question, Emily returned. Both men stood as she entered.

"Emily, is Lord Deming's bedchamber readied?"

"Yes, it is all prepared." Emily gave Marcus a warm smile. "Our footman Peter is waiting for you in the hall and will show you to your room. Please let him know if you have any other needs."

Gates set his empty glass down quickly and clasped his hands together. "Well then, if you will excuse me."

Marcus watched as Gates left the room without a care that Emily was being left alone with him. Then he remembered the footman's presence outside the open door. Regardless, with her father ill, he wished another chaperon was available to her.

"I should go to the stables to check on Jericho and retrieve my satchel," Marcus said, walking closer to where Emily stood.

"You shall be drenched in this downpour. When the rain lets up, a footman will retrieve it for you."

"I assure you, I'll not melt in the rain," Marcus gave her a crooked grin. Even in her plain day dress and her hair wrapped carelessly beneath her cap, his body reacted to her nearness. Her defiance of her cousin only made her more alluring. He had an immediate urge to take her into his arms and kiss her. Further, he'd spent the past couple of weeks moving from anger at her deception to desire for her body. Without the aunts about, he would need to rein in his lust.

Best to keep his distance.

Alone with her now, he could ask her about her lover. Make it clear that he would be pleased to know that she had someone to support her during this crisis.

Despite his own bruised ego.

"Once you are settled, Marcus, I shall enjoy showing you about the greenhouse and gardens," Emily said, snapping him out of his thoughts. "Father is quite proud of his plantings. His gardens are quite lovely and impressive. You will stay to see them, will you not?"

Marcus watched her as she bit into her lower lip. He realized that she was not unaffected by their moment alone together. He reached out and brushed a curl from her cheek. Her eyes widened at his touch. Seeing her anxiety, he compressed his lips and stepped back.

"I shall be delighted to see the greenhouse and your father's gardens," he said. "Though I believe your cousin would prefer that I wade through the mud tonight rather than wait until tomorrow."

"Ignore him and his incivility. He is self-centered and ill-tempered. He may attempt to control my father's house but he is master of nothing. Must you leave so soon?"

"Such family congeniality between you two," he said, not answering her question. He rather enjoyed seeing her eyes flash with anger when she referred to her cousin. Unlike the first moment when he saw her looking pale and tired, he saw evidence of the woman who had encouraged a ruse, defying convention. The woman who also, he reminded himself, lied about her reasons for the pretense.

"I despise him," Emily seethed, crossing her arms tightly below her bosom.

Marcus sucked in a breath. He'd been thinking about her for too long and in ways too ungentlemanly. *Does the chit have any idea how intoxicating she is?* He doubted it.

"If my father was aware of the way he has taken control…" Emily shook her head dismally. "I just cannot bring myself to tell him. Once he begins to improve, he'll most definitely handle Willard in his own way."

"And if your father's condition does not improve, Emily?"

"I refuse to think of it."

Her fierce look of determination made her even more desirable. He offered his arm and led her out the door and into the hallway where the footman stood a few feet away. Except for the housekeeper who he'd seen flitting about, there seemed no worthy chaperon to keep an eye on Emily's actions, or to keep him in line. He couldn't remain alone with her for another minute or he would crush her against him and demand the answers he wanted from her sensuous lips.

They walked together toward the main entrance of the house. The footman followed some lengths behind.

"Emily, you mentioned another interest, before you left London. I would be relieved to know that you have a diversion from the stress."

Marcus watched her expression change, as if an invisible veil floated down over her face.

"I have had little time for other interests. My focus is on my father's needs."

"But if you could receive a measure of comfort to relieve your stress?" Marcus waited, wondering if she would finally acknowledge a suitor.

"Oh, dear—" Emily's hands flew to her face. "With so much happening, I neglected to tell you. Aunt Delia plans to visit. In another day or two. Perhaps you could stay at least until she arrives?"

"She is coming then. Good," Marcus said, relieved but aware that Emily was avoiding his prodding. He wasn't going to find out anything today.

As he considered rephrasing his question, the housekeeper scurried over and bobbed a quick curtsy.

"Forgive me for interruptin'."

"It's fine, Heddy. What is it?"

"You said to find you as soon as your father wakes."

"Yes, thank you. I shall be up in a few minutes."

Heddy offered Marcus a cheery smile and left as quickly as she'd come.

"I must see to my father. Please, make yourself comfortable. Peter is at your service." Emily took a few steps toward the stairs. "I shall look forward to seeing you later this afternoon."

"Until then." Marcus remained in place until Emily disappeared up the staircase.

Although the footman offered to retrieve his baggage and check on his horse, Marcus refused, preferring to get out into the rain. He needed a good soaking after the way his blood heated in Emily's presence. The heavy rain would have to suffice for the time being.

Chapter Eleven

THE RAIN CONTINUED steadily for the rest of the day. Emily did not return, having sent a message that her father was having a difficult afternoon and that she would see Marcus at dinner. To occupy himself, Marcus asked Peter to show him to Mr. Hughes' library.

Scanning the bookshelves, he found impressive collections of histories and mythologies as well as a wide selection of classic and contemporary poetry. He smiled to himself as he remembered Emily spouting poetry in the corner of the bookstore. How could he forget? That was the morning she'd suggested the pretense. Even then he'd been captivated by her.

He put the memory aside and leafed through some early philosophical works by the poet William Blake. Blake's works weren't as highly regarded as some others but Marcus found his ideas quite stimulating. Eventually, he chose a collection by Keats and read for a time.

He couldn't concentrate. Emily's cousin's behavior disturbed him. Among other questions in his mind, he wanted to find out more about the man. The thought of leaving Emily in his hands unnerved him. Perhaps he would stay until her aunt arrived.

How did he become so involved? His only

issue had been to keep his aunt from meddling into his affairs. Now he was doing his own meddling. His heart had begun to rule his head.

He really needed to leave.

His thoughts were interrupted by a footman who announced that dinner would be served at six.

When he arrived in the dining room an hour later, he found Emily standing by the window watching the rain and looking solemn. Her cousin had not yet appeared.

She turned when Marcus approached, her face brightening. "I had so hoped to spend the afternoon with you. I just could not leave Father. I do apologize."

"Not necessary. I spent a lovely afternoon in the library."

"So that's where you were keeping yourself, Deming," Gates said as he entered the dining room. "I should apologize as well for not being a more accommodating host. I found myself caught up in paperwork." Gates turned to Emily. "How is my uncle?"

"I gave him some laudanum earlier than usual. His stomach was on fire this afternoon."

Gates' nod seemed to say that they should expect nothing less.

"I am wondering if the cook is using spices too rich for him," Emily said. "I plan to speak with her."

"You have much on your mind, and a guest to entertain. Let me talk to her later." Gates spread out a hand toward the table. "Come, let us sit, and see to our dinner now," he said, changing the subject.

As Marcus took a seat, his discomfort grew over the interaction between cousins. Though the topic of their discussion concerned Emily's father's welfare, their tone toward each other created a chillier atmosphere than the dampness caused by the rain.

The mood in the room changed little as dinner progressed. Even Emily's attempts to discuss events in London of a common interest to her and Marcus, including their aunts' friendship, did little to dissolve the undercurrent of unease.

When the meal concluded, Emily excused herself to look in on her father. She voiced the hope that the laudanum had taken effect and that she would find him sleeping. Marcus saw her brief absence as an opportunity to ask her cousin some searching questions. Gates, however, offered not even a pretense of hospitality.

"It's been a long day for all of us. I am sure you agree, Deming. You must be tired from your travel today and my cousin—she needs her rest."

Despite Emily's efforts to be congenial, Marcus had noticed her exhaustion.

"She gets little rest sitting by her father's bedside for hours and has reason to worry. Sadly, my uncle shows no sign of recovery. I, myself, find it unbearable to watch his decline. I visit him in the evening and try to serve him in other ways."

Marcus listened without comment. He sensed the man had little compassion or ability to empathize with another's pain.

"Speaking of my contribution, I should begin

my rounds of the servants to be sure they have completed their chores," Gates said with a hint of exasperation.

Marcus lowered his eyes as he dabbed his mouth with his napkin. Best to avert his eyes or he might not be able to hide his disgust over Gates' posturing.

Gates pulled back his chair and stood. "With my uncle so desperately ill and Emily distraught, someone must keep an eye out, lest the servants take advantage. No doubt in your position, you understand."

Marcus rose from his chair. He doubted that Hughes' servants were as problematic as Gates would like him to believe. Still, he was pleased that Emily's cousin was showing some concern for her tired state.

Gates walked to a window, his back to Marcus, and shook his head dismally. "Rain has a way of dampening our spirits as well. Would you mind terribly if we make an early night of it?"

"No, not at all." Marcus would hardly have expected any more from Gates.

"Well then, I bid you good night. I assume you will want an early start in the morning."

"Actually, I promised Emily I would stay for a tour of the gardens."

Gates lifted a brow. "Yes, of course. My uncle's gardens are vast. I shall inform Emily's maid to accompany you." With that he nodded and left the dining room.

Marcus stifled a snort at Gates' inconsistent sense of propriety. He stared after him just as a footman and a kitchen maid arrived to clear the long table.

He had thought to remain downstairs in case Emily returned or to fetch a maid to bring a message to her, but thought better of it. Somehow he doubted that Emily would be pleased that her cousin had made the decision for her to retire, rather than devote time to an unwanted guest.

As he climbed the stairs, a thought crossed his mind that, perhaps Gates had turned Emily's suitor away in the same inhospitable manner. If that were true and the man could be scared off so easily, he wasn't a worthy rival.

Once in his room, he shrugged out of his jacket. What was he thinking, a rival? Better to be glad that Emily might have a protector. He could breathe easier knowing that she would not be alone and bereft if her father should die.

But first, he needed to find out who this man was and if he loved her or was simply toying with her feelings. If Hughes dies, he could not in good conscience leave Emily in Gates' care.

If her lover is serious, so be it. If not, perhaps her aunt could take her in. Otherwise, he saw no other choice.

He must marry her.

HAVING CHANGED INTO her nightgown, Emily sat at her dressing table, brushing her hair. She knew she needed to sleep, but she felt too much disappointment that Marcus chose to retire early.

Her cousin had told her that Marcus wanted to rest for his trip in the morning. And it was understandable. He must be anxious to be on his way, she thought, but she had spent the afternoon anxious to see him again.

Her cousin had been so rude to him, and she could not, in good conscience, have left her father who had suffered an especially bad day. What must Marcus be thinking of their hospitality?

After speaking with her father's physician earlier in the morning, she thought she could take no more.

And then Marcus appeared as if in a dream.

He hadn't tossed off their relationship as simply a temporary indulgence, nor behaved as he did on their last night in London. *He cares*, she thought pensively, *at least as a friend. Why else would he have come?*

She set her brush down and drew a hand to her lips. She had thought Marcus had wanted to kiss her when they were alone in the parlor. And what if he had, would she have melted in his arms? And what if she had given into that impulse and someone walked in? Regardless of her desires, if her father passed, she would be dependent on her cousin's goodwill. She needed to walk a very narrow path. Just the thought of being at her cousin's mercy made her cringe. She felt as if she were in a vise with her own confusing desires and societal expectations crushing her and stifling all hope for her future happiness.

She pushed away her thoughts and rose. She needed sleep, but when she got into bed, she stayed sitting up, lifting her knees to her chest and folding her arms tightly about them.

Her father had been in so much pain this afternoon. Was she blinding herself to the truth? Her cousin said as much, though his words enraged her.

Her thoughts returned to Marcus. He had asked about her other interest but she could not bring herself to tell him. Was she being foolish? Other women wrote. It would come as no surprise to him. She grimaced. But few women were as obsessed to be published poets. And how many of them have written about romantic love? Even Jane Austin chose safer subjects in her poetry.

Lately, the muse had deserted her when she tried to write. Since meeting Marcus, she had begun to wonder if her love poetry was a mere substitution for a desire to love and be loved.

Her way of thinking and her chosen path had in so short a time taken a different route. She had been complacent, sure of herself and her destiny. Perhaps the poets weren't simply expounding about the possibilities of love. Perhaps they had discovered that one spark, when in the presence of the right person, could ignite a passion deeper than one could imagine.

She had been the naïve one.

She reached for a poetry book by William Blake that lay on her bedstand. Leafing through its pages, she paused at one poem, "Love's Secret." She pressed a hand to her heart.

I told my love, I told my love,
I told her all my heart,
Trembling, cold, in ghastly fears.
Ah! She did depart!

She snapped the book closed and held it to her chin. She wondered if Marcus would depart abruptly if she told him what she was feeling. Her need at the moment was not for the muse of poetry to nurture her mind. A much deeper need caused her body to quiver in her most intimate of places.

MARCUS STOOD BY the window in the guest chamber having given up on sleep. It was past midnight and the rain had slowed to a drizzle. No doubt his departure in the morning would please Gates. Regardless of the man's desire to be rid of him, he had decided to stay until Emily's aunt arrived. He could not leave her until he clearly assessed the situation and left her in secure hands.

Would he really marry her, if there were no other options? He thought of his father's death wish after his mother passed away. He had been a devoted husband who, as far as Marcus knew, would never have strayed. In the end his devotion had crippled him. But was his grief a small price to pay for the love they shared? He'd never thought of his parents' love in that way. Now it felt as if doors in his heart had burst opened and revealed a yearning for everything that love might offer that he had tossed aside.

And it wasn't as if he were in love with Emily. Yes, he'd found her difficult to forget, but she had used him to her own ends. If he married her because she needed his protection, they would most likely go their separate ways. She would have security and he would maintain the kind of freedom he had witnessed with so many other men of the *ton*.

Marcus turned away from the window, paced the room and returned to the situation at hand. What of Willard Gates? He doubted the man could be trusted. Marcus' thoughts created a restlessness that made it impossible for him to consider sleep.

Donning the borrowed robe left for him, he opened the bedroom door quietly. He'd eaten little at dinner, finding it impossible to consume a meal in the uncomfortable atmosphere. Perhaps he'd find a piece of fruit or a slice of bread in the kitchen to satisfy his hunger.

Stepping into the darkened hallway, he looked about and listened. The house was quiet. He walked to the staircase and looked toward Emily's bedchamber.

He stifled an improper urge to knock on her door. Instead, he descended the steps. Reaching the floor below, he stepped cautiously, appreciating the dense oriental carpet beneath his feet. He had no desire to be found roaming about the house.

As he moved closer to the kitchen, high windows allowed some moonlight to slip through. Approaching another hallway, he heard muffled voices. He stopped and considered turning back. His curiosity got the better of him and he took careful steps toward the voices. Peering around a corner, he spotted Gates and the cook, Mrs. Hanover, he remembered. Though the alcove where they stood was darkened, the small window above them allowed enough moonlight for recognition.

He remained still in the darkness, listening.

They were speaking in hushed voices and he could make out only a few words. The cook was dressed in her night robe and their meeting gave no impression of being about the business of the kitchen. The gist of their conversation concerned Mr. Hughes' loss of appetite. As they whispered, the cook's hand fiddled nervously with her robe pocket. Both seemed frustrated not at each other but at the situation at hand. Marcus heard the physician's name mentioned. He gathered their discussion centered on Mr. Hughes' treatment, but to meet in the middle of the night to discuss the patient made little sense. Damn, he thought, if he could only get a few feet closer.

Too late. Their conversation was coming to an end. Marcus watched as Mrs. Hanover reached out to touch Gate's cheek. Interesting, Marcus thought. Emily's cousin and the cook... It seemed Gates had found a diversion while he awaited his inheritance.

Aware that Gates would most likely be coming his way, Marcus slipped from his hiding place, moved quietly to the staircase and up to his room.

Closing his bedchamber door, he disrobed and stretched out on the bed while he ruminated about what he had discovered. He made little sense out of the clandestine meeting except that an affair was most likely going on between the two. From what was discussed at dinner, Emily's cousin had moved into his uncle's home just a few weeks before her return. To become so well acquainted with a member of the staff so soon was odd considering his purpose here. He had boasted at dinner of the responsibilities he'd taken upon himself since his arrival. Obviously he found time to satisfy his lust.

Marcus closed his eyes, envisioned the scene in the hallway and tried to string words together that he'd heard. He felt there was something significant that he could not recall. Something... The thought eventually dissolved as he drifted off to sleep.

Chapter Twelve

"MY LORD, YOU are an early riser."

Marcus was surprised by the appearance of the butler when he descended the stairs. Though the servant was dressed in neat livery and projected a distinguished air, he looked older than his butler, Jennings. "Good morning. Yes, I have a tendency to rise early most days."

The butler held a hand to his ear. Marcus realized the servant was hard of hearing. He leaned as close to the man's ear as possible to avoid raising his voice. "I need to send a message of my delay to London. Might I be shown to a writing desk?"

The servant squinted and appeared to be weighing Marcus' request. Eventually he turned and shuffled toward a nearby sitting room. Marcus followed. The servant approached a small mahogany desk. With arthritic fingers that shook slightly, he set out paper, pen and ink.

"You will find servants in the stables who might oblige you with the delivery or wait until Miss Emily awakes to send for someone," the butler suggested with deference as he moved aside so that Marcus could take a seat at the desk.

"May I ask your name?"

"Fitzsimmons, I am called Fitz," the servant perked up at being asked and lifted his slightly stooped shoulders.

"Thank you, Fitz, for accommodating me." He waited for him to leave the room before sitting down. The butler didn't suggest Mr. Gates as the one to ask, Marcus mused. *His loyalty remains with the lady of the house.*

As he prepared to write, he considered his quest. Prolonging his stay, despite Gate's desire for him to leave, was presumptuous but after what he had observed, leaving Emily did not set right. He trusted his feelings more than his manners. Telling Emily about the clandestine meeting he had witnessed the previous night didn't seem to be the right thing to do either. She had enough on her mind and he needed time to investigate the situation.

He wanted more information on Willard Gates and he knew just the person to ask. Marcus and his friend, Andrew Forrester, squabbled like brothers, but he trusted the man with his life. Forrester would know what avenues to investigate. He knew that Forrester's position in government office gave him the privilege of information on residents in London and its surrounding areas. He considered his friend's reaction to his request. Forrester owed him a favor, more than one, Marcus thought with an amused smirk as he prepared to write.

He wrote a brief but telling description of the situation and his questions. Remembering that Eva Hanover was introduced as the new cook, he added her name for investigation.

Sealing the letter, he questioned once again his own interference. Perhaps he was being overly curious and too cautious, but Emily's reaction to her cousin was enough for him to make certain that she had nothing to fear. The man was cold and calculating. Marcus suspected that he was simply waiting for his uncle's death so that he could gain his inheritance. He doubted the man would treat Emily with the respect she deserved after his uncle's death. If Mr. Hughes left it to Gates to house Emily or give her an allowance, he questioned his reliability.

He hoped that today would reveal more information. He shook off the thought that he might even learn more about Emily's other interest.

Walking out of the house into the damp morning air, he wondered how he'd gotten himself involved in Emily's circumstances. He was complicating his life. Yet he could not do otherwise. Perhaps it was simply that she was his aunt's dearest friend's niece. They'd played their games at their aunts' expense and now he felt responsible for Emily's welfare.

Dash it! I should leave today.

When he reached the stables, he found two men sweeping stalls. A strong smell of stale hay and horseflesh filled Marcus' nostrils.

Samuel stopped in his work, swept back his sandy-colored hair, and greeted him. "What can I do for you, milord? You'll see your horse is bein' well taken care of."

Marcus nodded at the burly built man and noticed his work-worn hands holding the rake. He'd met him briefly the day before when he had checked on Jericho. Could he be trusted to deliver the message?

"I have an urgent letter that needs to be delivered today. Is there a willing rider who could travel swiftly to London without causing too much disruption in his duties?" Marcus held coins in one hand and the letter in the other. He opened the hand that held the coins before closing his fist around them. Marcus saw Samuel's eyes widen at the sight of the generous offer.

"I might need to speak to Miss Emily, my lord," Samuel said, staring at Marcus' hand.

This servant, too, shows allegiance to Emily's authority. "She is still asleep. No doubt she would extend the hospitality needed to make my stay comfortable. I shall assure her of the necessity of my request."

"My orders used to come from 'er father but since 'e's been feelin' so poorly...and Miss Emily bein' busy with 'im, she might not mind me doin' a guest a favor at 'is request."

"She might even be disturbed if you refused," Marcus said, rubbing the coins together with his fingers.

The servant nodded his head in agreement and reached out a hand for the letter and the other for the coins, dropping the latter to his side when Marcus pocketed the coins.

"Later, when you have returned with a response in hand."

Samuel nodded sheepishly. "I know a quick way to London, I do, sir. I promise to be back in no time at all."

"This letter must be placed only in the hands of the person to whom it is addressed. Do you understand?" Marcus asked, his voice commanding. "I have written his name and his usual whereabouts on the envelope as well as his residence. You may need to search him out if he is not at home."

"I understand, my lord. Mr. 'ughes, 'e's sent me on like errands and I never disappointed 'im, unless the person were dead, o' course," Samuel snorted, then gulped when Marcus did not share in his morbid humor.

Marcus reached into his pocket and took out the coins. "If you follow my instructions and return with an acknowledgement to be handed to me, personally, I will double this."

Samuel gaped and offered a broad smile. "You won't be disappointed in me, sir."

"How long have you worked here, Samuel?"

"Goin' on fifteen years, since Miss Emily was as small as this," he held his hands to his waist.

"She has trust in your service, then?"

"Oh, yes, sir! She knows I can be trusted," he boasted proudly, puffing out his chest. "It's me she asks to deliver 'er mail. Ain't that true, 'enry?"

A groom who'd been watching and listening with his mouth open clamped it shut and nodded.

"Then saddle up and be on your way within the quarter hour," Marcus ordered.

"Yes, milord, no problem. Just need to change my shirt, going' into London and all."

Marcus nodded and went to check on his horse, staying long enough to see Samuel ride off. When he returned to the house, he guessed it was after six and that most of the servants would be up and moving about. He hoped that Gates would sleep late. He needed more time to figure out what to do next.

He walked into the breakfast room and found it empty. Just as he was about to leave, Heddy rushed in. "Good morning, milord. May I pour you some coffee? Breakfast muffins are on the way. Perhaps, you'd like some eggs today?"

"I had hoped to breakfast with Miss Hughes this morning. I understand that she rises early to check on her father. Is she up and about yet?" Marcus hoped for some time alone with Emily without being under her cousin's scrutiny.

"Yes, milord. She's up at the crack of dawn and sometimes earlier to check on Mr. Hughes. I keep tellin' her we won't hesitate to wake her if she's needed, but she won't listen." Heddy lowered her voice to a whisper. "Between you and me, I think she fears she might lose her father durin' the night. He was sleepin' soundly this morning when she looked in on him. I didn't tell her that he was up a good part of the night sufferin' from those pains he gets."

"She has returned to her bedchamber then?"

"Not missy, once she's up and about, there's no gettin' her to go back to bed. She left for a walk, which is often her custom before her father wakes. The rains have stopped and a bit of sunshine is appearin' below those clouds. She's most likely roamin' about in the back gardens or by the stream, 'gathering her thoughts' as she tells me."

"The stream is beyond the gardens?" Marcus asked nonchalantly, his thoughts returning to the love letter he'd found written in Emily's hand.

"Yes, milord, a lovely stream. It flows beyond the trees that line Mr. Hughes' rear gardens and trickles into the pond. Well now, I should be goin' to see what's keepin' those muffins from being set out." Curtsying, she left the room.

His thoughts returned to Emily's love letter. *By the stream where we first met… Perhaps she meets her lover in the early morning hours*, he thought as he strode purposely toward the rear gardens. Seeing them together would surely free him from his obsession over her.

Rather than follow a well-trodden path, he chose to find his way to the stream through the woods. Just as he neared an opening, he heard Emily's voice. He remained where he was, behind a large oak, feeling like an interloper.

"I have missed you so. Where have you been keeping yourself? Samuel tells me you visit on occasion."

Marcus' brow furrowed. Though he couldn't see anything from his vantage point, her scolding tone gave the impression that the man may have been avoiding her. He waited to hear his response, but none came.

"My cousin is a scoundrel. Not allowing you into my father's home. He cannot claim it yet."

Gates forbade him to visit? Her suitor was most definitely a coward if he allowed her cousin to scare him off, Marcus thought scornfully.

"Oh, Percy, how I have missed you."

Marcus cursed under his breath. Her voice sounded muffled as if the man held her against his chest. *Percy, what kind of name is that? Sounds effeminate.* He leaned forward, listening for her lover's voice. He heard only the sound of flowing water and birds chirping in the trees.

They must be sharing a kiss.

He should leave, or confront the two lovers — an embarrassing exposure for Emily's deception, Marcus decided.

"At night, I miss snuggling with you in my bed."

Marcus hands fisted at her words. She had truly deceived him. He had thought her to be an innocent during their pretense of a courtship, afraid of marriage and, perhaps, what it entailed.

How often had he imagined her in his own bed? *Damn, I am acting like a jealous suitor.*

He needed to stop this craziness and leave her to her lover.

Meeoow.

What was that? Marcus craned his neck to peer through the thick leaf-laden branches.

"Are you hungry? Your food disappears in your dish each morning. Perhaps, I should keep you in the cottage. You might feel more at home."

Meeoow.

Marcus' mouth fell open. A cat?

The meows turned to purring.

Feeling more like a fool than an earl, he stepped around the trees and through an opening in the brush.

Emily, perched on a low rock wall, looked up, startled. A large, furry gray cat lay snuggled in her lap.

"Is something wrong? Did they send you to find me?" The sudden jolt of her body caused the cat to jump from her arms.

Marcus stared after the cat as it disappeared into the woods, pressing a hand to his lips to avoid dissolving into laughter.

"Marcus?"

"No, all is well. Your housekeeper told me you were out for a walk. I decided on a walk myself. I, uh, see you have a cat." He hoped he'd sufficiently masked his embarrassment.

"Yes, Percy. He's a bit overgrown but quite affectionate."

"An odd name for a cat." Marcus hadn't yet cleared his head of his previous misconceptions.

"After Percy Shelley, my favorite poet."

"Hmm, I should have guessed." He walked closer to where she sat. "I remember the day I found you in the rear of the bookstore. You were reading a Shelley poem."

"The day we agreed to the pretense." Emily bit her bottom lip and lowered her eyes. "My time there seems like a dream. So much has happened since then."

Marcus didn't miss the sadness in her voice.

"I really should return to the house," she said, brushing off her skirt where her cat had lain. "I have been gone far too long and someone might..." She slipped down from the stone ledge, stepping on a root bulging from the uneven ground and losing her balance. Marcus lunged forward and grasped her arm with one hand while his free arm circled her waist, steadying her.

"Thank you…" Her breath caught as her hands pressed against his chest.

Marcus lowered his eyes to her lips, slightly parted in surprise. His hand tightened at the curve of her waist. Only moments before, he'd imagined her in a lover's arms. Now he wanted to crush her to him and hear her whimper in his arms.

"Marcus," Emily whispered as she lifted her eyes to his. "I… must return."

He looked deeply into her eyes and stepped back, loosening his hold. He couldn't take advantage of her vulnerability and his need was too great. She had risen early for a few moments of peace and to "gather her thoughts" as Heddy had told him, not for him to create more chaos in her life. He released her, offered his arm and led her back to the path.

As they walked toward the house, he came close to telling her about the letter he had given to Samuel to deliver but decided against it. He didn't want to add to her worries now.

"You seem quite attached to Percy," he said breaking the silence. "I found myself quite jealous when I saw him sitting on your lap." He gave her a devilish grin, deciding it would be better to lighten the mood.

Emily slanted her eyes toward him and broke into laughter. It was the first time Marcus had heard her laugh since his arrival.

"My cousin tossed Percy out when he realized his constant sneezing was due to my cat. It was a battle I chose not to fight with him when I returned, though it was difficult to hold my tongue.

My cat has a much more pleasant disposition than Willard."

Marcus chuckled. His own disposition had improved greatly since finding that Percy was a cat.

When they neared the house, Emily paused and looked about cautiously. "I should return alone. I look forward to showing you the gardens later this morning. You are staying until then, are you not? I do wish you would stay longer. Leave when you must, but please do not allow my cousin to make that decision for you."

"I trust that your father is still the head of this house. Perhaps, I may discuss prolonging my visit with him." He wanted to meet her father. He'd even wondered if it was really Mr. Hughes who refused all visitors. He'd begun to doubt everything Gates had told him.

Emily's tentative smile grew into a much brighter one. "You will stay longer then?"

"At least until your aunt arrives, if that would please you and if your father permits it." His visit was meant to be brief — to satisfy his need to know why Emily lied about her reasons for the pretense. Instead of getting answers and being on his way, he was intruding into matters that were none of his business. What had gotten into him? He was complicating his life for a woman whose heart was with another.

"No doubt he will approve."

"What?" Marcus realized he'd become distracted with his misgivings.

Emily looked at him quizzically. "My father, he

would be pleased if you extended your visit. He has always been a gracious host and you are… a dear friend."

Marcus gave an appreciative nod, while wondering why being called a dear friend stung.

"I must check on my father."

"Of course."

Marcus leaned against a tree, watching her as she walked up the path to the house. He shook his head in frustration at the turn of events.

When he walked into the house, he went toward the staircase when he heard the door open in the nearby sitting room. "My cousin, if he had any manners would be awake to greet you and see to your day. I do apologize."

Her downcast expression tugged at his heart. The Hughes' home before her father's illness had most likely been filled with warmth and hospitality, unlike the present cold and hostile atmosphere her cousin's presence fostered.

"The morning has been most pleasant. After all, I've met Percy," he said quietly, giving her a crooked grin. "Go to your father. I have some paperwork with me that needs review."

Emily nodded. "Until later then."

Marcus remained at the foot of the stairs until she reached the upper landing. His thoughts returned to his foolishness at the stream. Though his appearance had caused the cat to scurry away, he'd never been happier to see a fleeing feline.

Emily wanted him to stay. She seemed to have put aside his treatment of her on their last evening together in London. Their pretense was meant to come to an end, though perhaps not so harshly.

And she saw him as a friend, despite the intimate moments they shared in London. Why didn't that sit well with him? What was it about her that caused him to want more from her? No, not just want, need.

Shaking off his thoughts, he climbed the stairs to his bedchamber to retrieve his satchel before going to the breakfast room. He found Eva Hanover and the housekeeper he'd met the day before setting up coffee, breads and cheeses on the sideboard. Their backs were to him and they were squabbling.

"Mrs. Hanover, I am perfectly capable of setting up this table without your help. I have been doin' it for twenty years, long before you arrived," Heddy snapped as she elbowed her way past Hanover's taller and slimmer figure to place the silver down.

"Mr. Gates prefers that I do it. Your arrangement he finds unsatisfactory. Why don't you go off to your other duties, Heddy?"

"I am Mrs. Wilcox to you and I am the housekeeper here. It is not your place to tell me where my duties lie."

"We shall see what Mr. Gates has to say about that."

"And I shall take my orders from Miss Emily," Heddy hissed.

From a side view, Marcus could see the cook grit her teeth, surely ready to snap back when she turned to see Marcus standing there. She clamped her lips and quickly stiffened her spine.

"Good morning, ladies," he said calmly as he strolled in.

Heddy offered a nervous curtsy. "Lord Deming, we were... Please, young man, have a seat. Let me pour your coffee."

Marcus smiled at the servant's attempt to adjust the behavior he'd witnessed, while Mrs. Hanover remained stern and rigid, her lips pursed. Though the cook looked to be in her mid to late thirties and not terribly unattractive despite her servant attire, her severe and surly expressions created an uncomely and prudish appearance.

"Lord Deming, if you will excuse me, I must see to my duties in the kitchen," the cook said curtly. She turned to walk away but hesitated. "I understand, your lordship, that you will be leaving later this morning?"

Marcus sensed that she was fishing for a definitive response. He simply shrugged. The woman was a newly hired servant and her question, in his view, was inappropriate. He wondered if his stay created an obstacle for her to spend time with Gates.

The cook waited and when she received no reply, she lifted her chin haughtily and walked out.

Marcus turned to the housekeeper whose expression reflected enjoyment over his encounter with the cook. "May I call you Heddy, or do you prefer Mrs. Wilcox?"

"Heddy, please, milord," she said, offering a quick curtsy. "Mrs. Wilcox to that shrew," she mumbled under her breath.

Marcus hid a grin with his cupped hand.

"I do hope that you will stay for a time. Miss Emily is in such need of diversion and a handsome gentleman like you will do nicely."

Marcus laughed jovially. "I appreciate the compliment, Heddy."

"Why, I have not known what to do with her, always at her father's bedside and hardly eating. I must worry about them both."

"You have been in Mr. Hughes' employ for many years, I understand from your... conversation with the cook."

Heddy's cheeks grew red. "Yes, milord, I do apologize that you witnessed such a display."

"No need. I am glad to hear that Miss Hughes has faithful servants concerned for her welfare."

"I have tried to be like a mother to her since her own mother died, and now the poor dear is going through such a trial. Listen to me go on! Your coffee is getting cold and I am jabbering. Please, have a seat. I will see to Mr. Hughes and see if I might relieve Miss Emily for a time. She spends too many hours by his bedside. Many days she falls asleep in a chair with a book in her hand. Oh, there I go on again!" Heddy tossed her hands in the air. "I should leave you to your breakfast."

Marcus leaned back in his chair, grinning at the housekeeper. "What times does Mr. Gates usually rise?"

"He stays in bed 'til noon most days," Heddy answered with an expression of disapproval, "though I suspect today he will be up earlier. After all, he must show courtesy to you, milord. I dare not wake him. He is not a pleasant sort in the morning."

Marcus doubted that the man would rise early for an unwanted guest. "Is he ever pleasant?" he asked, leaning a shoulder toward the housekeeper.

Heddy smirked. She took a few steps closer, looked toward the doorway, then bent down to Marcus' ear and whispered, "Mr. Gates is the most disagreeable, intrusive, domineering man I have ever had the unfortunate duty to serve."

Her vehemence was unmistakable despite her hushed tone. Marcus decided he liked Emily's feisty housekeeper. He had found a willing confidante, perhaps more than one, in this bleak atmosphere.

Chapter Thirteen

"FATHER, WE HAVE a visitor," Emily announced cheerfully after helping him sit up in bed and fluffing his pillows. "He arrived yesterday. Marcus Deming, Earl of Pembridge. I met him while in London. He is the nephew of Aunt Delia's dearest friend, Agatha Trumbell."

"An earl, you say," her father replied, lifting his brows. "Am I to assume," his words were stifled by a dry cough, "that he is courting you?"

Emily lifted the water glass by his bedside. "Please, Father, you must allow me to do the talking while you rest."

Her father accepted the glass and took a few sips before attempting to place it on the bedside table, nearly spilling its entire contents.

Emily grabbed the glass from him and set it aside.

"Cannot even hold a glass of water," he grumbled in a hoarse, gravelly voice. "I need to get out of this damn bed." He clutched his blanket with angry fists.

"Father," Emily scolded, you are still too weak. You must eat your breakfast this morning or you'll not regain your strength." Emily looked over at the tray that the servant had left a few minutes earlier. "Let's see what you can keep down today."

Before she could retrieve the tray, her father

reached for her hand. "Tell me about this Lord Deming."

"I shall tell you all about him as you eat." Ignoring his grumbling, she reached for the tray and set it down before him.

"How did you meet him?" her father asked before taking a small bite of coddled eggs.

"Aunt Delia held a small dinner party. Both Lord Deming and his aunt were invited."

"No one else? It was an intimate gathering then?"

"Yes, on Sunday evening shortly after I arrived."

"Your aunt must approve of him. And did he visit again?"

"Actually we met quite by accident the following morning. Aunt Delia and I were out shopping. I stopped by a bookshop. Marcus... Lord Deming happened by."

"He, Marcus, just happened to be in the same vicinity? How interesting."

"Father, you have stopped eating. Please, eat some toast." Emily wanted to change the subject. Her father was eyeing her too closely and his expression went beyond mere curiosity.

"Tell me more." He obliged her by taking a bite of the toast.

"He extended an invitation for a carriage ride through the park the following day, his aunt and mine as well."

"I doubt very much his main objective was to take the aunts for a ride. And were there other invitations? Other rides in the park, other events?"

Emily brushed away a few crumbs that had fallen on the coverlet and adjusted her father's napkin that had slipped toward his plate.

"My dear, I am asking simple questions. You appear unsettled. Did the earl behave in an unseemly manner?"

"No, he was very much the gentleman." Emily hoped her smile covered the guilt that coursed through her. Her father must never know about the pretense. "We spent a most enjoyable evening at Vauxhall Gardens. The gardens were especially lovely and so much was going on."

"I am well aware of its allure, especially for young couples." Laying down his fork, he pushed the tray from him. "Take this away."

"Father, you've grown pale." She removed the tray hurriedly, reached for a napkin and wiped the sweat beading on his forehead. "The pain, it is bad?" She watched helplessly as her father's face distorted.

"Father?"

"It's… passing." He exhaled a shaky breath and settled his shoulders against his pillows before reaching for Emily's hand. "Don't fret, my dear," he said, offering a weak smile. "These attacks have lessened. I want to hear more."

"Later, you need to rest." She wasn't convinced of his bravado. She could see how much the episode had drained him.

Her father patted her hand. "The two of you spent a good deal of time together—rides in the park, other events? Now he's here. You left London too soon, Emily. He might have made an offer."

"We are only friends." She hoped her tone was convincing.

"Your view, perhaps. Do not think, even in my decrepit state, that I have forgotten your assertion not to marry." He cleared his throat again and pointed to the water. Emily held it to his mouth while he took a few sips.

"Enough." He waved her hand aside. "If the earl makes an offer, you must reconsider. I may not be here to protect you. My finances, they are not so great that I can promise you a life of leisure."

"Father, I doubt very much that the earl plans to make an offer. And, please, you must not concern yourself with my welfare. When you are stronger, we shall talk about future plans."

"Where is Deming? Have you seen him this morning?" he asked gruffly.

"Yes, I visited with him briefly. Her thoughts went to their time alone by the stream. *If only I were bolder and had kissed him.*

She shook off the wayward thought only to meet her father's questioning gaze.

Please, you need to rest." She rose from her seat and smoothed her gown.

"I want to meet this earl."

"I shall tell him." She forced a bright smile. "I encouraged him to extend his visit until Aunt Delia arrives. I plan to give him a tour of your gardens this morning."

"Ah, you told him of my gardens. They must be wasting…" he cleared his throat again, grumbled under his breath and continued, "overgrown with weeds."

"I have taken special care to speak to Shields. He is keeping them up quite handsomely."

"Good gad! That man cannot tell a weed from a seedling. Calls himself a gardener," he muttered as he twisted the bedcovers.

He was growing agitated and she could see the discomfort on his face. "You must calm yourself, Father." She reached to straighten the covers.

"Let me be. You should not be playing my nursemaid while I moan and groan. Go, have your breakfast with this Lord Deming."

"Soon, Father." She looked at the food tray on the side table where she'd placed it. "Look, you have eaten most of your meal. That is a sure sign that you are improving." She wanted to believe her words, but looking into his face, fear clawed at her insides.

"Tasted only slightly better today. Is that new cook improving on her skills and her manner?"

"She is still short with the other servants. I must admit I do not care for her at all. I do miss Ellie so."

"Too many changes. If I could get out of this damn bed and see what is going on under my own roof." He attempted once again to straighten up but overcome by weakness, slumped back against the pillows.

Emily nodded in silent understanding. "Perhaps if you eat lunch as well, you will feel stronger and can sit up in a chair this afternoon."

"Send Lord Deming in to see me," he ordered, taking Emily by surprise.

"Certainly, after your afternoon nap."

"Nonsense, I get nothing but rest in this bed. Ask this gentleman of yours to extend his visit."

"He is not my gentleman."

"Regardless, I want more time to get to know him. Tell him that we will have lunch together and tell my nephew to go talk to Shields. I want to know how many plants that idiot has lost since I have been cooped up in this room. Go now. You spend too much time in this sick room."

Emily nodded in resignation but remained standing beside his bed, her hand on his arm.

"Off with you, I said. Tell Peter to get in here. I want my bath and a shave." He waved her away again.

She retrieved the breakfast tray and turned to leave.

"Emily."

"Yes, Father?"

"Tell Willard to personally check all the plants this afternoon, every one, and look for mold or infestation of insects. I want a complete accounting from him before dinner. I do not want to see his face before that. When that weasel comes in here I feel as if he is looking for signs of rigor mortis."

Though Emily cringed at his last words, she began to smile as she walked toward the stairs. *I would like nothing better than to give Willard your order.* With their vast gardens and Shield's incessant chatter, it would take him most of the day to complete the task. She hoped that the rain and humidity had greatly increased the population of bees that enjoyed the nectar from her father's flowers. Perhaps more mosquitoes too... she thought as she reached the stairs.

Her father's request led her to believe, as well, that he wanted Willard away from the house when he visited with Marcus. Her father, even bedridden, hadn't missed the way Willard hovered about like a hawk seeking prey.

Emily gave a brief chuckle as she descended the stairs, tray in hand. She thought of the mosquitoes. *Perhaps, I shall instruct Mrs. Hanover to pick vegetables in the garden this afternoon.*

AFTER LEAVING HER father in Peter's care, Emily found Marcus in the library absorbed in his work. Rather than disturb him, she observed from the open door. His broad shoulders were hunched over a set of papers and his expression revealed a man in full concentration. As much as she wanted to spend time with him, she decided it best not to disturb him in the middle of his affairs.

Having no appetite for breakfast, she poured herself a cup of tea from the sideboard in the breakfast room and carried it to her favorite sitting room near the front entrance. She'd decorated the room to blend with the landscape she loved to view from the large windows framed with ivory silk. The paneled walls were painted a soft blue like a summer sky and brocade fabrics on the seating were of the same color, with swirls of gold and ivory to reflect the sun and the billowy clouds. Deep green ferns flourished in corners and other varieties of her father's plants graced the marble tables.

She sat staring out the window, sipping her tea.

She could hardly believe that Marcus was here in her home. She almost wished she had interrupted him. The anticipation to spend time with him created a restless feeling within her. She opened a book of poems that lay on a nearby table. A glimmer of sunlight spread across the pages, promising a beautiful day. Glancing through the pages, she stopped occasionally to read a favorite poem, drawing nourishment from each word as another person might enjoy a succulent sweet. She paused at one of Shakespeare's poems.

> *Take, O take those lips away*
> *That so sweetly were forsworn*
> *And those eyes, the break of day*
> *Lights that do mislead the morn;*
> *But my kisses bring again, bring again;*
> *Seals of love, but seal'd in vain, seal'd in vain!*

"Oh, Marcus…" She brought a hand to her lips, embarrassed that she had uttered his name aloud. How surprised she'd been to see him at the stream. Her stumble from the low wall was more from her emotional reaction than any obstruction. When he had drawn her close, she hadn't wanted him to release her. She felt safe in his arms.

She wondered if her father guessed her feelings toward Marcus. *I hope he is not planning an inquisition into his intentions. Marcus might well leave before the day is over, fearing entrapment.*

"Pardon me, Miss Emily."

Jolted from her thoughts, she looked up to see her butler standing at the door. "Yes, Fritz, what is it?"

"A carriage has just arrived. I sent for Samuel, but I was told he left for London early this morning on an errand for Lord Deming. Henry is attending the new arrival. Your aunt, I believe."

"Aunt Delia has arrived? And two days early. How wonderful! Thank you, Fitz. I shall be right along to greet her."

Setting her book aside, she rose and straightened her skirt, glad that she'd worn the peach-colored morning gown purchased in London. She had spent more time primping, admittedly for Marcus. She'd even added color to her cheeks, though she had been unsuccessful in taming her curls on such a humid morning.

Odd that Marcus sent a servant off to London without mentioning it. Putting her curiosity aside, she left to greet her aunt.

She approached the main entrance just as her aunt and Agatha Trumbell walked through the door. "Aunt Delia, I am so happy you've come!"

Her aunt reached out to her immediately and wrapped her in her arms. "I could not stay away a day longer. I have been beside myself with worry. My dear friend Agatha refused to allow me to travel alone. I promise our visit will be brief."

"I welcome you both and please stay as long as you like. I only wish the circumstances of your visit were of a more pleasant nature."

"My dear girl," Agatha cut in. "Seeing you once again is pleasure in itself. When Delia told me she was coming, I feared she might not take care of herself during the journey. With her arthritic condition, she must remember to stop occasionally and walk about, otherwise she stiffens up so."

"I'm thankful that you accompanied my aunt."

"I feared that I would be imposing, my dear," Agatha said, her smile cheery. "I have been terribly worried about you, having left London so suddenly. And Marcus, though he tries to hide his feelings, I can read him well. He was beside himself when he'd heard you had left. Why he left for his county house immediately, bereft. After all, the two of you spent much time together. I felt the need to reach out to you. A letter could not express my heart."

Had it truly upset him, Emily wondered, or was it Agatha's wishful thinking?

"Agatha…" Delia interrupted, her expression clearly indicating to her friend that enough had been said. She reached for Emily's hands. "How are you? And your father?"

"Please allow me to see both of you settled before we talk. I shall have Heddy prepare another room immediately."

"In no time at all, miss." Heddy chimed in, having been at the top of the stairs when Fitz opened the door for the guests. I've already sent Maggie to do just that." The housekeeper hurried down the remaining stairs. "Now I am off to the kitchen to order tea. Shall I bring it to the blue room, miss?"

"Yes, Heddy, just as I would have asked. You are well acquainted with my aunt, of course. Miss Trumbell is her dearest friend."

The housekeeper welcomed both of the older women with a curtsy. "If you have any special requests, ladies, you mustn't hesitate to ask."

"Indeed, may I come along with you to the

kitchen?" Agatha lifted a stout bag she'd been holding to her side. "I have cakes, specialties of my cook. I refused to arrive empty-handed, especially on such a difficult occasion and without notice."

Heddy's eyes gleamed at the short, plump guest with the wide smile. "Of course, Mrs. Trumbell, this way please."

As Agatha walked off with Heddy, engaging her in conversation, Delia drew her arm into the crook of her niece's. "Knowing Agatha as well as I do, I believe she wants to give us some time alone. Though she can be a bit too obvious in her intentions, she is a dear. Now tell me what is going on, child. After your last letter, I began packing immediately. I could not stay in London wondering how you and your father are faring."

"But your health, Aunt Delia..." Emily took her arm to lead her into the sitting room. "Come and sit."

"No, no, I have been sitting far too long in the carriage. Despite Agatha's pleas to stop every half hour, I was too anxious to arrive. My joints are stiff. Allow me to walk about with you a bit while you tell me of your father's condition. Your letters have left many questions unanswered."

"I too often write at my most anxious moments. I should not have troubled you with my worries."

"Stop that, young lady. He is my late sister's husband. I should have come with you on your return, but these old bones seldom behave themselves. Your father has always been so robust. I should have taken his illness more seriously."

"Neither of us would have expected such a rapid decline. I am so afraid for him." Emily's eyes grew moist and her chin quivered.

Delia wrapped her arms about her niece whose body shuddered in her arms.

Wiping her eyes, Emily pulled back. "Forgive me. I fall apart too easily these days."

"I highly doubt that. How long have you held in those tears?" Delia wiped away a tear from her niece's cheek. "You look pale and you've lost weight. Are you eating? Come, I am ready to sit. You must tell me all that has happened since your return."

Emily led her to the most comfortable sofa in the sitting room just as Maggie arrived with tea. Dismissing the maid after she set down the tray, she spent the next quarter hour telling her aunt of the most recent developments.

As Emily paused to pour tea, Marcus appeared in the doorway.

"Mrs. Fenning, I am relieved that you have arrived."

"And how pleasant to have you here upon my arrival," Delia said, giving him a broad smile. "Emily told me of your visit. Your aunt has come as well. I believe she shall be quite stunned when she sees you." She waved him closer. "I must say, without you in London to mother, Agatha has been forced to fill her time gallivanting about Bond Street and buying a whole new wardrobe. Our teas have turned into a show of fashion."

"Mother? You mean, badger," Marcus groaned. "I was on my way back to London, actually, to prod her into packing up. I decided to take a detour." He paused to acknowledge Emily with a nod before turning back to her aunt. "I planned to give you and Aunt Agatha a report when I returned."

"I have saved you the trouble," Agatha said as she entered the sitting room. "And I do not badger, I encourage. The housekeeper informed me of your visit. Indeed, it came as quite a surprise."

Marcus rolled his eyes before greeting his aunt.

"I have packed for the country and need only to send notice to a footman to bring my luggage to the estate, though I do want to accompany Delia back to London…"

"I have traveled here alone many times, Agatha," Delia interrupted. "I promise to stop along the way. If Marcus has no need to return to London, you must go with him."

"Well then, Aunt Agatha. We shall leave together and go directly to Hartwood."

His aunt skirted around Marcus and narrowed her eyes at her friend. "You must give me your word, Delia, that you will stop at least every hour." Agatha waved a finger. "You were quite rebellious on the drive here."

"And more anxious than I shall be on my return. Not another word about it, Agatha."

Marcus cut a glance toward Emily. "How were the roads? Were any impassable from the heavy rain yesterday?" He asked as Agatha took a seat across from Emily and her aunt.

"Not that I am aware. The ride was bumpy enough." Delia rubbed her backside to prove her point. "You were smart to delay your return. The sun may be showing its face to tease us, but more rain is not far away. I can feel it in my bones."

"Emily has graciously asked me to extend my visit until your arrival."

"Glad of that. I would have missed your company. I should hope you are not scurrying off now that we are here." Delia turned to Emily. "Would you mind, my dear, if Marcus stays a bit longer?"

"Of course not, and Father has encouraged him to stay as well. I am relieved to have all of you here though I must warn you, the atmosphere is quite depressing."

"Life has its bright as well as dreary times. We must accept them all, you know. Just being here with you warms my heart." Delia smiled at her niece before turning her gaze back to Marcus who stood only a few feet away with his hands clasped behind his back. "Young man, I am most pleased that you have demonstrated such concern for my niece." She settled back in her seat. "Tell me, have you met my brother-in-law?"

"Oh!" Emily jumped from her seat. All eyes turned toward her. "I became so absorbed in our talk that I lost track of time. I should have summoned Fitz to find you, Marcus. Luncheon will be served in less than an hour and my father expects you."

Marcus nodded. "I am honored that your father desires to see me."

"I wish you could have met him before his illness," Emily said, shaking her head as if to shake off her despair. She brushed her hand over the skirt of her gown and squared her shoulders. "If you will visit with our aunts for a few minutes, I shall be back in no time at all. I must tell Mrs. Hanover of father's request. She should prepare a heartier meal for you."

"Your housekeeper was looking for Mrs. Hanover to prepare the tea, but she was out in the vegetable garden," Agatha intervened.

"Indeed, it slipped my mind. I sent her out to gather fresh vegetables for canning."

"I would prefer to be served the same meal as your father."

"He eats little, perhaps some soup, a slice of bread, fruit at times."

"More than enough."

Emily nodded, pleased that Marcus displayed sensitivity toward her father's inability to eat the massive meals he'd once enjoyed. "And Marcus, you will agree to stay a few days longer?"

"How can I refuse? As your aunt has proclaimed, it seems there is to be more rain."

Chapter Fourteen

EVA SWATTED AWAY one mosquito and then another as she bent down between the tall rows of bean plants. "I don't appreciate your cousin ordering me out to the gardens today, Willard. She must have known the rains would multiply the insects. They are out in full force."

"You want my sympathy for pulling at a few vines? If my uncle thinks I am going to grovel around his immense gardens checking his overgrowth of plants all day, his mind has truly been affected. I've put Shields to work on the northern side for now and told him to be quick about it. After all, I should demonstrate my efficiency as the new master of the house."

Eva twisted her head toward Willard who stood above her. "I would not be surprised in the least if his daughter did not devise this distraction. After all, she has a male visitor. No doubt the servants keep a blind eye."

"At least the earl has created a diversion. The staff is busy making sure that he is comfortable." Willard cleared his throat. "I think we should increase the dose, Eva."

"No, not that again. It's too dangerous," she said with a slump of her shoulders. "We agreed his decline must be gradual. Increasing the dose could cause him to stop eating or make his illness suspect." She tugged at another vine almost viciously.

"His decline is taking too long. No one would be surprised if he succumbs soon."

"His death must appear natural." She rested a hand on her knee and looked up at him. "We have been patient this long, and you must know I want it over just as quickly as you do. Do you think I like playing the role of a mere servant?"

"I have no more patience. He has been bedridden for over three weeks, and my cousin still questions why I dismissed his physician." He paused to look about the vegetable garden, making sure that no one was in earshot. "What if I had not confiscated the letter she'd written to him? I told Emily his doctor was ancient and worthless, but now she questions Brandt's abilities."

Eva sagged back on her haunches and rested an arm on the handle of her basket. "Your uncle has weakened nicely. The problem is that the nausea causes him to eat too little of the meals I have prepared for him. He fears he'll vomit in front of his daughter. To make matters worse, Miss Hughes comes to the kitchen and takes him fruit, crackers and cheeses. He must eat what I bring him."

"Her return has caused more delay," Willard grimaced, wiping sweat from his forehead with his already damp handkerchief. "Deming may be a diversion at present but he makes me uneasy."

"We must stay focused." Eva snapped more beans off their stems and tossed them in her basket. "He should be leaving in a few days at most, but if

Hughes does not eat the meals I prepare him, the poison is useless. Rather than increase it, perhaps we should stop the doses until the visitors are gone."

"Why on earth would we do that?" Willard asked through clenched teeth.

"If Hughes has a couple of good days, it might demonstrate more confidence in Brandt." Eva wiped the sweat off her own brow with her apron. "If Miss Hughes tried to contact his other physician before, she may try again. What was his name? Dr. Howard? He must not return under any circumstances. His suspicions scared me half to death," she muttered, slapping her bare arm to kill a small spider.

Willard groaned. When his uncle's physician had suggested that Hughes might have ingested something from his array of gardening tonics, he'd had no choice but to insist on another opinion. He'd tossed Howard out just in time. "We cannot afford to wait much longer."

"Everything was going so well before his daughter's return." Eva slapped at another mosquito that landed on her forearm. "I have to get out of this infested garden. Pressing a hand to her back, she stood and lifted her basket with her other hand. "What do you suggest we do, Willard?" She reached out to touch his arm.

"Stop that!" He hissed as he brushed her hand aside and took a step back.

"It's been too long."

"We cannot afford to reveal our relationship. Once the house is mine…"

"Then what? How do you plan to transfer me from cook to wife?"

"Replace his servants, of course. Do not worry, my sweet." He lowered his chin and offered her a tight grin. "There shall be time enough after I rid myself of his daughter."

"You still have no idea what provisions her father has made for her?"

"Only the mention of the small cottage. He has said nothing of an allowance or a monetary inheritance."

"She cannot be allowed to stay on the property."

"I doubt she has any desire to live under my protection. Most likely she will go to live with her aunt or, perhaps, marry the earl. Hmm..." Willard paused and considered the benefits of the union.

"Go on. And if she does decide to remain here?" Eva gave him a look of exasperation.

"If she chooses to live in the cottage and a sudden fire erupts in the dwelling, she will need to find another residence. I assure you it will not be here. Do not worry, darling, she will not return."

Eva's expression appeared skeptical before she gave him a weary nod of acceptance. "A copy of his will must be somewhere in his study, unless he keeps it hidden in the library. With that nosey housekeeper about, it has been impossible to search for it."

"I searched through all his papers, those I could get my hands on, while my cousin was in London. I can find nothing." Willard swore as he swatted another mosquito that had landed on his neck. "We must take care of one situation at a time." He rubbed his sticky fingers on a nearby leaf. "I do not agree that we should stop the doses." As he pondered, he pulled at another leaf and crushed it within his fingers. "We might try another method to be certain he is getting the full effect of the poison."

"What are you suggesting?"

"Willard rubbed his jaw. "Yes, perhaps during my evening visits with my uncle we shall drink brandy together."

Eva's eyes lit up while the hand she'd been using to toss the beans nervously in the basket stilled. "Yes, a sprinkle of the powder in his glass before he sleeps. A splendid idea. Though with his sensitive stomach, he may refuse to drink."

"Brandy is good for the stomach. I'll tell him Brandt suggested I give his medicine in a drink. What better way to take it but in a hearty glass of brandy? If he questions the doctor later, well, we do know the illness has begun to affect the man's mind."

Eva grinned. "The damage can be done while he sleeps."

"And bring an end to him sooner. With Brandt's inexperience, the good doctor will not see my uncle's inevitable death as anything but natural." Willard looked toward the house before drawing closer to her. "Where are the vials?"

"Always in my pocket. I'll take no chance that someone might discover them." She reached into her apron pocket and handed him one of two tiny bottles, returning the second one to her pocket. He grasped it tightly and slipped it into his own coat pocket while his eyes scanned the garden walk.

"Remember, only a grain."

Willard smirked, turned away, and walked on ahead of the cook.

MARCUS STOOD TO the side of the tall window in his bedchamber, watching the distant scene. He took a step back when Gates walked toward the house. Raking his fingers through his hair, he pondered the scene. Although he could hear nothing of their conversation, Gates' expression and stance disturbed him. They were having a heated discussion, Marcus thought. A lover's quarrel? His instincts left him puzzled. He seemed too comfortable with the woman. Not at all like a man having a romp with a newly hired servant.

He grimaced as he straightened his cravat. Gates' behavior was odd, very odd, indeed. Casting a last glance in the mirror at his appearance, he left the room to meet with Mr. Hughes.

Peter, Hughes' manservant, met Marcus at the head of the stairs and led him to the sickroom. Hughes sat in a cushioned chair by his bed when the men entered. A small table was set up before him that held a tray of sandwiches, fruit and iced tea.

Marcus hoped his expression hid his dismay at the older man's appearance. Hughes' slouching shoulders were broad and his legs long though his robe covered them to his ankles. Marcus guessed that on healthier days, the man would have presented an impressive figure.

"Forgive me, Lord Deming, for not rising to greet you. I fear I am not at my best today." Hughes said in a gravelly voice.

"It is I who should apologize, sir, for intruding on your household without notice." Marcus drew closer and offered his hand. Hughes lifted his own, while meeting Marcus' eyes with a long stare. The weak handshake added to Marcus' concern for the man.

"Sit, young man, and tell me what brings you to my home, but first, we must eat." Hughes opened his palm to indicate to Marcus he should help himself.

Marcus obliged, remaining silent while Peter adjusted his master's plate closer to him and poured him a glass of iced tea. Hughes waved him off. "Leave us, Peter. I am sure that the earl will aid me if need be." He winked at Marcus as the servant bowed slightly and walked from the room.

Emily's father still had a sense of humor despite his ailment, Marcus mused, as he waited for Hughes' to begin his meal.

"Eat, Deming. I would have finished this entire tray of sandwiches a year ago. My appetite, however, has disappeared along with my strength."

"I appreciate your hospitality and your willingness to see me."

Hughes merely nodded and lifted his sandwich. They ate in silence. When Hughes wiped his chin and tossed down his napkin, Marcus noted the man had eaten barely a quarter of his sandwich before ringing a bell for his servant.

When the trays were removed, Hughes rested back in his chair. Marcus thought to suggest that he might be more comfortable in bed, but sensed the man's pride would be offended.

"Well now, Lord Deming, I understand that you spent much time with my daughter in London."

"My pleasure. My aunt and your sister-in-law are the closest of friends. Aunt Agatha was anxious to meet your daughter when she heard of her arrival in London."

"And you were not?"

"I... was delighted to make her acquaintance, of course."

"Sounds like you were less than pleased. Don't think I am not aware of the way women work to engage attention for their charges."

Marcus couldn't help but grin at the man's discernment. He could hardly be less than honest with him. "I admit I was hesitant to meet a new arrival. My aunt has made it her main objective in life to find me a wife."

"Yet you spent time with my daughter. A great deal, I understand."

"I enjoyed her company. I assure you, Mr. Hughes, we were well chaperoned."

Hughes grumbled and cleared his throat. Marcus waited as he appeared to hold back a breath as if he were stifling pain. *The man should be in bed, not holding an inquisition. What does he want from me?*

"Why have you come, Deming?"

"Your daughter left London quite suddenly. I

was concerned, especially after hearing of your illness."

"To offer her solace?"

"Yes... I hoped to find that all was well."

"Indeed. As you can see, I am not well. Not well at all."

Marcus noted that one of Hughes' hands was pressed to his stomach while the one that had been resting on the table formed a fist.

"Perhaps, I should call your manservant."

"Not yet." Hughes leaned toward Marcus, his pale eyes boring into his. "My daughter is a stubborn young woman. I have spoiled her—"

"She has been well brought up, sir. She is thoughtful, intelligent..."

"And quite lovely, don't you agree?

"Indeed."

"Then don't waste time with this old man. Get on with your visit." Hughes reached for his bell. Before Marcus could react to his sudden dismissal, Peter entered.

"I am ready for my nap, Peter. See Lord Deming out." He looked up as Marcus rose from his chair. "I want to see you again before you leave." He waved a hand, his expression a grimace that reflected a man, not angry, but in pain.

Chapter Fifteen

AT THE DINNER table that evening, Gates sat quietly though his insides were bristling at the inconveniences to his carefully thought out plan. Immediately upon his return from the gardens, a servant notified him that two more visitors had arrived. He'd been beside himself. To make matters worse, while he was in the hot sun being eaten by mosquitoes and gathering useless information, Deming was visiting with his uncle. He had spent the rest of the day simmering over the additional obstacles and wondering what his uncle and Deming had discussed.

He forced himself to listen to the conversation around the table while growing impatient for the dinner to end.

His cousin was chatting comfortably with her guests about their activities in London once again, all of which suggested an intimate relationship with Lord Deming. They'd certainly spent enough time together flitting about the town during her visit. *Soon I will be the one to enjoy the ton's affairs*, Gates thought as he patted his mouth with his napkin.

He was reminded of his own stay in London. With his mounting gambling debt, he could not afford to even rent a house for the Season. Fortunately he had met Eva. She turned out to be most generous. Her modest dwelling made it possible for him to take advantage of some of the city's enjoyments, mostly the gambling halls. He had no title, property, or admirable connections to be included in the grander events or to circulate in the more prestigious circles, but that would change once he inherited his uncle's estate. He paused in his thoughts when he heard Delia talking to Emily about their shopping trips.

"My dear, I so enjoyed those visits to the *modiste*. Madame Rochelle designed the loveliest gowns for you and your father would spare no expense."

"Gowns quite unsuitable for the country, I am afraid," Emily replied.

"Then you must return to London when your father's health improves."

Willard lowered his eyes, his teeth clenched. *Spared no expense, did he? Wasting my inheritance on foolish gowns. If I could only get my hands on my uncle's private papers.* He stabbed at another string bean on his plate.

He slanted his eyes toward the earl who was laughing at something Emily said. He wondered if Deming would take her off his hands. Their association might benefit him in the long run. His intimate relationship with Eva had played well into his plan, but he feared she might turn into a hazard in the long run. He would face that challenge later.

"Willard... Willard? Miss Trumbell asked you a question." Emily's address caused him to snap out of his thoughts. He lifted his eyes. All at the table were staring at him.

"Pardon me, I was thinking of some unfinished business," he said, straightening his shoulders. "I admit I find it difficult to revel in social activities at this time. What were you asking, Miss Trumbell?"

"Oh, not important, I simply felt that we were neglecting you in our conversations. Good Lord, we have spent most of dinner reminiscing about Emily's visit to London. We have hardly allowed you a word. Marcus mentioned that you spent time in London. I was saying that I did not recall ever seeing you at any affairs during the Season. Indeed, I try to attend as many as possible but too often settle into a comfortable chair and do not mingle as I used to when I was young and gay." She drew her head back and chuckled. Bunches of gray ringlets pinned back from her round cheeks bobbed merrily. "I asked if you had been in London long."

"I avoid social functions," Gates said, clasping his hands before him. "I doubt your enjoyments are my cup of tea." The corners of his mouth turned up briefly. "I actually left London shortly after my cousin arrived." He cut a glance to Emily. "To care for her father."

Emily flinched. Visibly stifling a retort to his insinuation, she changed the subject. "Lord Deming has agreed to extend his visit, cousin."

Gates' tightened his hands. He slanted his eyes toward Marcus who had obviously chosen to ignore his less than subtle comments concerning uninvited guests.

"I have accepted Emily's generous request to stay until her aunt leaves on Sunday," Marcus said. "Since Delia has brought Aunt Agatha along, she has saved me a London trip to retrieve her. We shall be able to go directly to my country estate."

After a pause, Gates nodded. "Ladies, your visit is quite convenient, is it not? You are worthy chaperones." He eyed his cousin. "I trust your father would agree, Emily, especially since he is incapacitated and unable to be a proper guardian."

Emily pressed her lips together and narrowed her eyes at him, but remained silent.

"My dear, your cousin is quite correct." Aunt Delia said, lacing her fingers together on the table's edge. "We would not want any undue gossip by servants."

"May I implore you to stay longer then?" Emily asked.

"Cousin," Gates interrupted, "you are being unduly thoughtless and inconsiderate of your aunt's plans."

"Please," Delia lifted a hand. "I am honored that she desires my company." She reached over to cover Emily's hand. "We can discuss this again tomorrow, my dear. London is only a few hours distance. On my next visit I shall pack more appropriately and return for a longer stay. That is if it would not be an inconvenience?" She turned her gaze back to Gates.

Inwardly cursing, he nodded in acquiescence.

"You could send for your things and remain for the summer," Emily pleaded.

"I must return to London for a few days. I left in quite a hurry, my dear. My next visit shall be longer, I promise."

Lifting his fork to his lips, Gates thought of the

week ahead. Damn if he would allow the woman to return for other than his uncle's funeral.

MARCUS SAT ON the edge of his bed, rubbing his forehead. He had hoped to have some time alone with Emily this evening, especially since her cousin left abruptly after dinner to visit with his uncle. Instead, out of respect for the ladies first night as visitors, he had spent only an hour with them before excusing himself. The aunts were here to console Emily and he felt compelled to leave them to share as women liked to do.

Samuel had returned a short time before and to Marcus' relief, Gates remained unaware of the errand. Emily seemed only slightly surprised when the servant arrived asking for him. He'd made a shallow excuse about sending a message to London concerning his delay and pocketed Forrester's note. He hoped he'd demonstrated its triviality to them.

As he took the note from his pocket, he wondered again if it would be wise to tell Emily about the meetings he'd witnessed between Gates and the cook. He tossed the thought aside. *She has enough to think about.* Regardless, something did not feel right. He felt impelled to investigate further. No doubt her cousin and Mrs. Hanover were carrying on an affair. That didn't warrant as much alarm, in his view, as something else indefinable about the meetings he'd observed.

He wondered if the other servants might be engaging in some gossip about the pair. He would have another talk with Heddy, he thought as he broke the seal of Forrester's note. While he read, he made a mental note to make his next fencing match with his friend especially bloody.

Deming,

Have you been dicked in the nob, old man, or has your aunt finally succeeded in her quest to have you leg-shackled? Your request is out of character, to say the least. Are you checking out future relations before being dragged to the altar? I suggest that you run rather than walk away from whatever you are considering.

You caught me just as I was making final preparations to leave London for the country. Since little time is left for correspondence, I will see what I can find out and make a side trip to Miss Hughes' home on my way to my estate. I should arrive on Saturday afternoon unless I hear from you or you should appear in London before then, having readjusted your crazed thinking. If I have nothing to report and you have wasted my time, I expect to receive appropriate compensation.

I have ordered that this note be handed directly to you. I trust you have chosen your messenger well.

Andrew Forrester

Resealing the note, Marcus returned it to his pocket. He pulled at his cravat, tossed it on a nearby chair and unbuttoned his shirt. Perhaps he should take Mrs. Fenning into his confidence. He discarded the idea for the time being.

"What am I doing preparing for bed before midnight?" he muttered. There was little else to do since the only other gentleman in the house did not demonstrate a desire for cards or for a drinking partner. He stood and rubbed the back of his neck. What were Forrester's words, crazed mind? Cursing to himself, he began to pace. "Why am I meddling into Emily's affairs? Shouldn't her lover be the one concerned with her situation? Where in hell is the man? I must be mad or close to it."

He thought of his brief visit with Mr. Hughes. The man was as pale as death, extremely weak, and obviously in pain. When Peter came to retrieve their trays, Marcus observed that even his brief stay tired him.

Though Hughes took only a few swallows of the food set before him, he had displayed his fatherly concern and his authority. He had wanted to assure her father that his visit was an act of friendship. He wondered if he had been at all convincing. He sensed that the man had hoped, perhaps, for a declaration.

He sat back on his bed and eyed the book on his nightstand about the life of Edward the First that he'd brought up from Hughes' library. He settled his back against the headboard and opened the book, hoping to clear his mind of his questions and concerns. After reading a few pages, he closed the book.

So old Edward ordered the extermination of all wolves in England. One must have escaped, he mused. Hadn't he arrived to prey on Emily, a wolf in the guise of friendship? Perhaps to grasp her from the hands of another predator, this elusive suitor?

Even in Emily's state of despair, he lusted after her. His desire for her was overshadowed by the question that pervaded his thoughts. Who was this lover? And did her cousin chase him off? Her father made no indication that he knew of a suitor. He sat up and clawed his fingers through his hair. *Forrester may be right. My mind has become muddled in madness. I could return to London and be free of this morose atmosphere. Except for Emily... The chit has bewitched me.*

He tossed the book aside and pushed himself off the bed. "Maybe I should go outside and howl at the moon. Or bring up an entire bottle of scotch. That should put me to sleep," he muttered as he rebuttoned his shirt. He had a feeling the next couple of days would be even more dismal, though the aunts' chatter would consume a better part of the day, he guessed. As it was, his reasons for staying confused him enough.

He tucked in his shirt and left the room. He might as well allow some liquid sustenance to either comfort or increase his insanity. As he walked down the stairs, he listened for any activity. The house was quiet with only a flickering light radiating from below the door of the room nearest to the front foyer.

Marcus passed the slightly opened door and heard what sounded like whimpering sobs. He hesitated until he was convinced that it was Emily in the room. He drew the door open slowly to see crumbled pieces of paper on the floor and Emily sitting alone, her hands covering her face as she sniffed into a handkerchief.

He wondered if he should intrude on her private moment. The strong, independent woman he had met in London was steeped in sorrow. He should stay uninvolved but instead he found himself even more enamored of her.

Her heart held so much love for her father and her grief was so genuine. He could only imagine her fear of the future if her father passed, though she refused to even broach the topic. Tossing aside his qualms, he walked into to the room quietly. She looked up from the settee, wide eyed.

"Marcus, I didn't expect to see you." Her eyes darted toward the door. "I thought everyone was asleep."

"The house is quiet. I believe we are very much alone."

Emily wrapped her thin robe more tightly about her and wiped away her tears. "I had trouble sleeping. You, as well?" She averted her eyes from his as she stuffed her handkerchief into her pocket.

"I was restless." He walked to her side and crouched down beside her, turning her face toward his. He wiped a tear from her cheek with his thumb. Her moist eyes glistened like dark emeralds in the candlelight.

"Emily, is there anything I can do?" He'd had little experience with grieving women. Women's tears from past dalliances were usually angry ones. He had promised them nothing and they'd wanted more. They had been better off without him, so their tears aroused little sympathy.

Emily's tears caused havoc within him. He wanted to protect her, to see the laughter he'd remembered in London, to lash out at anyone or anything that caused her pain. The reality shook him to the core as he gazed at her tearstained face. He would never have believed that his emotions could become so tangled up by a mere woman. He reached for her hand and clasped it in his.

"I am so sorry that a friendly visit has become

so wretched. Was it was wrong of me to ask you to stay?" Emily asked as she pulled her hand from his and pushed back damp, tangled curls from her cheek. "I am quite a sight."

He wanted to tell her she still looked beautiful to him, that the restlessness he felt was his constant companion since she'd left London. "I chose not to leave, Emily. Tell me what has caused such tears tonight? Has your father's condition worsened?"

"I looked in on him after our aunts retired. He was in a great deal of pain. I stayed with him until he fell asleep." She drew a breath. "I hold on to threads of hope but perhaps my cousin is right. I am refusing to face the truth. My father has shown no improvement."

"I still see hope in your eyes, Emily. That is the truth to hold on to." Unable to restrain himself any longer, he rose from his crouched position to sit next to her. He drew her into his arms. She didn't resist. He reveled in the warmth of her body and the scent of lavender in her hair. When she lifted her head, her moist lips were only inches from his. How he wanted to kiss away her pain. As quickly, he thought of her deception concerning the lover he'd yet to meet. He drew back. He wanted to wipe out the memory of the love letter, but he couldn't. Her lover was nowhere about and she was in a vulnerable place. He sensed he could take advantage, but his emotions had become too involved and he wanted more than a stolen kiss. He released her.

Emily lifted damp eyelashes to his, her lips parting in surprise before her expression changed to embarrassment. She leaned away from him, clasping her arms tightly about her waist. Uncomfortable moments of silence filled the space between them.

"I am sorry that you must see me like this," she said finally. "I find that I want to crawl into a corner and weep or snarl like a cat and defend my home from this calamity. And my cousin." She heaved a sigh. "He waits like a vulture."

"Your animosity toward each other is difficult to miss."

"I don't believe he holds any devotion toward my father, though he pretends to care. Tonight he visited him, wanted my father to drink brandy with him, insisting it would help his pain. He knows my father's stomach has been on fire. What was he thinking?"

Marcus' chest tightened. One thing was certain, Gates' presence was more a detriment than a comfort to the family and though he did not say it to Emily, he agreed with her assessment of him. Would Forrester's investigation be at all helpful, he wondered, as he searched his mind for other ideas.

"Emily, I know of a specialist in London, Dr. Bellingham. He is very well regarded. Would you allow me to send for him to examine your father?"

"Oh, yes, Marcus." She reached out, her hands clutching his arm, then pulled it back as quickly. "I would so desire another opinion. I had trust in my father's physician, despite his advanced age. Willard claims that Dr. Howard did not take my father's illness seriously. He dismissed him. I wrote to him when I arrived home, but he hasn't replied.

Willard had already called in Dr. Brandt to take over. My cousin has taken control of everything." Realizing that she'd raised her voice too loudly, she cupped her hand against her mouth and eyed the sitting room door.

Marcus followed her gaze, knowing it was best if they ended their conversation. "With your permission, I will send a messenger to London tomorrow to seek out the physician," he said quietly. "You remember my friend Andrew Forrester? You met in London. I've been in touch with him. He is traveling to his country house later this week. If I can contact him before he leaves London, he may be able to escort Dr. Bellingham here… that is if I might confide in him the urgency of the matter." Marcus realized an opportunity that had not occurred to him before. Forrester's visit on Saturday would need no other explanation.

"I would be most grateful." Emily hesitated. "If we might be able to keep this to ourselves and my aunt, of course, at least until we know if he will come."

"I understand. I shall have a sealed message ready for Samuel to take to London in the morning."

"I pray the doctor will come."

Marcus was pleased to see Emily's eyes bright with hope, though he could promise her no more. He wished her a better night's sleep and left the room.

EMILY RESTED HER head on her pillow, exhausted. The evening had been one of her hardest since

coming home but she did feel better, thanks to
Marcus. She wrapped her arms around her pillow
more tightly and thought of their time alone. She'd
been embarrassed, at first, that he'd found her
crying and dressed only in her nightclothes, but
when he held her in his arms… she didn't want him
to let her go. She pressed her lips together. She
must take care of her reputation. She must… Her
thoughts returned to the warmth of his arm
surrounding her. *Why must he be such a gentleman? I
hadn't thought that to be true in London.*

Chapter Sixteen

EMILY WOKE BEFORE daybreak, having slept soundly for at least a few hours. The thought of another physician examining her father had given her a measure of peace. Donning her robe, she left her bedchamber to check on her father. Finding him asleep and Maggie snoozing in a chair nearby, she heaved a sigh of relief. She had woken with the desire to ride this morning and too often of late had denied herself the enjoyment. She pulled out her riding habit and dressed hurriedly.

She was out the front door just as the sun began to rise. When she reached the stable she was surprised to find Marcus talking with Samuel. Or was she? She'd known Marcus was going to send a messenger to London early in the morning. A wave of shyness washed over her. She did want to ride and escape the house for a time. That was enough of a motive, despite what may have brought her here at dawn. She marched in and walked toward the men.

Both men turned at her approach. "Miss Emily, you're up early this mornin'. I was just talkin' to Lord Deming 'ere, 'e was askin' if I… "

"You need not explain, Samuel," Emily interrupted, offering a brief nod of greeting to Marcus. "I am well aware that he is sending you on a confidential errand to London. I suggest that you leave as soon as possible before my cousin rises and he demands other duties from you."

"Yer in your ridin' costume. Do ya want me to saddle up Sage?"

"You well know that I am capable of saddling my own horse."

"That I do, miss." Samuel looked to Marcus who stood with his hand clasped behind him, listening to the exchange and barely masking a grin. "Miss Emily's been ridin' since she were little. 'Er father and 'er, they use to go out together, that is before 'e took to bed." Samuel went on. "I'll be out of 'ere in no time, miss." Stepping through the hay strewn on the floor, he excused himself.

"It's barely dawn. Were you up again with your father?"

Emily avoided Marcus' eyes and instead walked over to her horse's stall. "No, I checked on him and he was resting comfortably. Maggie's with him and Peter is set to relieve her soon. I thought a ride might be a refreshing start of the day."

When she looked his way, she found him leaning against one of the stalls wearing a crooked grin, his eyes slowly roaming over her riding outfit. She was suddenly glad her aunt insisted she buy a new one. "I gather you are accustomed to going out riding without a groom?"

"Most definitely," she replied tartly. "Father has complete faith in my riding abilities."

"To some it would seem improper for you to go off on your own."

Emily shrugged a shoulder. "I realize in London, proper etiquette must be adhered to.

However, being my father's only child, he has not put such restraints upon me, perhaps because he never had a son. He has taught me how to swim and shoot arrows quite deftly. I have even gone hunting with him on occasion." Emily lifted her chin and smiled pertly, hoping she appeared more in control this morning and did not betray the discomfort she felt in his presence.

"Then perhaps you prefer to go riding on your own, though I would be pleased to join you."

Emily noted the mischievous curve of his lip. She couldn't possibly go out with him alone, though it was early. No one would be about. She looked over at the groom, hesitated, knowing that he had begun his morning chores. She gave the servant a beseeching look. "Henry, I realize it's quite early…"

"Not at all, miss. I'd be honored to accompany you and the earl. My chores will be done in plenty of time."

Emily quirked her head, surprised at his zealousness. Her groom appeared to show great admiration for Marcus in a very short time. She turned to Marcus. "You're welcome to join me." She turned away to attend to her horse.

"Then you must allow me to be chivalrous and help you saddle your horse."

"If it will feed your gallantry." She gave him a teasing smile. As she led Sage from her stall, she felt her heart fluttering within her breast like a dance of closeted butterflies.

"I believe the lady is showing the spunk I was a victim of in London," Marcus said while they worked together to saddle Sage.

Emily's lips curved in amusement as she tightened the stirrup to her liking. She thought to tell Marcus that she often rode astride, wearing breeches, when she rode in the early morning. Even her father approved when he took her with him to hunt since he found it to be safer for her. Her new riding costume would not allow for such disregard of propriety and as a member of the aristocracy, Marcus might be shocked.

Her thoughts trailed off as they led the horses out to the yard. Her groom helped her into her saddle. Once she was settled, her riding crop by her side, Marcus mounted Jericho and they were off.

They rode for a time, neither speaking, until they came to a wide meadow. Marcus pointed to a distant copse of trees. "Would you care to dismount and sit for a while? We've had little time to talk since I arrived."

Emily looked behind to her groom who stayed a respectable distance behind them. "It is best if we continue to ride, but would you care to race there?" She pointed to the distant trees.

"Let us race, then." Emily took off in an instant, leaving Marcus caught by surprise but soon chasing after her.

They arrived at their destination at nearly the same moment. For the first time in days, she'd been able to laugh and she was in no hurry to return to the somber atmosphere at home. She gazed back to see that they had left Henry a good distance behind but he'd be catching up soon. "There," she pointed to a brook that flowed nearby. "The horses must be thirsty after our race."

Marcus nodded. "I believe I shall join them."

MARCUS DISMOUNTED. WHILE his horse drank, he splashed water on his face before reaching for his handkerchief and patting his face dry. "Ah, refreshing. He looked up at Emily sitting tall in her saddle. "You are a confident rider. Few women attempt more than a trot, fearing a fall or a setdown by their peers."

"Do you think me less refined or find my behavior scandalous?"

"Not at all, rather I find it captivating," he said, giving her a wicked grin. "Are you certain you don't want to dismount? It would be rather pleasant to sit by the stream. He waved his arm in a flourish toward the large, rounded rocks at the brook's edge. Emily eyed her groom who had paused near the tree line. "Thank you, my lord, but it would not be appropriate." Despite her refusal, her eyes sparkled with humor and revealed a definite desire to join him.

Marcus remounted Jericho and they turned about riding at a slower pace and gazing at the meadow stretched out before them. Daisies were in full bloom and wild flowers swayed in the cool morning breeze dressing the meadow in cascades of vibrant, purples, pinks and yellows. Their petals still wet with dew sparkled as the sun rose above the trees. Its beams streaked through the leaf-covered branches and created a spattering of lights and shadows on the ground about them.

Marcus turned his gaze toward Emily and saw

a smile playing on her lips. "I believe this is the first time I have seen you smile with your eyes as well as your lips since I have arrived."

"I have had little to smile about—"

"You seemed to want to say more. Has worry already stolen your moment of contentment?"

"No, but I admit it is not far away. I want to thank you for your visit. I was losing hope. I should have stood up to my cousin, demanded another opinion. I was not thinking clearly. Each day I kept praying that I would see an improvement and willing my father to get better. Days just seemed to melt together."

"Just for this morning, or at least for this hour, let your mind rest," Marcus urged. "I admit I miss the sauciness I remember in London."

Emily slanted her eyes toward his. "You seemed glad to be rid of me the night of the Whittington ball. We had succeeded in our ploy. Were you not pleased that your aunt ceased in her attempts to bring you to the altar?"

Marcus looked searchingly into her eyes, wondering how much he should reveal. As his thoughts went to her deception, his expression grew serious. "Considering the circumstances at that time, I was pleased that we were of the same mind," he said finally, turning away to pull back on his reins when Jericho stopped to nibble on grasses.

With he turned back, Emily's gaze had dropped to his snug fawn-colored breeches, pulled taut as he pressed his foot into the stirrup. When she lifted her eyes, she flushed. He grinned, aware that she'd been caught. He wanted her admiration and much more.

"We were of the same mind, were we not?" Marcus said, returning to their conversation. His eyes settled on the smart blue hat she wore with an ostrich feather sticking out of its brim.

"Why, indeed. We accomplished our goal." Emily averted her eyes and turned to look back at her groom, appearing relieved that he remained a distance behind them.

"I remember well. You wanted to return to your other interest. I haven't had the pleasure of meeting him. Has your cousin chased him away?" There he'd said it.

"Him?" Emily glared. "You thought my interest was a man... a lover?"

"You had no desire to meet eligible men." He stopped short of telling her about the love note he'd found. "Your objection to finding a match was, well, questionable."

Emily's hand flew to her mouth before she tugged at the reins to urge Sage to pick up the pace. She rode ahead of him in a swift trot.

Marcus snapped his own reins and caught up with her. Her head was turned away from him and her shoulders appeared to be trembling. "What is it? Were you spurned?" He suddenly wondered if the man she'd written to had changed his mind about her, further adding to her grief. "I didn't mean to cause you more pain."

She turned her head. Instead of sobs, he realized that she was laughing almost to the point of tears.

"And what do you find so funny?" He said

angrily.

"You, Marcus," she giggled, covering her mouth to stifle another outburst. She brought her horse to stop. She waited for Marcus to do the same and peered back to be assured that the groom stopped as well. "I have no lover or male interest. Why is it that men always assume that a woman's only desire is to make a match?"

Marcus fisted the reins tightly in his hand, readjusted his position in the saddle and looked up to the sky. He felt as if someone had thrown a bucket of cold water in his face. All the wasted time he'd spent in jealousy over a phantom lover surfaced with incredulity.

It was his turn to laugh, and he did exuberantly.

"And may I ask what you find so hilarious? I made it clear I did not want to marry, had I not? Marriage is not the only means to happiness for a woman," Emily blurted.

Marcus stifled his laughter, swallowed hard and stared into her confused green eyes. "And what else would a woman possibly want? I have not yet met a young marriageable woman who prefers to become a spinster. Girls are groomed for marriage," he said with a grin that bordered on mockery. "I should know. I have spent years dodging manipulative mothers and their simpering daughters."

His grin turned to a cynical frown just thinking about his past experiences. "Women not only want, but need a provider and protector. They fear the humiliation of being left on the shelf. I simply refused to be snared by one so she could go about preening over her victory."

"You, my lord, are smug and egotistical. You assume women are needy creatures who can have no other passion to embrace than to be wedded and bedded."

Marcus' chin dropped. He drew his horse closer to hers and grasped Sage's harness, drawing them even closer.

Emily mouth dropped. She glared at him, but not before her head snapped back to see her groom's reaction. "What are you doing?"

The desire to pull her down to the ground and cover her body with his warred with the reality that they were not alone. He stared into her eyes and then at her moist, parted lips before reluctantly loosening his hold on Sage's harness. He was certain he saw need as strong as his own. He pulled his horse away from hers. Jericho whinnied, obviously annoyed at his master's rash movements.

What did she say about women having no other passion to embrace than to be wedded and bedded? He took a deep frustrating breath.

"You, my sweet Emily, have deep passion," he whispered gruffly, "and you do want to be embraced."

Emily lips compressed before she galloped away.

Marcus cursed. He hadn't meant to mock her.

He admired her independent spirit, lusted after her body, felt feelings he'd previously believed he could shrug off as easily as an evening jacket. And there was no suitor. She hadn't deceived him.

But what of the letter? He was more confused than ever.

He had wanted to confront her to heal his wounded pride, to free himself from thoughts of her, to resume his life as a carefree bachelor. He was confident he was above falling victim to love. Until Emily. He was beginning to understand his father's grief and how deeply a man could feel for the right woman.

Enough to make an absolute fool of himself.

EMILY LEFT HENRY to unsaddle and care for Sage. She needed time to herself before she could face Marcus again. Thankfully the house was quiet when she entered. She went directly to her bedchamber, shut the door behind her and leaned against it. Her shoulders sagged with humiliation at her own weakness.

Blast! The men in her life were driving her mad.

Marcus caused her to dream dreams she had tossed aside and to fulfill needs, yes, passionate needs that she'd banished from her thoughts. And now that she had come to realize her deeper desires, she fell in love with a man who wanted nothing to do with love. Then there was her cousin. The very sight of him appalled her and yet, she might have to depend on him for her livelihood. She should probably treat him with more deference if she did not want to be left destitute. Further, her father's illness was draining her of her strength. This last thought caused her to feel only guilt.

I must go check on Father... She looked at her

writing desk and inkwell. *My poetry, it seems almost trivial now. I thought my life secure. I was happy, wasn't I?* She pushed back the tears that threatened. "I will not cry!"

If only she'd confided in Aunt Delia long ago. She had feared being controlled and at the mercy of a husband's whims. She'd refused to become bitter like her mother. Her poetry had kept her needs at bay, had been her passion, her completion. Hours flew by during her creative spells. She couldn't deny now that her writing had been an escape.

She forced her thoughts away from self-pity. *I must stay strong, and decide what I am to do if Father does not recover.* A chill ran down her spine. *I must consider my future if he...if he dies.* She sucked in a breath.

She slumped onto the edge of her bed. If only the physician Marcus sent for would come and find a cure. Marcus was truly being a friend, despite his rakish behaviors—his devilish grin, his very presence.

She must not hope for more.

Could another physician make a difference? Her father grew weaker each day. How foolish she'd been to take her father's presence for granted. Marcus was right. Women expected a man to be their protector, their security. *I depended on my father.* He expected that she would live in the cottage and depend on her cousin's generosity. Why else would he put up with Willard's bothersome presence? He had said as much, hoping we would overcome our animosity. She'd left him with no other choice, especially with a stubborn daughter who refused to consider marriage.

She must talk to her father. *If I am to be left with a monetary inheritance, he must allow me to access it and not give my cousin authority over my portion.* She could stay with Aunt Delia, at least for a time. She could work as a governess if need be.

Emily opened a drawer where she stored her poems and pressed her hand against the pile. Her passion to write still flickered within her, but she wanted more.

Perhaps I'll marry. Emily drew a hand to her lips. *But only for love.*

Chapter Seventeen

MARCUS FOUND NO opportunity during the day to apologize to Emily for his arrogant remarks. She'd remained at her father's bedside most of the morning and lunched with him. She'd visited with the aunts for a good part of the afternoon and was pleasant enough at dinner. The day left no opportunity to be alone with her and she made no mention of showing him her father's gardens. It was obvious she didn't want to be alone with him.

Surprisingly, Emily's cousin was a bit more amiable, even offering to play a game of chess later in the evening. Marcus accepted his invitation more out of curiosity than desire.

After dinner Gates left to visit his uncle, the ladies retired to the parlor and Marcus headed for the stables. He suspected that Samuel would be returning soon and he preferred to meet him away from the house. Fortunately, Gates had spent most of the afternoon in his uncle's study and remained unaware that the servant had left for London. *If the man doesn't check on servants and their duties*, Marcus wondered, *what does he do locked up in Hughes' study most of the day?*

Pushing the thought aside, he entered the stable and greeted Henry who was feeding the horses. Samuel arrived soon after.

"Milord," Samuel said, slightly out of breath, as

he dismounted. "I came back as fast as I was able, though I did stop for a small pint, what with the long ride ahead o' me. I did just as you said, sir, got the message right to where it belonged and got this for you." Smiling proudly, Samuel opened a small satchel attached to his saddle and handed Marcus a sealed letter.

Marcus raised a hand. "You did well, Samuel. You should be able to buy a few more pints with this."

The servant looked down at the coins Marcus dropped in his hand and beamed. "Yes, sir, thank you, sir," he babbled as he bowed, wearing a wide smile.

Marcus left the stable and found a bench in a quiet garden alcove to read Forrester's letter. His friend acknowledged his request and promised to seek out the physician and encourage him to make the trip to the Hughes' residence. He would accompany him, even if he had no news to share concerning his investigations. Little more was written except for some concern over what his friend had gotten himself into this time.

Marcus folded the note and tucked it into his pocket. The feeling that something was amiss concerning Willard Gates gnawed at him.

When he returned to the house, the butler met him at the door. "Sir, Mr. Gates is in with his uncle. He has requested that you meet him in the parlor for a game of chess at ten."

"Thank you, Fitz, and the ladies?"

"Mrs. Fenning and Miss Trumbell have retired to their rooms. I believe Miss Emily is in the kitchen speaking with the staff. Would you like me to give her a message, milord?"

"No, Fitz, you can go about your business."

The servant bowed and walked toward his quarters while Marcus headed for the kitchen. As he drew closer he heard a ruckus. He found Emily standing between Heddy and Eva Hanover, her arms spread out to keep them apart. He took a step back to study the situation, questioning whether he should interfere.

"The two of you must stop your bickering!" Emily demanded.

"Tell her to stop takin' over my duties. I am the housekeeper here," Heddy hissed as she swung a wild arm toward the cook, managing to grasp only a piece of her apron.

The cook screamed and with both hands struggled to pull the material out of Heddy's grasp.

"Heddy, you have made yourself heard, now step back," Emily ordered.

"That woman should be discharged," the cook sputtered as she pulled and finally released the measure of material. "When I tell Mr. Gates…"

"Mrs. Hanover, you have been hired to work in the kitchen," Emily cut in, obviously attempting to keep her anger under control. "Cleaning in my father's study is not one of your duties."

"Mr. Gates requested that I dust the book shelves since they were done so poorly. I was following his orders," the servant harped back.

"Those shelves have just been done!" Heddy snapped back, her chin jutting out, her face crimson and hands fisted on her round hips.

"Heddy, go to your room. I shall take care of this," Emily ordered.

The housekeeper remained, glaring.

"Heddy."

The housekeeper let out a loud sigh. "Sorry, Miss Emily. She has no business doing my..."

"To your room, please."

"Yes, miss," Heddy mumbled. She left through the back door after offering a slight curtsy to her mistress and a scowl to the cook.

Emily glared at the servant who stood stiffly with her nose lifted and her hands pressed tightly against the large pockets of her apron.

"Mrs. Hanover, regardless of what my cousin has told you, he is not the master of this house. He is a family member visiting and helping out while my father is bedridden. You shall come to me for further instructions if you find that your kitchen duties are not enough to keep you occupied. Do I make myself clear?"

"Yes, Miss Hughes. I understand, perfectly."

Marcus observed that though the woman acknowledged the order, her pinched expression reflected her indignation at the setdown. He wanted to march in and chastise the impertinent servant. Emily was going through enough without having to deal with such pettiness. He refrained, knowing it was not his place to interfere.

He waited until the cook left her station and disappeared through the same door Heddy had exited earlier. He hoped their rooms in the servants' quarters were far apart.

"Emily, I am impressed at your voice of

authority."

Emily twirled about. "Oh, Marcus, you seem to find me at my worst moments. Were you looking for something?"

"For you, I did not want to intrude." He took a few steps into the room.

"So, you heard them," she sighed. "I suppose I should let her go, but I don't have the energy right now to go searching for another cook." She leaned back against a counter and shook her head despairingly as Marcus drew closer.

He drew her into his arms. Forgetting their earlier argument, she leaned her head on his shoulder and closed her eyes. Marcus took in the scent of her as the tension of the moment eased.

When Emily lifted her eyes, Marcus saw conflicting emotions in their depths. The time was not right to explain his earlier ill-mannered behavior or to expect her to understand his feelings, feelings he was not yet ready to acknowledge. At this moment, she needed a friend. "You should get some rest," he said abruptly, before releasing her and stepping back.

Emily bit her bottom lip, nodded and without another word, left the room.

MARCUS WATCHED EXPRESSIONLESS as Emily's cousin pondered his next move.

The man is a poor chess player. Marcus tried his best not to take advantage of his ineptitude. He could have ended the game a quarter hour ago, but was enjoying the man's determination to best him.

When Gates finished his move and sat back

looking smug, Marcus lowered his eyes to the board. He took his move. "Checkmate."

Gates glared, realized his king was trapped. "I bow to your cleverness, Deming." He offered a tight grin that evaporated as quickly as it appeared. He reached over to a nearby table for the bottle of whisky they had been sharing. "May I offer you another drink?"

"Yes, one more should help to give me a good night's sleep."

"Have you found your accommodations comfortable?" Gates asked as he poured.

"Most definitely."

"Deming, I prefer not to avoid issues or eventualities. As Emily's future benefactor, I would appreciate knowing your intentions toward my cousin."

Marcus had wondered when Gates would get around to questioning his intentions. He had not decided until that moment how to answer. He felt no compulsion to grant Gates, at present, the significant position of being in control of Emily's future.

Marcus lifted his glass and sipped slowly before answering. "Emily and I are friends. If our relationship is meant to go beyond friendship, it will not be until her father's health improves. Her focus is on seeing her father well."

"Come now, you have met my uncle." Gates set his glass down. "He has shown no improvement. His condition is grave. He has spoken to me of Emily and my responsibility for her welfare after he is gone."

Marcus nodded but remained silent. He wanted to hear more, while at the same time he doubted Gates' information held any truth.

"I appreciate that my cousin clings to a faint hope. I believe you to be a realist." He paused and took a gulp of his drink before going on. "My cousin and I, as you have surely noticed, do not get along. We never have. I suspect that my being her father's heir rattles her immensely. I fear she will find it difficult to remain at the estate."

"And you would like me to take her off your hands?" Marcus asked with a note of sarcasm.

"That sounds a bit harsh put in those terms." Gates shrugged, as he slid his glass to the side and twined his long fingers together. "I expect my cousin will bristle under my authority. However, I assure you that I will do my best to carry out my dear uncle's wishes."

Marcus didn't miss his pompous air nor believed a word of his declaration. He drew back his chair and stood, having had enough of the man's manipulative manner. Picking up his drink, he gestured in mock salute and took a final sip. "I prefer not to reflect on uncertain futures, Gates. I shall leave that to you. Thank you for a stimulating game of chess. Now if you will excuse me, the drink has fulfilled its purpose. I am ready for sleep." With an arch of his brow, Marcus set his glass down, turned and left the room.

FINALLY GIVING UP on sleep, Emily tried to write. Writing her thoughts or penning a poem had previously been her way to work out problems, but tonight nothing helped.

The servant issue would need to be addressed with her cousin. He was installing himself in a position that was not his, and she planned to tell him just that. She worried about the confrontation but she knew it was long overdue.

While Willard's behavior angered her and her father's condition terrified her, Marcus' presence turned her inside out. In the kitchen he had been thoughtful and concerned, while earlier in the morning, he'd mocked her.

He actually thought my reason to return to the country was a suitor. She couldn't help but smile. *Where on earth did he get that idea?* She pulled back defiant curls that were increasingly unmanageable in the humid weather. *I said only that I had another interest. For him to assume that it must be another man is outrageous. He cannot accept that a woman might have other passions as important.*

As important as love? Her eyes rested on the row of poetry books on her shelf written by Donne, Shelley, Lord Byron and Shakespeare. How often had she read their odes to love? It had been safe for her to think of love locked in words penned by poets as lovely illusions and its loss as the penalty of believing in false promises.

Suddenly the poets' verses held little magic. She thought of Marcus only a few doors away. She wanted to go to him, to have him hold her as he did this morning, regardless of the consequences. What if she told him about her desire to be a published poet? He would tell her only men strive to the business of publication. He'd certainly see it as a frivolous past time.

She picked up her journal and reread what she'd written.

Poets praise romantic love
And pine away its loss
Fill pages with its humbling power
And rail against its cost.
Thoughts of love spill on a page
A testament to the muse-
Fanciful imaginings,
Are they more ideality than truths?
Instead of soaring with the doves
In Love's celestial spheres,
My heart lies heavy in my breast
with unfulfilled desires.

She closed her journal and set it aside. How difficult it was to express the throes of love that reach far beyond expressions on a page. She couldn't express the new hunger she felt inside, especially knowing that the object of her interest slept in a bedchamber only a couple of doors away.

She rose from her chair, picked up her candlestick and prepared for bed. Once she was settled under her coverlet, she stared up at the ceiling and watched as the flicker of the candle created swirls of soft light and shadows. She needed sleep, she reminded herself, but still she did not snuff the candle.

Her aunt had insisted on sitting up with her father to allow her to get a full night's rest and instead she was dwelling on Marcus again and love as elusive as the changing shapes of light above her. She reached for the book of poetry by Shelley that lay on her bedstand, the one she had purchased in London. Opening it up, her eyes drifted down the page.

Our breath shall intermix, our bosoms bound,
And our veins beat together; and our lips,
With other eloquence than words, eclipse.

"Marcus..." she sighed as she brushed her lips gently with her fingers. Placing the book back on the bedstand and snuffing out the candle, she lifted the coverlet over her head and willed herself to go to sleep.

Chapter Eighteen

"THE RAIN WILL be here before the day is out. I have no doubt," Delia said, rubbing her knee. She and Agatha sat beneath the curved roof of the rear veranda to avoid the summer sun late Friday afternoon.

"Delia's bones are quite accurate when they act up, Marcus," Agatha said as her nephew joined them and took a chair unshielded by the roof.

Marcus nodded inattentively, looking out at the vast gardens and seeing clouds in the distance.

His thoughts were elsewhere.

To his surprise, Emily's father had sent for him before noon. He had spent over an hour by Hughes' bedside. He reviewed their meeting as the aunts nibbled on the assorted cakes set before them and continued their chatter.

Marcus felt certain Hughes had considered carefully beforehand every question he'd asked. He hoped his answers had set the man at ease. Hughes' concern for his daughter's future welfare had no doubt initiated the second meeting. It was also clear their discussion was meant to be confidential.

Sadly, Marcus noted the man appeared weaker than when he had seen him two days earlier.

After briefly touching on light matters, Hughes directed their conversation to his daughter, emphasizing her exceptional qualities, with only a brief mention of her independent nature. Marcus had clamped his lips together to avoid a guffaw.

Hughes turned the conversation to Emily's desire to remain single. In a somber voice, he told Marcus about disappointments in his own marriage that may have colored Emily's view of wedded life. Though Marcus sensed that Hughes found it difficult to talk negatively about Mrs. Hughes, he shared enough for Marcus to gain a picture of a bitter woman unhappily married.

How unlike my parents' relationship, Marcus thought.

He thought of Emily growing up without siblings and in a home where marital hostility reigned. He could only imagine the fear or even disgust of marriage that her mother may have instilled in her.

Marcus ran a hand along the black railing of the veranda and traced, absently, the scroll designs of the wrought iron with one finger.

Once Emily's father had freed his mind of what he wanted to share of his family, the conversation grew less strained between the two men. Hughes acknowledged that he had met and carried on cordial conversations years before with Marcus' father and mother at ton events. He shared some of his recollections. Marcus talked about his sister Felicity and her growing family and touched on his Parliamentary duties since inheriting the earldom.

It didn't take long for Hughes to turn the conversation again to what Marcus believed was the main point of the visit.

"No doubt you have given thought to the need of an heir, Deming," he'd said as nonchalantly as if he were discussing the weather.

Emily's father, Marcus decided, was a strategist and a wily one at that. *He is no less a matchmaker than my aunt*, Marcus mused. *The man has great hopes for his well-planned strategy.*

Marcus did too.

Settling in his seat, his lips curved into a grin. He found it interesting that whenever he used the word friendship to describe his relationship with Emily, Hughes conveniently went into one of his coughing fits.

Taking a deep satisfying breath, Marcus turned his attention to the aunts when he heard Emily's name.

"I wish your niece could join us, Delia. A little sunshine before the rain comes would be so refreshing for the girl," Agatha said, putting aside her empty cake dish.

"I asked her but the doctor had arrived. She wanted to wait and speak with him. I suspect she will be back to check on my brother-in-law once the doctor leaves."

"I don't suppose her cousin would take her place by her father's side so the girl could rest," Agatha replied. "What do you think, Marcus? You appear deep in thought."

"Gates plans his visit with his uncle in the evenings. He expects that Emily and the servants will take shifts during the day and through the night. Mrs. Fenning, I understand you have been sitting by his bedside during early morning hours."

"My brother-in-law is quite dear to me. I hope my time with him allows Emily a few more hours of sleep."

Agatha looked toward the house before leaning closer to Marcus and Delia. "Well, it just seems to me," she said in a hushed tone, "that his nephew spends the least amount of time possible with his uncle. He says he has too much to do, taking care of Mr. Hughes' affairs." Agatha put a finger to her chin and pinched her lips together before going on. "He spends an inordinate amount of time closeted away in that study, does he not?"

"Indeed, he does," Delia said flatly, lowering her lashes and taking a sip of her lemonade.

"I realize I speak out of turn," Agatha continued, "but the man is quite intolerable to be around. I find it impossible to carry on a normal conversation with him for more than a few minutes. I do believe he will be glad to be rid of us on Sunday."

Delia darted her eyes toward the house before setting down her glass. "Agatha, I agree with you that Emily needs some sunshine. I am going to relieve her."

Agatha clasped her hands together, her gray ringlets bobbing. "You must encourage Emily to leave that sickroom at once. I plan to enjoy the sun a bit longer. Indeed, I was eyeing that strawberry tart." Agatha reached for the tart and set it on her plate.

Delia rose and brushed a few crumbs from her skirt. She gave Marcus a brief smile and disappeared into the house.

"Marcus, would you pour me some lemonade?" Agatha asked once her friend had left. She held out her empty glass. "I must say your behavior of late is strange. And to find you here of all places when I arrived. You can imagine my surprise at…"

Marcus gave her a look that caused her to stop mid-sentence. He suspected she had been waiting for an opportunity to question him about his sudden visit. He set the pitcher down after filling her glass to the brim. "I would prefer to save this discussion for another time." He stood.

"I believe I'll spend some time in the library this afternoon. Hughes has some books that I am eager to peruse. He strode to the door, feeling his aunt's eyes boring into him. He turned and grinned. "Enjoy the sun, Aunt Agatha."

EMILY STAYED ON the front porch until Dr. Brandt's carriage disappeared down the drive. Her hands were clenched to her side. When she finally reentered the house, her aunt was standing in the foyer.

"Emily, what's wrong?" Delia could see from her high color and set expression that she was in a furious state.

"My cousin, how dare he not take the doctor's advice," she hissed through clenched teeth.

"What are you suggesting?" Delia held a finger to Emily's lips, urging her to keep her voice down. "First, you must calm yourself. I came in to relieve you so you can get some rest. Perhaps a walk in the fresh air might ease your anxiety."

"Heddy is with Father now. I left when Dr. Brandt came. When the doctor was finished, my cousin escorted him to the door. I waited in there out of sight." Emily pointed to the blue drawing room near the front door. "When my cousin went his way, I sought out the doctor as he was stepping into his carriage."

"Willard is always present during the examinations?"

"Yes, he insists as a woman I have no place being there. Later he hovers over any conversations I have with the doctor. This time I caught Dr. Brandt before he rode off."

"Brandt told me that on his last visit, he had recommended to Willard that another physician be called in for a second opinion. He even gave him a name. Willard requested that he not mention the idea of a second opinion to me because of my distraught state. The doctor told me only that my father had weakened more, and he'd made changes to the medication he hoped might ease his discomfort. Brandt is a country doctor, Marcus, an apothecary. I did not even know that! My father is not poor. He can afford the best of care."

"Oh, my dear." Delia rubbed away a tear that ran down Emily's cheek. "Is there anything I can do?"

"Just you being here helps. You are right. I need to go for a walk. Would you mind relieving Heddy so that she can get back to her chores? I won't be gone long."

"You take as much time as you need."

Emily pressed her hands against her aunt's and

walked out the front door.

MARCUS REMAINED IN the darkened hallway. He'd heard every word. He wanted to take Emily into his arms and hold her until all her fears subsided. He wanted to take her away from here, protect her. His hands fisted. And he wanted to grab Gates by the neck and lift his rail thin body in the air and pummel it.

He looked about. No one appeared and his aunt would assume he was in the library. He walked outside and looked about for Emily. He saw her in the distance walking along the path toward the side gardens. He waited until she entered the wooded area and was out of sight by any observer.

He followed the same path and caught up with her along the wooded path near a small cottage. He called out to her.

Emily stopped and looked back.

"Marcus, what are you doing here?" She looked about.

"I saw you leave. I know you're upset."

"I needed to be alone. Please, you must go back. At this time of day, the gardener is about. We might be seen."

"I'm not going anywhere. Walk with me," Marcus ordered. He grasped her elbow and urged her along. "Lashing out at your cousin today is not to your benefit, especially since a specialist may be arriving tomorrow."

"Everything in me wants to scream. How long have I been home, three weeks? Why have I allowed Willard to take charge of his care? And Dr. Howard, my father's physician, why hasn't he answered my letter? I have wasted precious time."

"Your time has been spent nursing your father, day and night, without enough rest."

"I trusted in Brandt's abilities. No, not, even that," she sighed. "I refused to believe my father would not rebound."

"Perhaps your cousin felt the same way. He may have hoped the medicine and the bed rest would make him well." Marcus did not believe a word of what he was saying. He imagined Gates rubbing his hands together in anxious anticipation of his inheritance. Still, he didn't want Emily to act rashly. He hoped that tomorrow some of the questions rattling about his own mind might be answered.

"Marcus, you do trust that your friend will bring the specialist?" Emily asked, her voice calming, while her eyes continued to be watchful of intruders.

"Most definitely, unless Dr. Bellingham is unable to get away immediately."

"But he will come."

"If I have to bring him here myself. I believe, however, that Forrester will do all in his power to escort him."

"You put much faith in your friend."

Marcus smiled. "Indeed, Andy and I have tried to best each other throughout most of our lives. We have also built a solid amount of trust."

"Does he share your view of wedlock?" Emily looked away as she asked.

Marcus was glad to see that Emily's mood had improved but was taken by surprise when she turned the subject to his previous views on marriage. "Forrester's father is a duke and enjoys good health and a large family. Andy's older brother and his wife are expecting a child soon. As a second son, he has no reason to rush to the altar. My aunt never fails to remind me that I do not have the luxury to remain free of the shackles."

"Shackles. That word makes little sense since husbands in our society have greater freedom than their wives."

"Has it ever occurred to you that most women want marriage and its benefits?"

"Perhaps they have not been given the freedom to nurture interests that might conflict with a wife's expected role, or a husband's expectations. As you have said, women are 'groomed' for marriage."

"Interests, now there's a word that I have been guilty of misinterpreting."

"Do you not agree that a woman must submit to her husband's rule if her interests are contrary to his expectations?"

"Titled gentleman hold positions in society that govern not only their behavior but that of their wives," Marcus said matter-of-factly before he slowed his gait and gazed at Emily curiously. "Is that your fear of marriage, that a husband would put undue restraints upon you?"

When she didn't respond immediately, Marcus found himself thinking of his earlier expectations — to marry someone compatible to his station, who knew her place, one reasonably attractive who would give him his heir, a woman he would respect but of whom he could never fall deeply in love.

EMILY DIDN'T ANSWER his question. How could she? She'd frowned on marriage because of her parents' dysfunctional union, but now she wanted more. She could see he expected an answer. A few raindrops saved her from a response.

"We should go back," Emily said, looking up at the sky. "Someone might come looking for me."

Frowning, Marcus stopped and turned toward her. Instead of moving on, he closed the gap between them. His eyes had darkened, like the sky above them.

Emily had seen that look on his face before. It was as if he was warring with himself. As if he wanted to kiss her and push her from him at the same time. She held her ground, leaning into him as the raindrops increased. *Let it pour*, she thought.

She got her wish.

The sky opened and a heavy rain pelted down on them. Marcus grabbed Emily's hand and ran with her along the path in the direction of the house. "The cottage we passed, we can wait out the rain there."

Emily bunched up the skirt of her gown, lifting it from the puddles of muddy water that formed on the path. By the time they found cover under the porch's roof, they were drenched.

"Welcome to my future home," Emily said breathlessly and with a note of derision. "My mother spent much time here."

"Did you spend time with her here as a child?"

"Seldom. She would say she needed time away by herself. "I came looking for her once when she'd been gone far too long. She was sitting by the spinning wheel she kept in there, simply twirling the wheel." Marcus followed her eyes as she stared into a window by the front door. "When I asked her what she was doing, she told me she was spinning dreams. She always seemed to be somewhere else in her mind, even when she sat right before me. This cottage will be left to me, that is if my cousin doesn't find a way to claim it," she said with scorn.

"Your future may be brighter than you foresee." Marcus grinned, arching a brow. "Our present, however, is creating a puddle on the porch."

Emily looked down and laughed. The laughter helped her to overcome a sudden shyness that rose up at the awareness that they were very much alone and away from any prying eyes. A pleasant defiance took its place but she pushed it away. They must return to the house. If only the rain would let up.

"Perhaps we could go in and wait out the shower."

Emily looked into his eyes. She wanted to say yes."

He reached up and drew a wet curl away from her cheek, caressing her soft damp skin beneath his palm. "Emily." His voice came out in a groan. He reached an arm about her waist and pulled her to him."

"Marcus, no. Someone might see us."

"It's pouring. Who would see us?"

"They'll come looking..."

"Before she could finish her sentence his lips came down on hers. He drew her closer, wrapping his arms more tightly about her. Her hands that were clutched to the front of his coat spread up and about his neck. His fingers combed through her hair dislodging her cap, the other drew her closer still, against his hardness. She returned his kiss, luxuriated in it, unable to resist the desire that pooled within her.

She stilled suddenly and pushed him away. What was she doing? Emily's lashes shot up. She bit into her bottom lip not realizing the effect that one gesture had on him.

He breathed out a ragged breath and drew her close again until he felt her warm breath mingling with his own. He kissed her lightly on the lips, then trailed kisses across her cheeks to the ridge of her chin.

"Marcus."

"We should marry," he said, drawing his face from hers." I can make the arrangements when I return to London." Her mouth dropped open. He lifted a hand, smoothing a thumb over her jaw. "It's for the best, for all concerned." He leaned toward her to capture her lips again.

She pushed him away and stumbled back. "And why do you assume that I will readily agree?" She snapped. "For all concerned? And what of my assent?"

"You must see the benefit, Emily. I could get a

special license. We could be married within the month. Here, if you would prefer, with your father present and, I believe, with his blessing."

Her shaking hands tried to wind her wild curls in some kind of knot at the back of her head — curls that he had only a short time before been twirling through his fingers as she allowed him to kiss her. She replaced her cap that had fallen to the porch floor. How could she have let down her guard? What if they'd been seen? She would be ruined, forced to marry.

"There is no need to offer marriage, of all things. My situation is not dire. Are we not aware of each other's position on the subject?" The rain has let up. I must go." She scrambled down the porch steps."

"Emily, listen!"

Ignoring his raised voice, she turned and ran down the path towards the house without looking back, stumbling over puddles that had been created by the heavy rain, and wiping tears that rolled down her cheeks. What was happening to her world of poetry and peace?

She'd changed, her life had changed and now she was running away from the one person that opened up a new world to her and offered her the life that she had been so certain she never wanted.

Chapter Nineteen

"BLASTED RAIN IS back," Gates said as he approached the main entry hall to find Marcus climbing the staircase.

Marcus looked over his right shoulder, having gained only a few steps. He'd hoped to go directly to his bedchamber without notice to change into dry clothes.

"It appears you could not find cover. Were you out walking?" Gates asked, having paused at the bottom of the stairs, his arm resting on the banister.

"Yes, the sun went swiftly behind the clouds," Marcus said, slanting his eyes toward Gates. He felt no need to explain his actions further, nor retreat down the steps.

"That first crack of thunder should have alerted you to return swiftly to the house."

"Did you want me for something? I'd like to change out of these damp clothes." Marcus cared little if his tone sounded surly. He needed time alone to think.

Gates seemed not to notice. "I thought, perhaps, a game of cards this evening? The women, we can be assured, shall be inexhaustible in their prattle long after the dinner hour."

Marcus lifted his gaze toward the upper landing, snickering at the man's sudden attempt at camaraderie. Lowering his eyes briefly, he gave a nod. "Cards, then." He continued up the stairs without looking back.

Once in his bedchamber, Marcus slumped into a chair and pulled off his boots, his lips tightly compressed into a scowl.

She'd looked so tantalizingly beautiful even drenched, her eyes shimmering like dew on a leaf of the deepest green. He had wanted to take her into the cottage and make love to her there. He could no longer ignore his feelings for her or return to his previous avowals. *Good heavens, she must realize we have gone beyond a mere friendship or even a virtuous courtship. She cannot deny the passion I saw in her eyes.*

Instead of agreeing or at the least being sensible, she had pushed him away. Grumbling at the memory, he tossed his boots and wet stockings in a corner followed by the rest of his clothes. At home, his valet would be blathering over his slovenly action.

He continued to mutter to himself while he pulled out his only other set of clothes, the ones he'd arrived in. Peter had taken care to have the shirt cleaned and his jacket and extra cravat pressed. Marcus breathed a sigh of relief that he had packed a pair of shoes and extra stockings in his satchel. He dressed, still simmering at Emily's stubbornness.

I must find an opportunity to talk to her. She must reconsider. He shook his head marveling at his change of heart. He had relished his freedom, feared losing it, even cringed at the thought of having the responsibilities of a wife. He had humored Aunt Agatha for the most part and went along with the parade of debutantes that she would gather like flowers to honor his father's final request. His fear of losing himself in love had ruled his actions.

He had avoided the truth and hardened his heart, believing he could control destiny.

Until Emily.

Love made the difference. He closed his eyes and sighed at the wonder of it. He would never let her go.

I must convince her to see reason.

He stood in front of the mirror, combed his hair and adjusted his cravat. Satisfied with his appearance, he looked at his pocket watch. It was close enough to the dinner hour.

He took a deep breath and walked to the door, realizing, suddenly, that he was quite famished.

GATES WAS RIGHT about one thing. The aunts did not let up on their chatter throughout dinner. Marcus was actually relieved to join Gates in the library for a glass of port after the women retired to the parlor.

To Marcus' disappointment, Emily chose to dine with her father and did not appear again. Emily was avoiding him and she was most likely still enraged at her cousin. If she faced Gates tonight, she might have reacted to his negligence for not telling her of Dr. Brandt's request or in her anger, tell him of Dr. Bellingham's possible visit tomorrow. It was best that Gates didn't know. He did not want him to become defensive in any way.

He found Gates subdued as they drank their port. A servant had set up a table for cards and they played for close to an hour before Gates approached the subject Marcus expected.

"Deming, you must be pleased that Mrs. Fenning's visit, and your aunt's as well, have allowed you to spend more time with my cousin. I admit, I had previously discouraged visitors out of my concern for my uncle, but I see that guests have been a welcome blessing for Emily."

Marcus kept his eyes on the cards he held in his hand. Gates had been falling over himself with attempts at smoothing over his earlier boorishness. The man was a poor actor. The look in his eyes and strained expression contrasted his conciliatory words.

Marcus decided to play along. "I found Emily to be a charming companion in London. Unfortunately, circumstances as they are have made it difficult to nurture more than a friendship at this time, you do agree?" He thought of Gates' relationship with Mrs. Hanover and wondered if the inference was evident to the man.

"It is unfortunate that my cousin chose not to join us this evening, but, indeed, there is the weekend," Gates said, after repositioning a couple of his cards and avoiding the question.

"True, there is the weekend," Marcus said, smiling at the royal flush he held in his hand.

EMILY PUMMELED HER pillow as she'd done a dozen times since slumping into her bed an hour before. Her heart ached, but not from regret. She loved

Marcus with all her heart but she could not marry him. She must plan her future, alone.

Marcus had taken for granted that she would agree to marriage, but he never spoke of love. He'd made it clear in London that when he chose to marry it would be out of necessity. Whether he considered her situation reason enough to offer for her hand, it wasn't enough.

Her mother's warnings flooded her mind. She had thought her mother's words no longer carried power over her. *He never spoke of love. I will not let him be my savior or feed his need to be honorable.*

He talked of marriage as if it were his duty… *set the date as soon as possible, special license, within a month…* After a time, she had stopped listening.

He would marry me out of duty.

If Marcus could not love her, her marriage would be no different than her parents'. She couldn't bear it. She needed to rekindle her passion for writing and make plans for a future without her father, if it must come to that. *If nothing else*, she thought as she wiped tears away and pummeled her pillow once again, *the experience may make me a better poet.*

MARCUS DRAGGED HIMSELF out of bed early Saturday morning. Emily's refusal to marry him kept him awake a good part of the night. He dressed hurriedly and focused on his expectations for the day—Forrester's arrival, hopefully, with information and Dr. Bellingham.

He entered the breakfast room to find Emily's aunt already seated and stirring her cup of tea.

"Mrs. Fenning, you are up especially early this morning. Aunt Agatha is seldom awake before ten."

"Damp days affect my bones. The weather today seems more like the fifteenth of March than the fifteenth of July."

"Hmm... the ides in the ancient Roman calendar," Marcus said as he poured himself a cup of coffee.

"Indeed. No grim predictions, I hope."

"I have no gift of augury, only concern for the day's events." He took a seat close enough to the aunt for a confidential discussion.

"We have had little opportunity to chat without ears about us," Delia said quietly. "I am quite pleased that you have taken the initiative to call in another physician. We can only pray and leave the outcome in God's hands."

Marcus nodded, while wondering if the outcome would cause more heartbreak for Emily. "As you probably know, Gates has not been told. With my added interference, he most likely would have created more problems for Emily these past few days. He'll find out soon enough."

"Emily chose not to mention the visit to her father as well."

"For the best. Dr. Bellingham may not be able to come as quickly as we may wish."

"I fear Willard will be most ungracious at not being consulted. He seems to have complete faith in Dr. Brandt.

Marcus grimaced. "I may be intruding without any better result. As a guest I have overstepped my boundaries."

"Not in my eyes or my niece's. In some instances we must listen to our hearts, rather than custom. No doubt you have formed a picture in your mind of the uncomfortable situation. The tension in this home is as thick as the fog that greeted us this morning."

"Not even a stranger could miss the hostility between Emily and her cousin."

"Marcus…" Delia hesitated and looked toward the door before continuing. "I've had some serious talks with my brother-in-law. He has asked me to contact his lawyer on his behalf when I return to London. He wants to be assured that the terms of his will are carried out if he should die." She sighed before going on. "Although he wants to believe the best of his nephew, he has concerns that he may not assume his duty to Emily."

Marcus' jaw tightened. He thought of telling Delia of his desire to marry her niece, but it wasn't his place to say a word and he had been refused. No, first he needed to convince Emily of her foolishness. He rubbed a knuckle against his chin. "Do you think Hughes has given up the fight?"

"He has tried to put up a grand fight has he not?" Delia's eyes grew misty. "I see the pain he suffers at night. I don't know how he bears it. If your friend arrives…" She stopped in mid sentence as Eva Hanover swept into the room carrying a serving platter.

The cook stopped abruptly, her eyes widening. She laid a platter down on the sideboard. "Mr. Gates requested fresh eggs and meats. He is to be down momentarily." She straightened her shoulders, folding her hands at the waist of her apron. "I could not help but overhear... Am I to be cooking for more guests?" she asked, her brows arched.

Marcus offered icy silence, while Delia ignored the question and turned to him. "Indeed, how irksome it is to carry on a conversation and be interrupted without regard to proper etiquette. Do you not agree, Lord Deming?" She dabbed her lips with her napkin without looking up.

Marcus nodded, masking a grin as he took a sip of his coffee while noting the fury in the cook's eyes as she walked stiffly out of the room.

"WILLARD, OPEN THE door, hurry," Eva whispered frantically. "I must talk to you."

Gate's bedroom door swung open. He glared at her. "How dare you come to my room, and I am Mr. Gates to you in this household." He scanned the empty hallway to be sure they were alone. "What is the meaning of this?"

"We must talk," she insisted, ignoring his surly tone. "The guests are in the breakfast room. I overheard them say that another visitor was coming today."

"What?" He stepped into the hallway and shut the door behind him.

"They stopped talking when I walked in and refused to answer my inquiry."

"You asked them? Are you addle-brained? You are a servant," he muttered, keeping his voice to a harsh whisper.

"I simply asked if I was to be preparing meals for more guests," Eva huffed.

"Oh, never mind. You heard nothing else?"

"No, that was it, but I fear more complications. We must do something."

"And what do you suggest?"

"To end it, now. You were right. It has gone on long enough. I cannot stomach that housekeeper much longer and catering to these intruders is beyond what I agreed to when I came here."

Gates scanned the hall again. "What are you thinking?"

She stepped closer. "I believe that Hughes has weakened enough for his heart to suddenly give out."

"And?" Gates cocked his head, his eyes widening.

"I've been thinking... a pillow drawn over his face tonight after he falls asleep, a cessation of breath," she whispered, every muscles in her face taut. "There, I have said it." Her shoulders sagged. She exhaled a strangled sigh as if her words had sucked the breath from her lungs.

Gates pressed his back against his closed bedroom door and brought a bent finger to his lips. If Hughes was given a sedative before he slept... "He has weakened enough." He paused, his eyes fixed on his accomplice. "And how advantageous for our guests." His lips curved into a satisfying sneer. "They will be available for the funeral."

His head jerked to the side at the sound of a door opening farther down the hallway. He watched as Maggie stepped out of a bedroom, humming, and hastening down the hall her arms filled with bed linens. Her eyes remained lowered toward the bundle she was carrying, oblivious to the encounter before her. She nearly walked into the cook. She stepped back and nearly dropped the sheets. "Excuse me, Mrs. Hanover... Mr. Gates. I was just makin' up the beds."

"Then go about your business," Gates said with a wave of his hand. "Mrs. Hanover, thank you for notifying me that breakfast is ready. I shall be down shortly. Oh, and your suggestion has merit. I will definitely take it under consideration." He gave a slight nod to the cook and returned to his bedchamber, closing the door firmly behind him.

When Emily did not appear for breakfast, Marcus made the decision to find her even if it meant knocking on her bedroom door. He had escaped the breakfast room soon after Aunt Agatha arrived and just as Emily's cousin entered. He figured the aunts' chatter would keep Gates busy for a time.

He found Emily leaving her father's bedchamber. He caught her arm and urged her toward a private corner. "Emily, we need to talk."

"Is something wrong?" Emily asked, startled.

"We need to talk about yesterday."

"I have hardly had a chance to prepare for the day. Later, Marcus, I have much on my mind."

"Now."

Emily looked at him warily, before visibly collecting her wits. "I visited my father early so that I would be available to speak with the physician, if he comes today. I have been most anxious. Are the aunts up and about?" Emily spoke rapidly.

"Stop it." Emily's nervous chatter only added to his frustration. "Today will take care of itself. You and I have a future to discuss."

"Today is my only concern," Emily said, crossing her arms tightly. "Please, let us remain hopeful that the specialist arrives today, shall we? We can talk tomorrow." She cast her eyes from him and glanced down the hallway.

Marcus opened his mouth to protest but clamped it shut angrily when he heard footsteps.

"Maggie, I was just coming to look for you," Emily said too brightly at the sight of her maid.

Damn. Marcus turned about as the maid walked toward them. Emily obviously did not want to be alone with him or discuss their future.

"Yes, miss. I have changed all the beds, 'cept your father's. I need Peter to help me. He'll be joining me any minute now."

"Actually, Peter is already in with Father. I want you to come to my room with me. I... I have a gown that needs mending. Marcus, do send a message if there is any news." With that, Emily, maneuvered around him, took Maggie's arm and walked with her down the hall.

Marcus stared after them, cursing under his breath.

THE LADIES SAT quietly in the parlor doing needlework while Marcus struggled to keep his mind on a book about the French Revolution. He had finally given up on having a moment alone with Emily. Though she had been quite civil to him in front of the aunts, she had made no effort to speak with him without other ears about.

It was already past three in the afternoon and there was still no sign of Forrester. He feared that his friend might not have been able to contact Dr. Bellingham and, perhaps, his investigations had proved fruitless as well. His thoughts were interrupted when Emily's cousin walked into the room.

"Greetings, I see that you are all having a congenial afternoon despite such a raw day. The July weather has been a disappointment," Gates said almost cheerfully. "I talked to the gardener earlier, Emily. He complains that your father's plants are starving for sun. Some warm sunshine would be welcomed, I dare say." Clasping his hands together, he smiled at the gathering.

Emily eyed her cousin suspiciously. His sudden exuberance seemed to have taken everyone by surprise.

Gates turned his attention to the guests. "I suspect all of you will want an early start tomorrow morning. I will tell Mrs. Hanover to have baskets prepared for your journey."

"We would appreciate that, of course," Delia replied politely.

"A game of cards later this evening, Deming?"

Marcus, who had been watching the man clasping and unclasping his hands, gave an affirmative nod.

"Until dinner then?" When no one offered a word, Gates bowed his head slightly to the ladies and left the room.

GATES HEADED FOR Hughes' study, shrugging off the cold reception from Emily and her guests. He felt remarkably at ease. What had been months in the planning was finally coming to an end.

And no one was the wiser.

He and Eva had confirmed the plan. She would bring his uncle his usual cup of tea after dinner, but it would be laced with an extra dose of laudanum. During his own nightly visit, he would make certain that his uncle drank the tea and drifted off to sleep. When Eva arrived to remove the tray, he'd leave to join Deming for a game of cards. The servants would be busy with evening chores and his cousin should still be in the midst of entertaining her other guests on their final evening. Eva would have enough time to complete the task without interruption.

Eva, my foolish lovesick puppet, I may soon need to clip your strings.

Gates walked into the comfortable study that would be his by morning and sat at Hughes' desk, stretching back pleasurably. *Indeed, it is better that our guests stay until the end. They can better deal with my cousin's grief.*

Chapter Twenty

"HEDDY, WHAT IS it?" Emily looked up from her needlework when her housekeeper rushed into the parlor.

"A carriage is comin' up the drive. I saw it from the upstairs window," Heddy said, her chest heaving. She paused to catch her breath. "I didn't tell anyone there'd be more visitors, just like you said. Someone is riding on horseback alongside too."

Emily tossed her needlework aside and gripped the arms of her chair. Her eyes darted toward Marcus.

Marcus held up his hand, signaling her to remain seated. "Let me talk to them before they make their appearance." He turned to the housekeeper. "Are you certain no one else saw them coming?"

"As certain as I can be, milord. The other servants are either in the scullery or in their quarters takin' a rest before their evenin' duties."

"And Gates?"

Heddy humphed and tossed a hand in the air. "He is where you can always find him, in Mr. Hughes' study or in the kitchen talkin' to the cook. If he'd seen them comin', he'd already be stalking through the house, swearin'. You can bet on that."

Marcus gave the housekeeper a knowing grin.

"Do your best to keep the servants unaware of the visitors for as long as possible."

Heddy lifted her chin proudly. "Glad to be of service, milord." She looked to her mistress. "I can't promise that witch of a cook won't start cacklin' if I keep her caged in the kitchen."

"Now, Heddy..." Emily raised a scolding finger.

"Indeed, I shall help as well," Agatha cut in, scooting up from her seat and setting down her tatting. "I shall have a long chat with Mrs. Hanover. I do have some questions about the herbs she uses in her dishes."

"You are a godsend, Agatha," Emily said, reaching out to her and grasping her hand briefly.

"Emily, it would be beneficial if you would keep your cousin occupied," Marcus suggested. "I need to find out who has come and what to expect without interruption."

She nodded, her eyes meeting his, before turning away.

"I shall see what I can do as well." Delia said, looking uncertain of how to proceed.

"I know how to deal with my cousin. If the physician has arrived, Aunt Delia, please take him to my father."

"Yes, my dear," Delia said, reassuringly.

Marcus waited until Emily left before leaving. He was grateful that most of the activities took place in the rear of the house and that the butler was hard of hearing.

Exiting the house, he approached the drive just as his friend rode up with the carriage following behind.

"Forrester, where the hell have you been?"

"Damn you, Deming," Forrester swore as he swung off his horse and tossed the reins to Marcus. "Do you have any idea how you have interrupted my schedule?"

"Complain later," Marcus grumbled, while he gripped his friend's hand solidly. "You've brought the doctor?"

"Two of them, as a matter of fact," Forrester said smugly. "What have you gotten yourself into?"

"Later. Two of them?" Marcus watched as the coachman opened the door and dropped the step. A slightly built, elderly man wearing a long black coat, too warm for the time of year, was the first to step down. He reached into the carriage to retrieve a small black bag. The next to descend was a taller, more dignified middle-aged man that Deming recognized as Dr. Bellingham.

"Dr. Howard, may I introduce Lord Deming, Earl of Pembridge," Forrester said, walking toward the older man. "Deming, I believe you know Dr. Bellingham."

Marcus gave Forrester a questioning look before taking a step toward the men. "Howard, Bellingham. Thank you both for coming at such short notice."

"I understand your surprise at seeing me, my lord." Dr. Howard offered a warm smile as Marcus shook his hand. "Bellingham and I are longtime friends. When you mentioned my name in your letter, he sought my counsel on the patient."

Marcus had forgotten that he'd referred to Dr. Howard as Hughes' previous physician in his letter to Forrester. "I appreciate that both of you have come at such short notice."

"Mr. Hughes had been my patient for years," Dr. Howard replied. "I attended to him weeks ago but was dismissed when his nephew arrived. I admit I was concerned, especially when Mr. Hughes did not contact me further. I assumed that he found this new physician to his liking or had improved and no longer needed my services. His nephew, I suspect, felt that I was too old." He grinned and rubbed his short gray beard, the corners of his pale blue eyes crinkling. "Mr. Gates appeared to distrust my diagnosis."

"I apologize for not bringing both of you in the house immediately, but if we could take a few minutes... what was your diagnosis?" Marcus asked, listening intently while keeping an eye on the house.

"Mr. Hughes has always been in the best of health, he seldom needed my care. I spent more time caring for his wife before her death and looking in on his daughter on occasion. I could find no reason why he should suddenly be experiencing his symptoms. I knew Hughes to be an avid gardener. I asked about his plant tonics. I thought perhaps some contamination in handling or inhaling fumes may have sickened him. I suggested to his nephew that Mr. Hughes avoid puttering in his gardens for a while and have him drink plenty of liquids. I would have looked in on him again, but I was dismissed.

"Mr. Gates felt my diagnosis was 'pulled out of the wind' as he put it. Yes, I remember his reaction. He was quite put out, told me that he wanted a second opinion and that I would be sent for, if needed." Dr. Howard frowned. "I admit I was offended by the dismissal. When I didn't hear from Mr. Hughes, I could only trust that Mr. Gates had acted in my former patient's best interest. I fear I may have been mistaken."

"Do not second-guess yourself, Reginald," Dr. Bellingham interrupted. "We are here to be of service when asked." He turned to Marcus. "I asked Howard to accompany me when I heard of his previous involvement with the patient. Unlike this Gates fellow, I have extreme confidence in my friend's expertise. Use him myself." He raised his eyes to the house. "Enough talk."

He pointed to the larger black satchel tied to the top of the carriage and signaled to the coachman to take it down. "I had other patients to see this morning. Late start," Bellingham grimaced. "I hope to be back in London by midnight. May we see the patient?"

"I must make you aware that your visit will most likely be unwelcomed."

"Explain, Deming, I have come all this way on the assumption that I had been requested." Bellingham gave Marcus a wary look.

"You have… by Hughes' daughter, but we have not informed her cousin, Willard Gates, that I sent for you. Miss Hughes returned recently from a trip to London only to find her father in a dire state. She has lost faith in the doctor that her cousin chose. I found out only yesterday that Dr. Brandt encouraged Gates to call in another physician. He chose not to act on the doctor's advice."

"Brandt, ah, yes. I checked on the man when I heard who replaced me," Dr. Howard said. "He is young, trained as an apothecary, adequate medical expertise for many patients. Let us hope he did not wait too long to admit his limitations." He rubbed his beard. "I made my mistakes when I first began... but we do not know yet, nor do we know when he suggested obtaining a second opinion, do we? We cannot question his care until we examine the patient."

Forrester, who had remained in the background listening to the exchange, drew Marcus' attention and took him aside while the doctors gathered their belongings. "I have some news for you on the investigation. While the doctors are seeing the patient, we should talk."

Marcus sensed from Forrester's expression that besides bringing the doctors, he had significant news.

Samuel's voice caused a distraction. The stable hand ran toward them flustered and practically tripping on his boots.

"My apologies, gentlemen. Didn't see anyone comin'. 'Enry and I was... well, we was... "

Marcus smelled the liquor on Samuel's breath. No doubt they were enjoying some rum after a day's work. "Take care of Mr. Forrester's horse and direct the coachman to the stables. Samuel, it is best that the coach and coachman stay out of sight of the house for a time. Can you see to that? Perhaps you can offer the coachman whatever you have been drinking in the stables?"

Samuel looked at Marcus oddly at first when he'd suggested that the coach and coachman be kept out of sight, but at the mention of his libations, he dropped his head and nodded. "Yes, sir, I'll do just as you say." Taking the reins of Forrester's horse and waving to the driver, he stumbled off. The coachman handed Bellingham his satchel, climbed up to his seat and followed Samuel with the carriage.

Marcus led the visitors up the steps. When he opened the door, he found Delia standing alone in the entrance hall. Relieved that he wouldn't have to deal with Gates just yet, he made the introductions.

"Thank you, doctors, for coming. Would you prefer to rest before seeing Mr. Hughes or, perhaps, have a beverage?" She asked.

"Later," Bellingham said. "I prefer to see the patient first."

"Please, come this way." Delia led them toward the stairs.

When they were out of sight, Marcus waved to Forrester to follow him into the blue sitting room, shutting the door behind them. "We may not have much time alone to talk."

"Not even a butler to greet us? I am offended."

"Swallow your sensibilities, Andy. The man is older than my butler Jennings and deaf. He would not have heard you if you had kicked in the door. Now tell me, what have you found?"

"No offer of a drink?" Forrester asked with a flourish of his hand, only to receive a scowl. "Do you mind if I sit? I need a soft cushion after being in the saddle for hours."

Marcus waved toward the couch. "Will you get on with it?"

Forrester gave him an amused grin and took a seat. "You do owe me, Marcus."

"No doubt," he conceded as he took a chair across from him and leaned forward, waiting.

"It seems Willard Gates has built up quite a reputation as a loose fish in London," Forrester began. "He's a gambler and not a very good one. I asked around at the clubs and among some of my other connections. A few men who play the tables regularly bristled at his name and called him a cheat. One of the club owners wanted to know where to find him. Gates left London without paying substantial debts."

"Is that it?" Marcus shook his head. He had hoped for more. *The man obviously needs his inheritance and would mostly likely lose it within a year.*

"There is one more thing," Forrester said, leaning back on the cushion and bending one long leg to rest a boot on the opposite knee.

"Damn, spit it out!"

"Such surliness does not become you. I have never seen you worked up over a damsel in distress. I won't keep you in suspense any further. You asked me to check on Eva Hanover. You said she was the cook?"

"Yes, Gates hired her after accusing the previous cook of thievery and firing her. I thought the entire situation suspicious."

"Indeed, especially since Gates lived with a widow while in London, a Mrs. Hanover."

Marcus arched his brow. "He knew her before coming here?"

"As the gossips have it, he was her lover. Turns out she left London shortly after Gates left. She told a neighbor woman she had acquired a position in the country. The woman thought it was odd since Hanover seemed to have been left comfortable enough when her husband died. I asked her if Hanover had ever served as a cook. The woman laughed, said she was too stuffy, that it would be beneath her.

Marcus clenched his teeth. He thought of the questionable meetings he had observed between the two. "Why the pretense?" Marcus murmured more to himself as thoughts raced through his mind. Could Gates simply have thought it convenient to give his lover a position in the household? Or could she be waiting for Hughes' death so she could become the lady of the house? More dire suspicions crowded into his thoughts as he absorbed Forrester's news.

"Something certainly smells foul," Forrester muttered, "and it looks like you have sunk yourself into the mire right up to your heart, Deming."

EMILY LOOKED THROUGH the slightly opened door of her father's study. The sight of her cousin sitting comfortably in her father's chair enraged her. She pushed the door open further and strolled in.

"Cousin." Willard frowned. "It would be polite to knock before entering."

Giving Willard a brief, cold glare, she walked over to a wall of books and fingered some of the volumes. "This room is my father's. I see no reason to announce myself. I have come to look for one of his books."

Willard stretched back in the chair. "I am done here for the time being. I shall leave you to your search," he said as he dropped the paper he had been reading, straightened his cuffs, and prepared to stand.

"What do you do in here hours at a time?" Emily asked as she turned about. "My father will be enraged if he finds that you have created havoc with his private papers."

"I have done my best to keep your father's household affairs in order, as I pledged to him that I would do. He understands that I am looking out for his best interests. During the past few weeks, I have met regularly with his steward to be certain that bills are paid, repairs are current, and supplies are ordered. You have not had to deal with any of these issues while in London or since you have returned."

"I trust that my father's steward and our servants are capable of handling their duties while Father is ill. Father has directed them well in the past and has had faith in those he's hired."

"You are naïve, Emily. All servants need an overseer. I have felt it my duty as your only male relative to ensure that the estate runs smoothly."

"Since it is your inheritance?"

"Partially," Gates replied. "We both know that is a future reality. Let us hope and pray that it is far into the future."

Emily held her tongue, despite her desire to lash out at him. Her purpose was to keep her cousin engaged not to be antagonistic and lose her quarry. Though she wanted desperately to know who had arrived, she needed to trust Marcus and allow him time to evaluate the situation without interference.

She walked over to the desk and looked down at the scattered papers. Despite her best intensions, the sight of her father's usually neat desk in such disarray infuriated her. "My father's desk has never been so disorderly."

"What do you want, to harass me?"

"For you to leave. If my father is to pass… " She swallowed hard. "I expect you will return within a day to take up your place."

"My dear, you must prepare yourself." Wearing a sympathetic expression, he leaned forward and rested his folded hands on the desk. "Dr. Brandt tried to prepare you on his last visit. Your father's heart and lungs have grown weak. The doctor said that without signs of improvement, he may have little time left."

Emily took a step back. "When did he say that?"

"On his last visit. You were so shaken when he told you there was no improvement. I couldn't bring myself to tell you about the details of his examination." He stood, walked around the desk and laid his hand on Emily's shoulder.

She shrank from his touch as if scalded. "You are lying!" she spit out. Stricken by her cousin's news, she turned away and covered her face with her hands.

"We have both seen him in severe pain, his breathing difficult. Do you want your father to go on like this, day after day? Forgive me if I appear unfeeling, but I believe it may be a blessing if he passes. Your father has not asked me to leave. He must realize that the end may be soon."

Emily took another step back and covered her ears. She wanted to slap him for his directness and for his pitying looks, but his words held truth. And her cousin would most certainly become her provider. Her father had permitted her cousin to take up residence and, no doubt, her father expected her to show him a measure of respect.

In reality, she should, if she had no choice but be dependent on him for her livelihood. She'd witnessed her father's decline. She saw the terrible pain that gripped him and left him sweating and exhausted. Was she being selfish in wanting him to hang on to life despite his suffering? She closed her eyes in an attempt to hold back the sorrow that threatened to consume her. She wanted, needed, to hold on to hope.

No! Her mind screamed. *I will not give up yet. Less than three months ago, he was in perfect health.* She turned to her cousin, her eyes flashing with anger. "Why didn't you take Dr. Brandt's advice and call in another physician?"

"What?" Gates' eyes narrowed.

"Dr. Brandt told me yesterday that he urged you to call in another doctor for a second opinion."

Gate's jaw tightened. She could see she'd

surprised him. He hadn't known she had spoken to the doctor.

"Dr. Brandt had administered a new medication," he said finally, regaining his composure. "I told him if your father didn't respond to it in a few days, then another doctor would be called. Ask him, if you don't believe me."

Emily opened her mouth to argue when they heard a crash.

"What the devil?" Gates headed for the door before Emily could stop him. The noise came from the kitchen. When they entered the kitchen, they found Heddy and the cook standing in a pile of broken dishes. Mrs. Hanover held a frying pan in front of her face as a shield against the housekeeper's assault.

"What is the meaning of this?" Gates shouted.

Heddy dropped the dish she held at the sound of his voice.

Agatha, who had pressed herself into a corner by the door, opened her mouth but was cut off by the cook.

"Willard," Mrs. Hanover said, quivering. "She attacked me. She refuses to allow me to leave the kitchen."

"Willard, hmmm," Heddy huffed. "Knew there was somethin' going on between the two of you."

"A ridiculous assumption," Gates growled. "I have had enough of your idle tongue and disrespectful behavior. You'll receive no pay until you have covered the cost of these dishes. When you have paid your debt, you can find other employment and with no references from me."

Emily whirled about to face her cousin. She'd had quite enough of the dictatorial position he'd assumed. "You will not replace another servant in my father's house. You have no authority to do so."

"Emily, consider your guests," he seethed before turning his eyes on the servants. "Both of you, clean up this mess. I expect to have dinner served on time and without any shards of china in my meal." Scowling, he marched out of the room. Agatha scrambled from the corner and followed him out, calling after him.

"Miss Emily, I am so sorry. I shouldn't have interrupted Miss Trumbell," Heddy stammered. "She was doin' fine. I merely was checkin' and the witch started stompin' off the minute I walked in."

"Heddy, enough," Emily said, pressing a palm to her forehead and exhaling a weary sigh. "I want this kitchen back in order."

"What does she mean, 'she was doin' fine'?" the cook asked, her brows knitted together. "With guests coming into my kitchen chattering away, I can get nothing done. What am I to do about these interruptions?"

"Nothing," Emily replied in an even tone, "except to expect more company for dinner."

Chapter Twenty-One

AFTER LEAVING THE kitchen, Emily found Agatha standing quietly in the darkened hallway near the entry hall watching as Gates confronted Marcus and Forrester.

"I was unable to stop Mr. Gates in time," Agatha whispered regretfully.

"You were most helpful and I thank you." Emily took in the scene. She saw no sign of a physician. "Agatha, would you mind going upstairs to see if my aunt is with the physician?"

"Not at all. Whatever I can do. I feel so inadequate. I...

Emily brought a finger to her closed lips. "It may be better if you went around to the back stairs," She said quietly.

Agatha nodded, pressing a hand against her mouth. She turned and scurried away.

Emily was relieved that both aunts might be uninvolved in what could turn into a violent argument. She had no idea what to expect from her cousin. Remaining out of sight, she listened to the exchange.

"As I said, he is my friend from London."

Gates ignored Marcus' explanation. "Mr. Forrester, we have a critical illness in the house. Unfortunately, it is a difficult time to welcome visitors." Gates' voice sounded frayed.

"Please show more hospitality, Willard," Emily interrupted, joining the group. "If you bring our new visitor into the parlor, I shall see to refreshments." Ignoring her cousin's sharp glare, she gave a welcoming smile to Forrester. "How nice of you to visit. May I offer you a cold drink?"

"Something stronger than lemonade, I hope." He quirked a grin, before his expression grew thoughtful. "It is a pleasure to see you once again, Miss Hughes. I understand that your father remains unwell."

"Yes, we continue to pray for his healing," Emily replied, while her eyes searched Forrester's and then Marcus', hoping she could see some acknowledgement that the physician had come. She read nothing in them and instead sensed her cousin's impatience. She stepped aside to allow her cousin to guide the new guest to the parlor.

Marcus lagged behind with Emily until Gates and Forrester were out of sight and they were alone. "Mrs. Hanover must be the one to serve."

She jerked her head up. I don't understand."

"I shall explain later. The physicians are in with your father."

"Physicians?" Emily's mouth dropped open.

"Dr. Bellingham and Dr. Howard."

Emily pressed a hand to her breast. "Dr. Howard is here?"

He nodded. "Emily, is there a constable nearby?" His tone grew serious.

"Yes, in the village." She looked at him curiously.

"Send one of the stable boys to fetch him,

immediately."

"But... why? What are you thinking?"

"Will you trust me? I am most likely being overly cautious, but now is not the time to explain." He hadn't planned to send for a constable. It was a sudden decision, but if his intuition proved true, he may be needed, even if it was simply to remove unsavory imposters.

Emily's faced paled before she nodded and walked away.

THANKFUL THAT EMILY would not be present during the confrontation, Marcus entered the parlor, pausing briefly to listen to the ongoing discussion. He noted Gates' agitation as the man engaged Forrester in a dialogue bordering on interrogation. Forrester maintained his nonchalant demeanor while remaining evasive when asked why he had come.

"Are you aware that Deming plans to return to London tomorrow?" Gates asked before shooting a glance toward Marcus.

"I had no idea," Forrester answered giving Marcus a weary look.

"I thought we might wait for my friend to enjoy a refreshment before we discuss the purpose of his visit," Marcus said as he walked to the hearth, leaning an arm on the mantle. Forrester joined him and rested his elbow on the other side.

Gates glanced sharply at both men.

"You seem tense, Gates," Marcus said. "I suspect that it is the thought of more guests at such a trying time."

"Indeed," Gates replied, clearing his throat. "The increasing severity of my uncle's illness has caused much anxiety, especially over the past few days." Gates settled his eyes on Forrester. "I do not mean to be inhospitable. I am sure you planned only a brief visit."

When Forrester gave no response, Gates heaved a sigh. "Visit with your guest, Lord Deming. I must take care of some business before dinner."

"Actually, Forrester has brought me some disturbing news."

Gates, who had nearly reached the door, stopped and gave the men a sideways glance. "I see, most unfortunate. I shall leave you then to talk in private. If you need to have your horse saddled and ready, just ring, and Forrester, a fresh horse will be at your disposal as well."

"I am afraid Forrester's news concerns you."

"I beg your pardon?" Gates stiffened.

"I understand the gambling halls are your favored haunts while in London," Marcus said.

Gates appeared suddenly relieved. He looked curiously at Forrester as if trying to recall if he'd met him before. "Gentleman, no doubt the two of you enjoy betting on a round of cards on occasion."

"No doubt," Forrester replied.

"From what I understand, Gates, you have lost a great deal at the tables," Marcus added.

"Is that what your visit is all about, Forrester?"

"Left some debts behind, I hear," Marcus answered.

"Rather large ones," Forrester echoed.

Gates glared at Marcus. "If I have business with Forrester, it is no business of yours." He turned to the visitor. "Perhaps you and I can have a private discussion. If I have a debt that needs to be covered, I assure you that it will be paid in full."

"Just one?" Marcus cut in. "From what I understand, you would not be welcomed back in London's gambling halls."

"What are you implying?" Gates asked angrily.

Marcus gave Forrester a casual glance before turning back to Gates. "If, however, you were to come into an inheritance, you might be most welcomed, I would imagine."

Gates took a step back as if he'd been physically attacked. "What are you insinuating?"

Before Marcus could answer, the door opened and Emily entered followed by Mrs. Hanover. The servant carried a tray with a brandy decanter and glasses to a side table.

The cook addressed Gates. "I told Miss Hughes that you most likely have bottles of brandy stocked in the parlor, but she requested that I bring a fresh decanter."

Gates opened his mouth then shut it. "Just set it down, Mrs. Hanover."

"Please excuse me, I need to check on my father," Emily said, catching Marcus' eye before turning to the new guest. "I have asked cook to set another plate for dinner, Mr. Forrester. I am so pleased that you have come." Not waiting for a response, she left the room.

"Mrs. Hanover, would you pour for us?" Marcus asked politely as the servant set the tray down. "We are in the midst of an enlightening conversation with your employer."

With pursed lips, she poured brandy into each glass. When the men remained where they were, she carried the tray to where Marcus and Forrester stood. She waited as each gave her a slow appraising look before taking a glass. Turning her back to them, she carried the tray to Gates.

As he lifted a glass, they exchanged wary glances. "Get on with your evening duties, Mrs. Hanover."

"Gates, do you mind if I ask the cook to join us?" Marcus asked, taking a sip of his brandy. "I suspect that she may be able to contribute to our inquiries."

Chapter Twenty-Two

"I DO NOT understand, Dr. Howard, I sent you a letter at least three weeks ago."

"My dear Miss Emily, I would have attended to your father immediately if I had received your letter," the doctor assured her as they stood outside her father's bedroom door.

Emily shook her head, puzzled. "When my cousin told me that you were no longer treating my father, I questioned it. I wrote to you asking for an explanation. I gave it to…" Emily paused, her face distorting into an angry grimace. She knew suddenly why he did not receive her letter. No doubt, the same reason she was not notified of her father's failing health when she was in London. Willard wanted no one to counter his authority or interfere with his decisions. She looked at her aunt who stood beside her. "My cousin," she said through gritted teeth.

Dr. Howard took both of Emily's hands in his. "My dear, I know how worried you are about your father. Dr. Bellingham is giving him a thorough examination. There is no one better at diagnosis." He stopped abruptly when the door opened behind him and Dr. Bellingham walked out carrying his black bag.

Shutting the door carefully, Bellingham eyed the group wearing a grimace. "Miss Hughes, is there somewhere private where we can talk?"

"Yes, doctor, of course." She motioned down the hall and led them to her own private sitting room adjacent to her bedchamber.

Delia hesitated at the door. "Agatha has gone to her room. I'll just go and sit with her until dinner."

"Please stay," Emily pleaded. "You can hear anything the physicians have to say."

Once they were gathered inside the small sitting room, Emily confronted the doctors. "Do not spare me from any details. What is wrong with my father?"

Bellingham put out a hand signaling Emily and her aunt to take seats.

Emily remained standing. Her aunt took her arm gently and urged her to the settee. Emily reluctantly obeyed.

Bellingham turned to his fellow physician. "Dr. Howard, my tests confirm your diagnosis. I have given the patient one dose of the coal extract. We shall discuss the administration of the antidote and other remedies we might pursue. I have not revealed to the patient my suspicions. I will leave that to you."

Howard nodded grimly.

"What have you found?" Emily's hand grasped her throat.

Dr. Howard took a seat beside her. "When I examined your father a few weeks ago, I suspected that he may have been exposed to a toxic agent, perhaps his gardening tonics."

"Toxic?" Emily's breath caught, every muscle

in her body gripping her with fear. "Do you mean poisonous?"

"My dear, you must remain calm," Dr. Howard patted her hand soothingly.

"Calm? I have tried to remain calm during all of Dr. Brandt's administrations. I have waited and watched my father grow weaker every day." She covered her mouth with her hand, realizing that she was spewing anger at the kind doctor. "I apologize. I am so grateful that you are here." She looked up at Dr. Bellingham. "Both of you." She forced herself to settle back in her seat. "Please go on."

"Initial symptoms, Dr. Howard had noted in his records, resembled those of cholera," Bellingham interjected.

"Cholera?" Emily stared at him confused.

"Yes," Dr. Howard confirmed, "but upon further examination, I changed my diagnosis. Other symptoms suggested something else. Your father's stomach problems, slight confusion... the slow progression of his various complaints. I questioned his use of his plant tonics. After all, I knew your father to be in perfect health on previous examinations. I expressed my suspicions to your cousin. At that time, of course, your father felt ill, but he was not bedridden—"

Bellingham cut in authoritatively, his arms folded firmly across his chest. "After reviewing Dr. Howard's report and discussing the case, I came prepared to do toxicity tests to confirm my colleague's suspicions. Unfortunately much time has elapsed since his original examination." His gaze dropped toward the floor.

Fear clutched at Emily's heart at the doctor's grim stance. Bellingham's medical expertise might be more exceptional, Emily realized, but Dr. Howard exuded a more empathetic manner. She drew her eyes expectantly to Dr. Howard.

"We have concluded after reviewing the progression of symptoms that your father has exhibited..." Dr. Howard paused to take Emily's hands in his own, "that he has somehow ingested, in miniscule doses we suspect and for an extended time, a lethal toxin. Perhaps an accidental contamination..." He gave a deep sigh, his eyes darting toward Bellingham.

"Poison, Miss Hughes," Bellingham said without hesitation. "An investigation is in order."

Delia wrapped her arms immediately about Emily as her niece shrank back and gasped in horror.

MRS. HANOVER GLARED at Marcus. Frozen in place, she turned stiff-necked to Gates. "If we are to have another guest for dinner, I must return to the kitchen and alert the staff."

"We were not discussing dinner, ma'am," Marcus said as he studied her reaction. He had expected an indignant response from Gates when Marcus had requested that the cook stay in the parlor, rather than follow his direction. Gates, however, had turned a ghastly shade of gray.

Marcus took a slow sip of his drink before resting the glass on the mantle. Despite his outward control, his insides simmered with rage at the pair's devious behaviors.

"Deming, I doubt I would want to stay for dinner," Forrester announced, filling the momentary silence. "The present atmosphere I find to be oppressive."

Forrester's offhand remark helped Marcus to shake off his own turmoil. "Tell me, Mrs. Hanover, how did you come about being a cook in this household?"

Eva gawked at Marcus defiantly. "I was hired by Mr. Gates, and I am quite uncomfortable being asked such an absurd question by a guest," she snipped.

"Indeed, I have no business interfering, but I find myself in an awkward position," Marcus continued. "Since my arrival I have felt much like an intruder once I realized the state of affairs. It appears, however, I may not be the only intruder in the household." He moved away from the hearth and took a few steps in the cook's direction. "Some pretenses may be harmless but I do not find yours to be so."

"Pretense?" Her eyes darted to her employer. "Mr. Gates, what is the meaning of this interrogation? And by a guest!"

Marcus watched as Gates shrugged his shoulders in the cook's direction, but remained silent.

"I understand the two of you lived together in London," Marcus said, "which begs the question. Why are you here in service as a cook?"

"You had me investigated?" Gates snapped, ignoring the direction of the question. "How dare you."

"Regardless of my inquiries, you owe Miss Hughes an explanation," Marcus said as Emily marched into the room.

"YOU LIVED TOGETHER?" Emily gasped, having heard the last bit of conversation.

Gates swerved toward Emily's voice, spilling the glass he held in his hand. "Emily, my dear, you must understand. Mrs. Hanover and I had a relationship before I arrived," he admitted while he brushed off the liquid from his coat. Setting his glass down, he squared his shoulders. "When I left London to attend to your father, Mrs. Hanover, Eva, was distraught. You must realize love detests separation." His face distorted into an awkward grin.

Emily, who had barely managed only a quarter hour before to retain a semblance of control after hearing the physician's diagnosis, could barely speak. She thought of how her father had worked in his beloved garden for years and had never experienced ill effects. She remembered that he had often shooed her away when she was a child if he or the gardeners were working with fertilizers or other plant tonics he deemed poisonous. How could his garden tonics be to blame?

Poisoned? Her desire to accuse her cousin shivered like a scream in her throat. She pressed a hand to her collarbone and swallowed hard, fearing that she'd be sick from the revulsion that welled up within her. Both the doctors and her aunt had urged her not to make rash accusations until an investigation could be undertaken.

But her cousin and Mrs. Hanover, lovers? She stood stunned, glaring at both of them.

"Eva and I were not content to be separated," her cousin stammered on. "And your father needed me here. Indeed, you must understand, especially since you were unavailable to care for him."

Emily remained speechless. Her cousin's reference to her absence resurrecting the guilt she'd felt at leaving her father before he had fully recovered.

"When I found your cook stealing from my uncle, I was forced to find someone quickly. Eva came to my aid." He glanced in the cook's direction. "It would have been egregious for me to bring her here, outwardly, as my lover. I admit the concealment of our relationship was highly improper. I feared servants' gossip, and a cook needed to be found without delay. You must admit that she has carried out her duties and we have shown great restraint."

Emily's eyes blazed with contempt at his excuses. She spoke barely above a whisper. "What have you done, Willard?"

Gates' body arched back. "I have done nothing but my duty. I have taken care of my uncle's affairs and given him appropriate care. You lack appreciation for all my efforts. I will not let you blame me for his decline."

Emily took a step closer. "Did I say I was blaming you?" She asked in a low, even tone.

Everyone else in the room listened in stony silence during the confrontation. Marcus and

Forrester kept their positions near the fireplace, while Eva Hanover retreated behind a nearby chair, clutching the folds of her apron.

"You have just come from your father's bedside," Gates said, regaining his composure. "You are obviously distraught. I admit I was dishonest about my relationship with Mrs. Hanover, but I have not let my relationship with her deter me from my responsibilities. You well know I spend most days in my study doing paperwork and maintaining order with the servants. If you want to place blame, look to the staff."

Marcus eyed Mrs. Hanover, who flinched at Gate's words.

"My father's study, not yours. Nothing is yours yet," Emily spit out. She took a step closer to her cousin. "You visited my father before I left for London."

Gates swallowed, causing his Adam's apple to bob in his long neck. "Yes, my visits were cordial at that time. My uncle was in good spirits. When I returned for a second visit I saw, as you did, that he was not well. Unlike you, I chose not to leave. I offered to help him with his affairs. Your father agreed."

"Help him? You have taken over his affairs." Emily hands fisted against her skirt.

Marcus moved closer to her side. She held up a hand and waved him away with a brusque toss of her hand.

"Indeed I have. I've done my duty," Gates shot back.

"As his heir presumptive."

"I accept that I have not been totally selfless, Emily. I should not have brought Eva here, but apart from this one transgression, I have done my best." Gates crossed his arms tightly across his chest, his expression cold and unyielding. Only his quivering chin gave a clue to his discomfort.

"If it is proven..." Emily clenched her teeth, forcing herself to gain control of her rage. She caught Marcus' eye. *I must tell him.*

Marcus moved to her side. "Emily, let me handle this."

When he reached for her arm, she accepted it and allowed him to lead her to a nearby chair. Leaning closer to him, she whispered the doctor's diagnosis in his ear.

Marcus' eyes darkened at Emily's words. Returning to his full height, Marcus walked to where Forrester stood by the fireplace. "Please tell the other guests to join us," he said in a low voice.

From her seat, Emily watched Gates' expression change from arrogance to apprehension as Forrester walked to the door. He glared at Marcus. "What are you up to, Deming? My debts and my personal life are none of your business. You have no right getting involved in our family matters. This entire situation has been blown out of proportion."

Mrs. Hanover interrupted. "Did I hear you say more guests?" Her face had grown a shade paler. "I must return to the kitchen." She brushed past Marcus, but her attempt to leave failed when Aunt Delia, who had been standing near the open doors, entered, followed by the two physicians.

"I have informed Heddy of our additional guests, Mrs. Hanover," Aunt Delia said politely. "She has taken charge of the final dinner preparations and guestrooms." She drew closer to Emily's side as Marcus greeted the physicians.

"Dr. Bellingham, Dr. Howard, you have completed your examinations?"

Bellingham glanced around the room before answering Marcus' question. "I am very glad that you contacted me. A few more days and it may have been too late. As it is, I cannot promise… "

"What is the meaning of this?" Gates cut in as he looked anxiously from one man to another. "Dr. Brandt is my uncle's physician."

Bellingham looked to Deming, his irritation obvious at being interrupted.

Emily, refusing her aunt's plea to remain seated, stood and gave her cousin an icy glare. "I accepted Marcus' offer to bring in a specialist, Willard. Dr. Bellingham, please inform everyone of your diagnosis."

Bellingham nodded. "From our examination, Dr. Howard and I concur. More tests are needed however, the identifiable symptoms strongly suggest that the patient has ingested a lethal substance. Poison, we suspect," Bellingham paused, "possibly arsenic."

Gates visibly cringed, while Mrs. Hanover, standing on the opposite side of the room gasped.

"Poison?" Gates finally choked out. "A misdiagnosis, to be sure!"

Bellingham lowered his eyes. "We have

another physician in the room?"

Gates clamped his hands together and gripped them to his chin. "Forgive my overreaction," he stammered. "Indeed, I certainly did not mean to disrespect your expertise. I am just taken aback. After all, Dr. Brandt believed it to be a critical infection. I will notify him of your findings, of course."

"Dr. Brandt, yes," Dr. Howard interjected, stroking his beard. "I met him once, a gentle sort, pleasant manners but quite young, very much a novice, I fear. I suggest we focus on a possible source."

Gates eyed the older doctor. "As I remember, you had suggested that his garden tonics might be the cause," Gates conceded with a sigh. "Perhaps we should call in Shields, the gardener."

Gates turned to Emily. "After Dr. Howard's diagnosis, I sought a second opinion. I believed I was doing what was best for my uncle. You must understand my quandary. Dr. Brandt did a thorough examination. I put my faith in him. I realize now I may have misjudged your father's physician. His age, you know..." He held out a hand helplessly. "Could I have unintentionally allowed my uncle to suffer needlessly?" He appeared mortified.

"We must discover the source," Gates continued. "I shall demand that a thorough investigation of the garden supplies be done immediately." His fingers tugged at his cuffs. "Who knows what might have been used for insect infestation or for pesky animals that roam the gardens?" He raised his eyes to Bellingham. "Do you believe my uncle may recover?"

"Perhaps," Bellingham answered cautiously. "I would prefer to take him to London to be hospitalized, but he is too weak to be moved at this time. Therefore, as Howard said, we must try to discover the source while we administer an antidote. Only time will tell."

"Source?" No longer able to contain her suspicions, Emily charged at her cousin. "I believe you are the source. "Marcus grabbed her shoulders from behind and held her back.

"My cousin is mad," Gates said, shirking back. "Doctors, she needs a sedative."

"I do not need a sedative," Emily snapped, trying to pull away from Marcus' grasp.

"I will not stand here and be accused," Gates growled. "You have no proof that I have done anything but look after your father's welfare."

"And your own," Marcus cut in just as the butler made himself known by clearing his throat.

"Yes, Fitz?" Aunt Delia asked amidst the turmoil.

"The village constable has arrived with two officers."

Emily whirled about to face the bewildered butler. "Show them in."

Marcus shot a glance to Forrester. "Inform them of what has transpired."

"Done," Forrester answered and followed the butler out.

"WHY CALL IN the constable?" Gates stammered. "I

will investigate immediately. The gardener, he's worthless, he may have caused a contamination."

"Shields has been in my father's employ for years," Emily bit out. "He has no reason to harm my father. How dare you accuse him of foul play?"

"Not foul play, a lack of caution. My uncle believes that the man is careless. He asked me to report to him on plants that have withered and died under Shield's care."

"My father feels helpless. He does not believe anyone could nurture his gardens as he does. If he were well he would never call Shields worthless or irresponsible."

Gates ignored Emily's argument and turned to the doctors. "I promise that I will get to the bottom of this within the hour." He turned and walked briskly to toward the door.

"Stay right where you are," Marcus ordered. While Gates and Emily had argued, he'd been watching Mrs. Hanover's reaction. Her eyes had been wide with fear, her hands splayed against her apron pockets.

Realization struck. A blur of a memory had been niggling in the back of Marcus' mind, but he hadn't been able to put a finger on it. Suddenly he recalled the cook's meetings with Gates. Each time she had fiddled with something in her pocket. He remembered that she gave Gates something in the garden. At the time it seemed trivial, perhaps a key to her room.

"You have no right to order me around. You are only a guest in this house," Gates answered Marcus indignantly before turning his attention back to Emily. "Cousin, you must believe that I have my uncle's best interests at heart."

"I am sick of your repeated boasts," Emily shot back.

As they argued and all eyes were on them, Marcus moved along the edge of the room and closer to where the cook stood.

Engrossed in the interchange, the cook remained unaware of Marcus' movements.

He stepped quietly behind her.

Before she realized what was happening, he thrust an arm across the front of her shoulders and held her firmly in place against his chest.

She shrieked and grasped at his arm with both hands. While she tried to wrestle from his grip, he reached into an apron pocket and pulled out a small vial.

"Forrester!" Marcus tossed him the vial just as his friend entered the room followed by the constable.

Forrester caught the small bottle in one hand. "Deming, you are full of surprises. Who would have thought the country to be more exciting than London?"

Marcus rolled his eyes as he released the cook only to have her flail her arms at him and claw his face with her nails. "Give it to the doctors, Forrester," he shouted, as he grabbed her hands.

Gates eyes widened in horror as Forrester passed the vial to Howard. The physician twisted off the cap and examined the white powder before handing it to his colleague.

The room held its breath as Bellingham

fingered the ingredients, touching a grain to his tongue. He hesitated before looking across the room to the constable who stood at the door with his men. "The content needs to be examined. I believe it to be poison and from what I have witnessed, I suspect foul play."

"Eva," Gates bellowed. "What have you done?"

"Me?" she screamed. "You blame me?" She tore away from Marcus' loosened grip and rushed toward Gates, her eyes wild.

As she lurched forward, her foot caught on the edge of the thick carpet. Losing her balance, she stumbled. One of her arms swung wildly in the air. She fell forward, her head slamming against a center table edged in marble. A large crystal vase wobbled and crashed. A cry escaped her lips as her body crumbled to the floor.

Gate's face paled in horror at his lover's lifeless body. Blood seeped from her skull and pooled around one of the table's clawed feet. Gates staggered back, his hands clutching his chest.

Dr. Howard rushed forward and bent down to examine the fallen woman. The others in the room watched the ghastly scene as Gate's eyes darted from one startled face to another.

"She expected me to marry her," he blurted out, "lusted after my inheritance. She had no patience." He raised a shaking hand to his forehead. "She served my uncle his meals. I do not want to think of what she must have done." As he ranted on, with all eyes on him, the woman moaned.

Gates gaped at the body on the floor.

The cook reached up a hand and grabbed the lapel of Dr. Howard's coat. "He planned it, bought the poison," she choked out. Releasing her hold, she pointed a finger toward Gates. "He lost my money... what my husband left me. Gambled it away. He promised me..." Her voice grew weaker with each faltering breath as more blood oozed onto the carpet.

"She's hallucinating!" Gates bellowed.

"His inheritance, he promised... if I helped him..." Her arm fell limply to her side as her eyes settled on Gates. "Tonight, it would have been over..." Her body jerked and became still.

Dr. Howard felt for a pulse as everyone watched. He looked up and shook his head.

"She lies. There is no proof I took part." Gates' tall figure seemed to shrivel as his thin arms pressed into his sides.

"You monster, may you rot in hell." Emily's voice rasped with rage.

"She was deranged. Cousin, you must believe me."

"His coat pockets," Marcus said suddenly as he took a step toward him.

Gates drew back and bolted toward the door. The constable's men greeted him, pulling his arms behind his back. Marcus approached and reached into his pockets, pulling out an identical vial. He stepped back before the officers threw Gates to the floor.

In seconds the men tied Gates' hands behind his back while he squirmed like a trapped snake.

AFTER FURTHER INQUIRIES, the constable seemed satisfied. He ordered one of the officers to take Eva Hanover's body to the morgue while the other kept watch over Gates. Securing the vials for further tests, he assured everyone that the prisoner would be brought before the magistrate in the morning.

As the constable talked with the physicians, Forrester bid Marcus and the others farewell. "I believe that extending my visit would be anticlimactic," he said, as he patted down his collar and cuffs.

"But certainly you will stay the night," Emily urged, still shaken but overcome with gratitude for his help.

"I appreciate the offer, Miss Hughes, but I am off to my country house. I must say, my visit held more interest than fencing with Deming."

Marcus smirked before offering his hand. Though no words were spoken, Marcus' solid handshake said enough.

"I can think of no way to thank you." Emily gestured helplessly, holding out her hand. "Marcus is fortunate to have such a friend."

Forrester reached for her hand and kissed it with purposeful ardor. Raising his head, he offered her a warm smile before looking over her shoulder to Marcus. He acknowledged Marcus' glare with an affable snicker. "I wish your father well," Forrester said, returning his gaze to Emily. "I look forward to hearing good news."

"All right, Forrester, you have been thanked," Marcus ground out when his friend continued to hold Emily's hand and look into her eyes meaningfully. "You must want to be on your way."

Forrester grinned broadly. "Remember, Deming, you owe me. I promise I shall collect one day."

"Indeed. I have saved your neck before. Unless you change your ways, I will again."

"Mrs. Fenning." Forrester offered a bow to Emily's aunt before striding out with one of the officers close behind, the bound prisoner in tow. Marcus followed them out.

"My word," Heddy said as she rushed to Emily's side. "What in good heavens has happened?"

Emily, who had barely recovered from the horror of the past hour, turned to see the housekeeper staring at her wide-eyed and expectant.

"Shall I... call our guests to dinner?" the housekeeper stuttered.

Emily hesitated, gazing about at the solemn faces that had witnessed the scene. Folding her arms, she let out a deep sigh.

"Our guests could use some time to freshen up, Heddy," she said finally. The doctors have graciously agreed to stay at least for the night. Dr. Howard may stay longer. Have Maggie prepare rooms."

"Rooms have already been prepared. Maggie will see that the doctors are settled upstairs."

"I should have known that you would take care of everything."

"Just doin' my job, missy," the housekeeper

beamed.

"Heddy," Emily paused, biting her bottom lip. "There has been a... fatality in the parlor."

The housekeeper gaped.

"Mrs. Hanover has succumbed. I am afraid you will have quite a mess to clean up."

"Is there a body?" Agatha choked out, having reached the bottom of the staircase.

Delia rushed to her friend who appeared to be in shock and grasped her arm.

"No, it has been removed," Emily answered, thankful that Agatha had been in her room at the farthest end of the house. "Heddy, if you would see to the cleaning and hold dinner until I tell you to serve."

Still wide-eyed, Heddy bobbed a curtsy before rushing off.

Emily pressed her hands to her temples before turning to the physicians who had been talking together privately a few feet away. They looked up as she approached. "Doctors, I am at a loss for words. I would never have imagined that my cousin was capable of anything so evil. Vials with poison..."

"Ah, yes, the vials." Dr. Bellingham cleared his throat, putting aside his formal demeanor.

Emily looked at him oddly. "What is it?"

"I confess I had no way of really knowing if the vials contained the poison. Arsenic has no odor and is tasteless," Dr. Bellingham admitted.

Emily tilting her head in confusion.

"I suspected the worst and my observations of the guilty ones left little doubt in my mind."

"You tricked them," Emily snorted.

"Physicians do have investigative abilities, Miss Hughes. We often must use various tactics to gather information," Bellingham said with a shrug of one shoulder.

"Their guilt convicted them," Howard added.

Emily shuddered.

"Arsenic has been called inheritance powder, an apt moniker for a deadly poison, and used for centuries by the ruthless to gain power or wealth," Bellingham said grimly. "If the vials do contain arsenic, the antidote should be taking effect soon."

"Is there any doubt?"

"Not in our opinion," Howard answered. "We have both witnessed it in our practice over the years, though its use has declined. Methods of detection through bodily fluids have improved. The pair obviously hoped that they could mask the cause of his illness by using a miniscule amount, most likely a grain or two over an extended period. Fortunately their method allowed time for discovery."

"Without intervention, your father would have expired with what would have seemed to be natural causes," Bellingham added.

"The way the two reacted when the vials were found," Aunt Delia shook her head in amazement. "I thought the woman was going to scratch Willard's eyes out when he tossed the blame to her."

"She said tonight... what were they planning?" Emily murmured, pressing a hand to her chest to calm her pounding heart.

"Poison? Will someone please tell me what is going on?"

"Do not agonize, Agatha, I shall explain later," Delia said, patting her friend's arm.

"I must go to my father."

"I administered a strong sedative, Miss Hughes. You should find him sleeping quite soundly. We will check on him later this evening and talk of the recovery process," Bellingham said, smiling for the first time.

Emily's eyes brightened. "You do believe then, that he will recover?"

"We must take it a day at a time, my dear," Dr. Howard answered. "Tomorrow I shall speak with your father. Explain his situation, the antidotes and outcomes. He has a strong will, as you well know. Once he realizes there is hope of recovery, I suspect his determination will be his greatest asset." He smiled reassuringly.

"Doctors, I cannot thank you enough," Emily said, perhaps for the third time and just as Maggie appeared offering a deep curtsy. "Maggie, please lead our guests to their rooms."

After they walked away, Emily dropped her face into her hands.

"My dear, look in on your father if you wish, then go to your room and rest," Delia pleaded, reaching for her niece's hand. "If you prefer dinner in your room, Agatha and I shall visit with the doctors and Marcus."

"The thought of eating sickens me. How can I express my gratitude to everyone? And to think of what my cousin and that woman had been doing in my presence."

"Enough now, you must rest." Delia waved her niece off in the direction of the staircase.

"I should check…"

"Go, everything is under control."

Seeing the uncompromising look on her aunt's face, Emily gave her a hug and climbed the stairs to her room.

Chapter Twenty-Three

MR. HUGHES SAT on the veranda enjoying the late September sun with Delia and Agatha. Percy the cat was snuggled on Agatha's lap. She had accompanied Marcus on his return visit a few days earlier. Delia had stayed on to help care for Emily's father and to support her niece. Her presence was a godsend to Emily and her father as they reestablished the household to its prior state, including rehiring the cook unfairly discharged by Gates.

Once the physicians declared their patient out of danger, Delia and her brother-in-law had restored their old friendship and seemed on the brink of a courtship. The evidence against Gates and the witnesses' accounts left no doubt that he would be locked up for an interminable amount of time.

Marcus had spent the last few weeks at his country estate trying his best to be patient while the Hughes' put their house in order. His time away from Emily turned out to be more difficult than he had imagined.

When lunch was over and Mr. Hughes and the aunts were settled on the porch, Marcus asked permission to walk through the gardens with Emily. Her father practically shooed them off. Marcus sensed that Hughes was enjoying the extra attention that the two older ladies were giving him.

"Shall I accompany them?" Delia asked.

"They'll be in the gardens for God's sake. Let them be."

Marcus grinned widely at Mr. Hughes, who he'd come to respect immensely.

"So, your passion is poetry," Marcus said as they walked along the path toward the back gardens.

Emily's father had boasted of her pastime during lunch without regard to her narrowed eyes glaring at him.

"Yes, it has been my greatest passion," Emily teased, remembering what Marcus had assumed earlier.

"And I thought you had a love interest."

"But, why? What did I do that would have caused you to believe such a fallacy?"

"The night of the ball, I saw a note in your writing... a love note."

"Perhaps, a poem?" Emily tilted her face to his, her eyes sparkling with humor.

Marcus lowered his head, shaking it slowly from side to side. His own folly had caused him grief beyond words. "I was cruel to you that night."

"I thought you were relieved that our pretense would end with the close of the Season."

Marcus stopped and turned to her. "I was jealous, and judged you wrongly. I beg your forgiveness, Emily."

Emily nodded, before lifting her eyes to the blue sky above them, her smile as radiant as the brightness of the day.

They walked on.

"Tell me about your poetry."

Emily hesitated, biting at her bottom lip. "I have been writing poems since I was a small child. Those are hidden away for good reason. I continued to write and found it to be my most enjoyable past time. I... have dreamed of being published one day, *A Selection of Poems by E.G. Hughes.*" She glanced at him briefly before looking away past the gardens.

"If it is the name you prefer," Marcus murmured, rubbing his chin. He led her to a stone wall that bordered a section of the gardens.

"I doubt I would be published using my given name."

"Really?" Marcus tried to maintain a serious expression.

"Women, as you well know, must follow the dictates of society or work around them without causing a stir," Emily expounded, brushing loose auburn curls off her shoulder. "A book of love poems by a woman would be scoffed at by society."

"Love poems?" Marcus lips creased into a sideways grin as he watched her nose crinkle and her lips purse. "I hope I have influenced your art."

Emily suppressed a smile.

"Why didn't you tell me about your hobby?"

"For just that reason!" Emily huffed. "You see it simply as a hobby."

"I see I would have misjudged you again. It appears that I need proper guidance in the care and understanding of independent women."

Emily looked at him, her mouth parted in pleasant surprise.

"*A Selection of Poems by E.G. Hughes*," Marcus repeated. "Would I cause a stir if I suggested another name?" He reached for her hand and brought it to his lips.

"Another name? Using initials would be the only way. A publisher will assume I am a male poet. Though I must say, I have no understanding of why women cannot—"

"Might you consider E.G. Deming?" Marcus interrupted before she had a chance to go on a rampage about women's rights. "On the other hand, if you insist on using Hughes as your pen name, I suppose as my wife I would have no objection." He kissed her hand and raised his eyes to hers, wearing a lopsided grin. "Well?"

"But you desire a marriage of—"

Marcus drew her into his arms and kissed her full on the lips before she could start any nervous chatter. When he withdrew his lips, he said softly, "I love you, my darling, and it is my deepest desire to be married to a poetess."

Emily lifted her hand and smoothed her fingers gently down the side of his face and over his lips, still warm from their kiss.

"Are you going to answer me, Miss Hughes, or must I spout poetry?"

"You must ask my father," a smile played on her lips.

"Already done. We have his blessing."

"When did you ask him?" she asked surprised.

"The second time I met him."

Emily gaped at him. "The second time? Before we found out the cause of his illness?"

"I thought the first time might seem presumptuous." Marcus grinned as he led her to a nearby bench. "When I realized there was no suitor about to vie for your hand, I told your father of my intentions."

"And if there had been a suitor?"

"I would have found a way to discourage him. Perhaps I would have told him that you have a tendency toward pretense and deception."

Emily reddened at the reminder. "And what did my father say when you approached him?"

"He quite approved. I believe that I brought him some peace of mind, though he warned me that you had been a precocious child and were still accustomed to doing as you please." Taking her into his arms once again, he lifted her chin and gazed deep into her eyes. "Will you please give me peace of mind? Tell me you love me, and say yes."

"Yes, oh, yes. Marcus, my dearest darling. I love you more than words could ever express."

"My sweet poetess, you must promise to write a love poem for our wedding day."

Emily nodded, her eyes bright with happiness as Marcus' lips came down on hers. Her arms curled around his broad shoulders as she returned his kiss. When their lips parted, she snuggled in his arms.

Emily's thoughts went to her ethereal poems about love, a love she had believed to be only in the eyes of poets and dreamers. She closed her eyes and breathed in the scent of the man who had awakened her beyond the passion of words. True passion so soul wrenchingly beautiful, she doubted words could ever grasp and hold and express the depth of her love.

Perhaps not, but she'd try... After all, that's what poets do.

TO MARCUS, MY LOVE
From Love Poems by E.G. Deming

Keats waits to 'hear her tender-taken breath
And so live ever-or else swoon to death.'
Spenser hallows his love's virtues in his verse,
While other poets pine away in love's remorse.
Shakespeare, Donne, Sir Walter Scott,
Grasped to find the flowery words
That I believed love was not.
I read, I wept; I wrote words as sweet,
Idylls of romantic minds,
Simply put, creative rhymes, until we met.
Shakespeare's sonnets came to life:
'So are you to my thoughts as food for life,'
I lay entwined within your arms, dear husband mine.
My doubts have fled, my soul is fed,
And as I write with quill in hand,
I smile at my once foolish stand.
For if all the sentiments of poets
Could be wrapped in one bouquet,
The love burning in my heart for you,
Would consume to ash, the penned array.

Regal Reward

One

"I REFUSE TO move from this spot, Gerald. Your pleading is futile."

"Please, milady, consider the danger!"

"I'll not leave Beatrice here to be mauled by some wild animal and have her babes eaten up. Why, she's just given birth." Marielle looked down at her cluster of pets, her hands clasped firmly about her trim waist. "Oh, look! There's another one beneath Bea's hind leg…"

Marielle smiled as her faithful hound cleaned her pups and welcomed the new little one as it nuzzled its way into the crowded horde. The dog, swollen with her impending litter, had taken to the hills earlier in the day and they'd gone in circles trying to find her. Now with night closing in, she regretted being the cause of Gerald's anxiety. The evening dampness caused his arthritic bones to ache and she could see his discomfort as he limped back and forth scanning the shadow-draped woods.

"Milady, return with me. We'll send the grooms to find her. She'll be back home in no time at all."

"And, dear Gerald, when they arrive, they'll be carrying you back also. Your limp has worsened. You cannot stay out any longer in this night air waiting for a search party. You need to direct them. Bea chose a safe, secluded spot under this big oak and I'll not leave her.

"But, Milady, your father will have my head if any harm comes to you."

"The night will protect me." Marielle patted Gerald's arm and smiled, hoping to placate him. "The grooms need only to keep a sharp eye for the stone markers we've placed near the road. You'll see. I'll be home with our new little family soon enough. I'm truly sorry for pushing you to continue searching past dinnertime, but we've found them. I wouldn't have had a moment's rest worrying about Bea's whereabouts. You must understand."

"Knowing you as well as I do, I most certainly understand. As your caretakers, Matty and I have coddled you and your behavior tonight confirms it. If only your mother was still here. You would not have been allowed to prance about the estate unsupervised since you were old enough to wander."

"Both you and Matty have been wonderful caretakers, but this night I must care for my pets. Do not fear. You know I've walked and ridden about the estate lands in perfect safety. This night will be no different from any other. Now, off with you. I'll not hold you accountable if my father rages."

"If your father took more interests in your whereabouts…" Gerald mumbled, then caught himself. "Since I cannot change your mind, here…take my cloak to fend against the night's chill and my knife too," her servant grumbled. "Pray, do not move from this spot and keep alert to any sounds that might warn you of intruders."

"I will keep it securely by my side," Marielle promised.

"It's not right, milady, not right at all," Gerald replied, shaking his head as he wrapped the cloak about her, turned and slowly limped away. He knew if he stayed a search party might take hours to find them. "Oh, milady, this is most unsettling, most unsettling..."

Marielle listened to her servant's voice fade into inarticulate mumbling as the distance grew between them. *How could he possible think I would leave Beatrice alone? Let my father rage. He most likely hasn't even noticed my absence. Poor Gerald. I should have set out on my own to find Bea. I've only caused him more worry.*

Having made peace with her decision, she wrapped the cloak snugly about her and struggled to find a comfortable position against the ancient tree trunk. Her cherished dog, nestled between two gnarled roots, slept blissfully with her new brood.

The sounds of night became more distinct and despite her efforts to stay awake and alert, her eyes grew heavy and sleep took over.

YORK BLACKSTONE STOOD above the sleeping miss nestled beneath the large oak, rubbing his chin. He and his partner had recently stopped a carriage that held all sorts of rewards. The wealthy occupants were most generous and amendable, despite the one who attempted to run off into the woods. York couldn't blame him. Having followed the carriage from the gaming house, his pockets held the most sizable win.

As he and his partner Braum headed homeward at a comfortable trot, the moon's glow created a dim spotlight over the strange bundle. While his partner watched the road, York checked out the site, surprised to see the young woman wrapped in a heavy cloak. As he moved stealthily around the tree, he was even more surprised to realize that she was completely alone except for a dog and its new litter snuggled next to her.

While he meditated on what to do with her— he certainly couldn't leave her in the woods without protection—she began to stir.

MARIELLE SIGHED AS she sifted through the strange dream that interrupted her sleep. She stirred, unconsciously wrestling with the tightly wrapped cloak. Her green eyes, glazed from sleep, opened, attempted to focus. The full moon cast an eerie glow on a shadowy figure before her. Boots, high boots, worn, supple. While her mind tried to make sense of the dream, her eyes followed the lines of the boots upward from the sight of leggings stretched taut against large, muscular thighs to the stranger's bulging manhood.

"Oh my…" Marielle's eyes bolted upward. A mocking smile met her horrified gaze. The moon's glow created a ghostly aura around the tall stranger's mass of charcoal hair and broad shoulders. For a brief, profound second, Marielle thought she beheld the image of a god or a devil.

The effect was surreal, until the sound of deep laughter broke into her terrifying trance.

Another voice joined in, jolting her into full awareness of her surroundings, where she was and why. Gerald's warnings and the events of the day swirled in her mind. Her glance flew to Bea then scanned the darkness for Gerald or her father. Her body instinctively shrank deeper into the folds of Gerald's heavy cloak while forcing herself to look directly up at the tall stranger and into the blackness of his eyes. This was no dream. She tried to speak, but no sound escaped her lips.

A gruff voice broke the silence. "York, I think we've found us a tasty morsel to dine on tonight."

Marielle's head snapped toward the sound to see a shorter, stockier man crouching, leering, his squinting eyes almost hidden by full cheeks.

Her body shook involuntarily. Despite the tremors, she ignored the shorter man and glared at the taller one just addressed as York. "What are you doing here? You're trespassing on my father's land. His men are on their way, will arrive at any moment... you must leave, *now!*" Marielle reached protectively toward Beatrice who'd begun to growl in a low, steady rumbling as her litter of pups, looking more like squirming mice, snuggled against her damp, speckled coat.

The tall stranger reached down slowly, smiled and patted the dog's head. Beatrice quieted and returned to cleaning up one of the pups. Marielle watched, momentarily paralyzed at the stranger's audacity and her pet's meek response. She gripped her fists beneath the cloak as her anger took hold.

"Who are you? My father, Lord Henley... he'll have your heads for trespassing. You must... "

"*Silence,*" the tall stranger snapped, then gave her a crooked smile as he bent down closer, meeting her glare. His voice softened. "I find your inane chatter annoying."

"Wh-what...?" she sputtered. "You have no right to speak to me in that tone."

Her attempt at boldness drew more laughter as she watched the tall stranger turn to his partner to mock her. "We've found ourselves a spunky little fox, Braum. A lady of the estate and she even comes with her own hound."

Marielle suddenly remembered Gerald's knife. She reached beneath the cloak for the leather scabbard only to have the shorter man, Braum, grab her arm and pull the cloak aside. Finding the knife, he sneered, waving it before her face.

"What else might you 'ave under that cloak?" He reached down to grab the cape. Marielle lashed out, clawing. She grabbed his arm and bit fiercely into his flesh.

"You little witch," Braum howled, pulling back and wincing in pain. "I'll do more than... " He lunged towards her, but was instantly pulled back. York's hand caught his collar, yanking him up and away from Marielle.

"Leave her be," York ordered while his partner stumbled, cursing as he fell back into a nearby bush. "We've come upon much more than a tasty snack. We may be able to secure our future with this midnight miss."

Marielle, fearful but fuming, attempted to

stand but became tangled in the long cloak. Stumbling over a gnarled root, she tripped, grasping at what she could to block her fall. Her palms landed on York's steel-hard chest. Without firm footing, she lost the battle for balance. Her hands slipped further down his frame over his belt to the bulge beneath.

York's breath caught in his throat, his manhood reacting, rising to the occasion. "Ooh, my sweet, if that is what you're after, I will be happy to oblige."

"*Despicable demon*," Marielle hissed, pulling at the cloak and wrapping it more securely about her.

"Such language, you behave more like a wench than a well-bred lady," York jeered, while admiring her courage. "I would have thought, though you seem quite young, that you'd be more refined and with such beauty, even in the dark, certainly worthy of more ladylike actions. Might I ask why you're out here alone in the middle of night and without a guardian? I promise you, we'll do a much better job of keeping you safe."

Marielle wrapped her arms more tightly about her ignoring his query.

"The chattering miss has grown silent," York said, still smiling down at her. I find that much more agreeable. Now, I think it's time that we were off."

"Off? Off where? You must leave. I am safeguarding my pet and her litter. My father's men will arrive at any moment and you'll pay for trespassing *and* your crude behavior."

"Then we should be on our way. I refuse to leave you here unprotected," York countered, while leaning down to lift her off the ground.

Marielle tried to pull away only to have the stranger lift her up effortlessly and toss her, like a rag doll, over his shoulder. Struggling against his powerful hold, she pounded his back. "*Put me down*. Do you hear me? I cannot leave Beatrice... *Please*, I must stay with her. Let me go!"

"Braum, grab a horse blanket and some rope. Make a harness for the animal and its brood. We'll bring them along. It seems the young lady takes her responsibilities quite seriously."

His partner shrugged his shoulders, muttering as he followed York's direction. "While my partner makes your charges comfortable, you, Miss Henley, will ride with me."

Marielle screamed, slamming her fists into his back, but to no avail.

"You may choose to ride upside down or right side up, whichever you prefer, but you will ride with me, so I advise you to stop struggling."

Marielle barely heard him as she screamed hoping someone might hear her in the darkness. The stranger heaved her onto his stallion and mounted, adjusting her flailing body. The ribbon that held her hair unraveled, releasing her thick, auburn curls that now fell recklessly brushing the ground.

Staring down into the darkness, fear crawled through her until she thought she might retch. Her attempts to push her body forward, away, grasp at the brush nearby, succeeded only in amusing her captor as her derriere, padded with petticoats, squirmed wildly.

"You don't seem to be enjoying the view, Miss Henley."

"You animal, you…" Against her will, tears sprang forth as her face rubbed against the horse's firm side.

In an instant, York lifted her, settled her firmly between his legs, her body pressed against his chest while his free arm clasped her waist tightly.

"I suggest you calm down and stop your babbling, or I'll gag your mouth shut."

"You wouldn't *dare*."

Hearing her iron will emerging, York pulled the black scarf from around his neck, preparing to use it if needed.

Marielle covered her mouth with her fists.

"That's much better. I see you're a fast learner." He pulled the reins, easing his horse closer to his partner. "Braum, is everything attended to?"

Having lifted Bea, Braum was busy grabbing some of the pups that had loosened their hold on their mother's teats. Once he'd gathered them all, he wrapped them securely in the blanket, placing the pups atop their mother. He tied the heavy bundle to his saddle, leaving an opening large enough for air to circulate. "Aye, the pups are secure," Braum grumbled as he mounted his horse.

Bea, her pups now hidden in the makeshift sling that hung half off the horse and partly on Braum's lap, whimpered. Marielle tried to call out her name, but their fate was out of her hands.

"We should o' stayed on the road and minded our business, Yorkie," Braum said as he pulled at his horse's reins. "We were havin' a fine night.

Now, we're loaded down with trouble. A little play would o' been enough. We don't need anybody followin' us home."

"Let's be gone then, before we're forced to entertain unwelcome company." York said as he led his horse onto the main road.

Marielle attempted to wrench away from York's firm hold. He in turn, held her closer. As he picked up speed, she felt his body move rhythmically in the saddle. Being a rider herself, she could tell that he was an expert horseman, sure of his movements, despite the extra weight of his passenger. Screaming or fighting, she realized, was futile.

AS THEY RODE further away from her home, she prayed that someone would come along, another rider, or, perhaps a carriage returning to the country from a night in London. She heard nothing except for the sound of the horses' hooves and York's steady breathing. Scattered thoughts crept in. Numbing fear held a tight grip. She worried about Bea and wondered if the pups would be alive when they arrived at wherever they were going. Her back, stiff from her attempts to stay rigid and away from her assailant, ached.

York sensed her weariness, as well as her stubbornness to make herself more comfortable. He pulled Marielle to him and rested her upper torso against his chest. He was accustomed to keeping his mind on his purpose, but the softness and scent of the young woman he tucked into his arms was disconcerting and stimulating.

"Rest, my midnight miss. You won't come to any harm this night."

Marielle tried to protest, but knew she had no options. Fighting him only sapped her strength. She must save it for the opportune time when she could find a means of escape. She tried to keep her eyes on her surroundings, but the time seemed endless. As time passed, despite her grandest efforts to stay alert, her eyes grew heavy.

With York in the lead and Braum following close behind, they traveled through the night. As they drew closer to their destination, the sights and sounds of a new morning replaced the darkness. An ethereal coral glow emanated from the horizon casting off drapes of heavy mist that covered the distant mountains. York pulled the reins taut and led his horse into the brush and down through a gully.

Marielle woke with a start. She tried to lift her head only to have him push it down while he bent his own head over hers. Only a muffled squeak escaped her lips.

"Keep still or the brush will scratch you like cat's claws. We're almost there," he whispered hoarsely.

His faced was pressed so near to her own that Marielle could feel his breath on her cheek. They passed through a wooded area down an uneven, stone-stubbled path, causing the horses to tread with an unsteady gait. Soon a rush of fresh mountain air brushed Marielle's face.

York loosened his grip, allowing his captive to lift herself up and view the surroundings. The horses knew their way as they followed a creek that threaded through the rocky plain leading to a larger stream. He covered her head once again as they turned into more brush.

As soon as Marielle felt the cool air again, she squirmed from his grip. This time she could see a small thatched-roofed cottage in the distance with smoke curling from the chimney. The serene picture-book landscape softly lit by the new dawn was breathtaking. Simple beauty lay before her but she refused to allow herself to appreciate it. She adjusted her thoughts to the bleakness of her situation. The reality of the moment was no longer a hazy nightmare, but shone clear as glass. She felt powerless and knew it was useless to plead for release, but she could think of no other alternative.

"Where have you taken me? You *must* let me go. How far from home am I and where is Beatrice?"

"When your tongue wakes up, it chirps and flutters like mother birds skittering in the grasses to find food for their young," York teased as he brushed aside her tousled curls.

"I beg your pardon," Marielle hissed, pulling herself away from his grasp.

"I beg you to hush and save your strength for more productive exercise. Your dogs are safe and have been well behaved on our journey. Braum's left us many times through the night's ride to scramble our tracks and he's returned with the dogs in tow. I suspect he's become accustomed to the extra weight and may even have grown attached to his cargo."

The hint of satisfaction in his voice only increased Marielle's irritation. She grumbled something unintelligible as they rode up to the porch of the small cottage.

Meanwhile, Braum rode up behind them, dismounted and tethered the horses while a younger version of York stepped out on the porch, his eyes widening in wonder as he spotted Marielle.

"Well, big brother," Martin exclaimed, "I'm not certain whether your night's journey was a success or not, but it sure looks like a heap of trouble to me. Could it be you've found us a maid to tidy up the place?"

"Not a bad idea, Martin, but I'm considering other plans for this prim package."

Marielle tried to protest but before she could utter a sound, York lifted her up into the younger man's arms.

"Ah, light as a feather yet well rounded if my arms do not deceive me," Martin said, grinning.

"How dare you. Put me down!"

"She's a hot spark of fire too. Where on earth did you find her?"

"Be patient. Right now I could use a hot cup of coffee." York led the way through the cottage door. "Once we're rested, I'll tell you all about our profitable adventures. Braum, bring in the mutt and her brood. Then find old George to rub down the horses."

A freshly fed fire warmed the cottage and the rich smell of strong coffee permeated the air. Martin carried Marielle, despite her protests and once inside, stood her on her feet. She pushed him from her, but her legs, unsteady from the long ride, caused her to lose her balance. He grabbed her by the waist to steady her.

"Don't touch me! I am perfectly able to…" Unable to keep her knees from weakening beneath her, she reached out for support, unconsciously grasping York's arm.

"Ah, haven't had enough of me yet?"

Regaining her balance, Marielle gave him a look that could fry bacon. She pushed away and took a few steps before spotting Beatrice and her pups. Braum had placed them near the fire wrapped in the horse blanket. She could see the pups squirming and suckling while Bea busied herself with washing each of the scrawny babes. She rushed to them and bent down to count each one. She sighed with relief. They'd made the trip safely and when Marielle stroked her head, Beatrice seemed content. She marveled at their ability to adapt, despite the circumstances.

Her own insides were turning cartwheels and she feared she might be sick. Her predicament was beyond belief and what of her servant? *Poor Gerald, he'll be so distraught and will most likely blame himself and Father – he'll never forgive him for leaving me.* She stared up at her captives, her fists clenched. It was obvious they were not considering her distress, but only their own stomachs.

The men were comfortably seated around the large table that filled the center of the room. Marielle looked about, noticed a small bed along one wall and a washstand nearby. A large black stove with a few pots that hung above it and an open-shelved cabinet with assorted dishes took up another wall. An open door revealed a pantry to the rear of the small cottage. Turning about, she noticed the large front window that looked out onto the front porch. In the distance she could see overgrown grasses, wild flowers and clusters of trees that wound about an open field. The mountains she'd seen earlier were now splashed with sunlight.

Sitting on the worn rug, her arms tightly clasped around her knees, she continued to examine her surroundings. Two worn, but comfortable-looking chairs were placed near the large stone fireplace, with a small table and lamp between them. Off to the left, a half-opened door revealed a small bedroom with two roughly made beds. She guessed that was probably the extent of the living space. It was neat, warm and would be considered welcoming if it weren't for her dire situation.

Her gaze returned to the men sitting around the table. The younger man, whom they called Martin, sat engrossed as her two kidnappers filled him in on their night's exploits. Angered by their conversation, she returned her thoughts to Beatrice's needs. Concern grew, outweighing her fear. She stood and walked to the table interrupted their animated conversation.

"I request water and rations for my pet. She is, no doubt, thirsty and probably starved."

"And, so are we, love. I suspect that you are not up to fetching water from the well or helping with breakfast." York stood too close, his words and expression taunting.

Marielle took a step back, her breath caught. His formidable presence filled the room. Then she stopped, held her ground and challenged him with a frosty glare.

York didn't miss her repositioning, her recalculation. He admired her courage. She knew how to stand against fear and he understood the force of will behind it too well. He smiled, glanced over to the animals. "Actually, your dog and her new family have settled in quite nicely. I think they are going to enjoy their stay."

"Aye," Braum cut in, "as long as they don't begin to get underfoot. I may be forced to stomp on 'em or toss 'em out for the wolves though they ain't much to feed on. Of course, the bitch will be a bigger mouthful."

Marielle clutched her throat ready to snap at him, but held her tongue, recognizing his distasteful humor. Instead, she watched silently, surprised at York's actions as he searched for a bowl and filled it with water from a nearby jug. She would not allow them to intimidate her, nor feel any gratitude for her pets' care. This man riddled her mind, one minute a brute, yet in another, almost human.

While York set the bowl down near Beatrice's head, he brushed her arm. She backed away, narrowed her brow, glared, as he smiled knowingly.

This was the first time she could actually observe him in the light of day. She had to admit to herself that she'd never seen a man quite as handsome. His eyes, so black in the night, in the light of morning were the deepest blue she'd ever encountered, his dark lashes, thick and long. His hair, the color of mahogany and still damp from the night air, fell in reckless waves about his face. Wet curls clung to the nape of his neck. She guessed he was probably in his late twenties, perhaps older. His face reflected a naked strength she'd not seen before. His lips, she'd noted earlier, were beautifully formed. The deep cleft in his chin, now covered with at least a day's stubble only enhanced his sensual masculinity.

She couldn't help but notice, for she'd been kept too isolated on the estate to meet men other than the work hands and, of course, Richard her betrothed. Despite her precarious situation, her captor's few acts of kindness left her with an unsteady sense of security for the time being.

As she watched York out of the corner of her eyes, she readjusted her thoughts. *I'm a prisoner. He is a ruthless kidnapper, a highwayman. His appearance proves that good looks do not make a gentleman but may only hide the cruelest of men, as her Aunt Cornelia had often said.*

She looked down at her wrinkled gown, the dirt on her hands and the scratches, surely from her attempts to fend him off. *Why, my thoughts are as disheveled as my appearance. I must find a means of escape.*

She'd given little thought to Richard, her betrothed, until now. *Oh dear heavens, what will he imagine? He's most likely rounding up all his men and my father's men are probably scouring the woods. I must believe that they will be able to follow their tracks.* As she made useless attempts to evaluate her dilemma, York held out a glass of cool water.

"You seem to be in deep thought, my sweet. I can feel those lovely green eyes of yours piercing into me like hot coals. Mine may begin to smolder with lust if you keep staring at me like that."

Marielle's face glowed crimson.

York, aware he'd humiliated her, reached out with the drink urging her, in silence, to take it.

Her first inclination was refusal, but her thirst won out. She took the glass, begrudgingly. The water was cool, refreshing and she could turn away to hide her embarrassment. He was right. She'd become mesmerized and lost in her thoughts as she took in his appearance. *It must be exhaustion. It had to be.* Her thoughts swirled as if at sea, her mind doing battle with her senses.

York noted the change. Her guard was down. He reached out, took her arm, felt her stiffen, but urged her to come to the table. "Come, eat some bread and cheese. You must be as hungry as your pet."

Marielle grasped at one of the large chairs to pull herself up and away from his touch. "I need to take care of private matters," she managed, almost politely, setting the glass down on the table.

"Ah, yes. You might want to freshen up before breakfast. I'll accompany you to the pond."

"You *must* realize I have need for time alone. Please, you have humiliated me enough."

"I worry that you might do something foolish if

I left you to yourself," York replied, "but I'm sure that you wouldn't want to become lost in this valley or to have your pups suffer from lack of your tender care."

Marielle bristled at the truth of his words. She couldn't run off, leave Beatrice. She had no idea where she was or where to find help. She needed to think, consider a plan and wait for an opportune time.

Biography

Elaine Violette's first published works were poetry, book reviews, and articles. Her debut Regency Romance, *Regal Reward*, was a NJRW Golden Leaf finalist. Her second Regency, *A Convenient Pretense*, illustrates not only her ability to create emotional depth in her characters and an intriguing plot, but also her skill at writing poetry that can be both heart-wrenching and humorous. Her third historical, A Kiss of Promise, continues the story of the Blackstone brothers that readers meet in *Regal Reward*.

Elaine is a veteran English teacher and holds a BS in English Education from the University of CT and an MS in Educational Leadership from Central CT State University. She presently teaches public speaking part time at a local community college. She is a member of Romance Writers of America, CT Romance Writers (CTRWA), and Women's Fiction Writers Association. She resides on the Connecticut shoreline with her golfing husband, Drew, and delights in being a wife, mother, and grandmother.

Visit Elaine on her Website
www.elaineviolette.com

Her blog: Talking about Writing
http://elainevioletteblogs.blogspot.com/

and on Facebook
www.facebook.com/elaineviolette.author